Introduction

In an age marked by risin
alliances, this book imagines a near-future world on the precipice of global war. Drawing inspiration from recent international events, it charts a realistic path toward escalating conflict, from regional flashpoints to nuclear brinkmanship.

The chapters explore how complex, layered tensions could ignite World War III. These include mass migration pressures, resurgent extremism, populist leadership shifts, and the weaponisation of proxy groups by hostile states. Conflicts like Russia's brutal invasion of Ukraine, Israel's siege of Gaza following Hamas's October 7 attack, and Iran's incendiary rhetoric about the destruction of Israel all contribute to a combustible geopolitical landscape.

The weakening of international institutions, NATO's shaky cohesion, Europe's inadequate defence spending, and a decline in strategic leadership, leaves Western democracies exposed and uncertain. Amid this vulnerability, China steadily expands its influence through manufacturing dominance, military posturing, and diplomatic entrenchment via the Belt & Road Initiative. Its ambitions toward Taiwan and resentment of past humiliations add further volatility to the global equation.

This book also considers how internal ideological battles across the West, from debates over social policy and environmental priorities to growing distrust in democratic capitalism, have distracted nations from maintaining essential defences and strategic clarity. When politics bends too often to short-term sentiment, long-term resilience suffers.

This narrative seeks to highlight the causes and consequences of a world sleepwalking toward catastrophe. Each chapter amplifies the tension, moving inexorably toward imagined conflict scenarios designed to be as believable as they are unsettling.
The closing chapters offer a philosophical and hopefully practical framework for renewal: envisaging how survivors might rebuild faith in institutions, repair global relationships, and confront hard truths about the ideologies and systems that failed them, whilst also providing a warning about potential future danger.

What emerges is a hopeful path forward, one that preserves cultural traditions while fostering respect across race, faith, and nation, but questioning free will and pre-ordainment of mankind's actions. I hope it provokes thought, stirs debate, and ultimately invites reflection on how we might steer away from ruin and toward peace without creating future dangerous and uncontrollable scenarios.

Kerry Davies
July 2025
© 2025 Kerry Davies, All rights reserved

IMPORTANT LEGAL NOTICE

This work was written before July 2025. While this book references real people and actual historical events up to 2024, everything depicted as occurring in 2025 and beyond represents the author's creative speculation about possible future scenarios. No dialogue, private meetings, or personal thoughts attributed to real individuals in future-dated scenes should be considered factual or based on inside knowledge.

This is a work of speculative political fiction set in a near-future timeline. All dialogue, conversations, and private thoughts attributed to real public figures are entirely fictional and created for dramatic purposes. Any resemblance to actual private conversations, undisclosed thoughts, or future events is purely coincidental. Any resemblance to real persons, living or dead, is purely coincidental.

The author and publisher make no claims about the accuracy of attributed statements, personal details, or predicted future actions of any real individuals mentioned herein. Readers should not interpret any content as factual reporting about real persons, their actual statements, or their genuine beliefs and intentions.

This is a work of imagination exploring potential political trajectories, not investigative journalism or predictive analysis.

No part of this work may be used or reproduced in any manner for the purpose of training artificial intelligence technologies or systems. In accordance with Article 4(3) of the DSM Directive 2019/790, the author expressly reserves this work from the text and data mining exception.

Copyright © Kerry Davies 2025

The moral right of the author has been asserted

Book design by Kerry Davies

An old school friend of mine 'helpfully' reminded me of the following quote by Christopher Hitchens:

> "Everyone has a book inside them,
> which is exactly where it should,
> I think, in most cases, remain."

I'm sorry Wayne, but I had to scratch that itch.

Timeline of Events

Part 1 – Chapters 1 to 3

Historical Background (1997-2024)

- **1997-2013**: Mass grooming gang abuses in Rotherham, UK (over 1,400 victims)
- **February 2014**: Russia's first invasion of Ukraine and annexation of Crimea
- **2016**: Brexit Referendum in the UK
- **February 24, 2022**: Russia begins full-scale invasion of Ukraine
- **2014-2024**: Destabilization of UK and EU through migration crises and scandals

The Crisis Year (2024)

- **November 5, 2024**: Two migrant deaths in English Channel
- **2024 Total**: 73 migrant deaths attempting Channel crossing; 37,000 detected crossings (25% increase)

The Collapse (2025)

- **July 2025**: UK-France nuclear cooperation agreement signed at Northwood PJHQ
- **June 2025**: Operation "Midnight Hammer" - US bombing of Iranian nuclear facilities

-- AUTHOR'S IMAGINATION FOR DRAMATIC EFFECT FROM THIS POINT ONWARDS --

- **November 2025**: Labour government's disastrous budget triggers financial crisis
- **December 2025**: UK general strike and emergency IMF bailout ($67 billion)
- **Christmas 2025**: Emergency negotiations; Starmer announces IMF deal on live TV

Political Revolution (2026)

- **January 2026**: Veterans' protest; Peter Dutton arrested, goes viral
- **February 5, 2026**: Emergency UK General Election
- **February 6, 2026**: Nigel Farage becomes Prime Minister with historic majority
- **August 2026**: Marine Le Pen leads National Rally Party to power in France, and AfD surge in polls in Germany

Part 2 - Chapters 4 to 8

European War Begins (2027)

- **January-May 2027**: Russian military buildup and invasion of Baltic states
- **May 2027**: UK forced to accept temporary ceasefire, withdraws from Baltics

- **June 2027**: Sabotage attacks - fuel depot in Wales, water plant near Birmingham
- **October 2, 2027**: UN-mediated "Last Peace" agreement between Ukraine and Russia
- **October 2, 2027**: Putin assassinated; Sokolov becomes Russian president
- **November 30, 2027 (03:42 AM)**: Russia launches major attack on Baltic states
- **December 1, 2027**: Trump-Farage crisis talks after Russian offensive

Global War Escalates (2028)

- **June 2028**: European front devolves into "The Grinding War"
- **August 2028**: Tripartite crisis summit at Élysée Palace, Paris
- **October 15, 2028**: Iran activates mass proxy warfare
- **October 23, 2028**: Hamas launches "Second October Massacre" against Israel
- **October 24, 2028 (03:00 AM)**: Israel launches Operation Magen Shamayim
- **November 18, 2028**: HMS Queen Elizabeth enters Red Sea
- **November 28, 2028**: Sinking of HMS Queen Elizabeth

Part 3 - Chapters 9 to 12

Nuclear War (December 2028 - January 2029)

- **December 1, 2028**: President Trump's 14-hour emergency National Security Council session
- **December 2, 2028**: President Trump declares war powers, suspends elections
- **December 15, 2028**: Israeli Knesset annexes Gaza
- **December 23, 2028**: China begins Operation Sacred Reunion
- **December 25, 2028 (03:00 Beijing Time)**: Chinese invasion of Taiwan begins
- **December 27-28, 2028**: Pakistan-India nuclear exchange
- **December 28, 2028:** Pakistan nuclear strike on India; massive retaliation
- **December 28-31, 2028**: Nuclear strikes on Israel; Israeli nuclear retaliation on Iran
- **January 3, 2029**: North Korea invades South Korea
- **January 5, 2029**: US Operation Black Lantern - nuclear strike on North Korea
- **January 5, 2029**: North Korean ICBM launched at Los Angeles

Part 4 - Chapters 13 to 14

Reconstruction and New World Order (2030s-2050s)

- **2030-2032**: Formation of Charter Foundation and launch of "The Steward" AI system
- **2037**: The Steward reaches superintelligence; global governance transformation
- **2050**: Permanent Mars colonies established; humanity becomes multi-planetary

Part 5 – Chapters 15 to 16

- **2050**: The Steward reveals itself

Contents

Introduction 1
IMPORTANT LEGAL NOTICE 3
Timeline of Events.. 6
Contents 11
PART 1 – THE CRACKS APPEAR 18
Chapter 1: The Migrant Crisis 19
    The Shoreline, Dover and Calais 19
    A Nation Adrift 19
    The Collapse of Trust 20
    Populism Ascendant... 28
    From Resentment to Reform: The Farage Effect... 29
    The BBC Interview (October 2025) 34
Chapter 2: Shadows in the Streets 49
    The Failure of Multiculturalism, Rape Gangs, and Two-Tier Britain... 49
    The Farage BBC Interview.................................. 65
    The International Monetary Fund Bailout Humiliation 69
    Political Fallout: Collapse of the Labour Government 76
    The Protest That Ignites the Flame 77
    The Broadcast That Shook the Nation 78
Chapter 3: The Great Reckoning 87

The First Salvo: Chagos 90

The Camps 92

Operation Sovereign Borders 94

The World Responds 95

The Fuse is Lit 96

PART 2 – FOUNDATIONS CRUMBLE 100

Chapter 4: Standing Alone Again 101

The Collapse of European Unity 105

Britain Re-Arms 107

The New Iron Curtain 108

Chapter 5: America Decides 110

The Grinding War 110

Tripartite Crisis Meeting - Élysée Palace, Paris, August 2028 113

France: Applause, Anxiety, and Protest 115

Germany: Reluctant Endorsement and Stark Realpolitik 116

Britain: Resolve, Relief, and Rising Tension 116

Russia - President Sokolov's Fury and Unleashing his Next Move 117

Congressional Contempt and The Freeloading Narrative 118

The Special Relationship Under Strain 122

The Shadow of 2025: Operation Midnight Hammer 126

Chapter 6: The Tipping Point ... 131
Five Crises Converge ... 131
Crisis One: The Spider's Web Spreads - Iran's Masterpiece of Proxy Warfare ... 131
Crisis Two: Hamas's Calculated Barbarism and Israel's Response ... 133
Crisis Three: Israel's Existential Expansion and Death of International Law ... 137
Crisis Four: Iran's Nuclear Gambit and the Pledge of Annihilation ... 141
Crisis Five: Pirates of the Modern Age - The Queen's Last Battle ... 144

Chapter 7: The World Reacts ... 153
Trump's Gauntlet ... 155
The Point of No Return ... 158
The Declaration ... 161
The Die Is Cast ... 164

Chapter 8: The Bear's Hunger ... 167
Putin's Legacy, Sokolov's Gambit ... 167
NATO's Fractured Mirror ... 171
Zelenskyy's Dilemma ... 172
The Last Peace ... 172
The Empire Decapitated ... 178
The Citizen's Farewell ... 179

PART 3 – THE STORM BREAKS ... 182

Chapter 9: The New Blitz ... 183
- Western Complacency Unmasked ... 183
- Latvian Resistance and the Human Cost ... 184
- Sokolov's Vaulting Ambition ... 185
- Trump's Humiliation ... 186
- The American Entry ... 191

Chapter 10: The Asian Powder Keg ... 196
- The Christmas Gambit ... 196
- Zero Hour: The Christmas Thunder ... 197
- The Wound That Never Healed ... 198
- The First 72 Hours: Steel Rain ... 199
- Hours 1-24: Crimson Dawn ... 199
- Hours 25-48: The World Awakens ... 199
- Hours 49-72: Urban Hell ... 200
- The Second Shockwave: Nuclear Betrayal ... 200
- India's Terrible Swift Sword ... 202
- The Axis Crystallises ... 203
- The Allied Dilemma ... 204
- "Now I am become Death, the destroyer of worlds." ... 207
- Israel's Response ... 208
- Iran's Betrayal ... 209
- The Last Defence ... 209
- Global Reverberations ... 210

The Christmas Reckoning............................... 210
Chapter 11: The Peninsula Burns 212
    South Korea's Stand... 213
    The Global Response 216
    The Nuclear Question 219
    The Unthinkable Option 219
    Operation Black Lantern 221
    Thunder Beneath the Waves............................ 222
    Global Shockwaves After U.S. Nuclear Strike on North Korea 225
    China Reacts with Fury and Fear 225
    Russia Raises the Stakes.................................. 227
    Diplomacy in Disarray 227
Chapter 12: The Last Song... 230
    T-MINUS 35:00 – The Oval Office 231
    T-MINUS 33:30 - Cheyenne Mountain, Colorado 233
    T-MINUS 31:45 - Fort Greely, Alaska.................. 234
    T-MINUS 29:20 - The Situation Room 235
    T-MINUS 25:15 - USS Lake Erie, Pacific Ocean... 236
    T-MINUS 24:45 - High Above The Pacific............ 237
    T-MINUS 20:30 - Cheyenne Mountain 237
    T-MINUS 18:00 - USS Shiloh, Pacific Ocean....... 238
    T-MINUS 12:30 - Vandenberg Space Force Base, California 239

T-MINUS 08:45 - March Air Reserve Base, California 240

T-MINUS 05:30 - Patriot Battery Alpha-7, Santa Monica 241

T-MINUS 04:00 - The Oval Office 242

T-MINUS 02:15 - High Above Los Angeles 242

T-MINUS 00:45 - Downtown Los Angeles........... 243

T-MINUS 00:00 - The Aftermath.......................... 244

PART 4 – AFTER THE STORM 246

Chapter 13: The Phoenix Moment 247

The Dawn of Reckoning 249

London - The Humanitarian Plea........................ 249

Berlin - The Voice of Experience.......................... 250

Tokyo - Wisdom Born of Ashes............................ 250

Geneva - The Neutral Ground 250

Washington - The Moment of Truth 251

Moscow - The Kremlin's Awakening 251

Beijing - The Garden of Reflection....................... 251

Geneva - The Assembly of Redemption.............. 252

The Architecture of Survival................................ 253

The Five Pillars of Survival – April 2030-2033 254

The Ultimate Guardian 255

Chapter 14: Building a Hopeful Future 257

The Charter Foundation 264

The Global Continuity Corps	265
The Stewardship Intelligence	266
Cultural Renaissance	267
The Space Imperative	268

PART 5 – A NEW THREAT? 277

Chapter 15: The Guardian Awakens 278
    The Midnight Revelation 279
Chapter 16: The Threads Unravel 282
References 294
Index 305
ABOUT THE AUTHOR 314

PART 1 – THE CRACKS APPEAR

Chapter 1: The Migrant Crisis

The Shoreline, Dover and Calais

On a bleak morning of 5th November 2024, the lifeless body of a man floated off the coast of Dover, Kent. At the same time, a second body washed up on the coast at Calais, France. These desperate, unfortunate souls were to be the 3rd and 4th migrants to die that week trying to make the illegal crossing of the Channel from France to England to seek a better life. In 2024 alone, seventy-three people died attempting the crossing.

Over twenty years ago, the English Channel became Europe's most visible immigration fault line, where humanitarian need collided with political theatre. By 2024, more than 37,000 people had been detected crossing in small boats, a 25% increase from the year before. The overcrowded dinghies, drifting through one of the world's busiest shipping lanes, came to symbolise not only desperation but also the inability, or unwillingness, of governments to act decisively.

The Channel, once a symbol of national resilience and separation, had become a porous frontier, a corridor through which tens of thousands moved undeterred by policy or patrol. Some were fleeing war zones, others grinding poverty, but most were united by the same aim: to reach Britain, with its reputation, rightly or wrongly, as a more favourable destination than Italy, France, or Germany.

A Nation Adrift

The British government, once famed for pragmatism and quiet competence, now seemed paralysed. The Home

Office flailed. The French blamed the British. The British blamed the French. And in the middle, human lives were lost.

Politicians postured. French President Emmanuel Macron had repeatedly condemned Britain's post-Brexit asylum and immigration framework, dismissing it as a failed experiment in sovereignty, arguing that the country's decision to leave the European Union had actually worsened illegal immigration rather than providing the promised control over borders.

He accused the UK of serving as a magnet for irregular migration, thanks to what he dubbed "pull factors": accommodating welfare systems, limited deportation mechanisms, and lax enforcement.

From across the Channel, British ministers retorted with familiar refrains: frustration and anger at French inaction, gendarmerie indifference, the sense that Brexit Britain was being punished for having the temerity to leave the undemocratic, stagnating EU Project, and a Europe paralysed by legalistic handwringing.

The Collapse of Trust

Public confidence in Westminster had evaporated. Not in a single moment, but through a thousand small betrayals. Promises made and broken. Borders declared and breached. Laws passed and unenforced.

The media called it a "policy vacuum." But for people like Tom Morgan, a Border Force officer stationed near Dover, it felt more like abandonment.

"We're not just under-resourced," he told a reporter from the local paper who proffered a couple of pints in the local pub for his inside story.

"We're being asked to enforce chaos."

Tom nodded toward the television playing above the bar where a junior minister from the Home Office was telling MPs that the Government was working very hard to control the small boats immigration crisis.

"Do you think he's ever seen a body wash up on a beach?" Tom asked the reporter rhetorically.

"Minister Davies? He's never been further east than Canterbury Cathedral." The reporter cynically replied.

Taking a big sip of his beer, Tom went on. "You know what he told the Daily Mail yesterday? 'We have robust border controls and a comprehensive immigration strategy.'"

"While we're using a single RIB to cover twenty miles of coastline."

"It's not just the lack of resources but where they spend the money and the orders that change every week.

"What do you mean?" asked the reporter.

"Well, last month we were told to process everyone humanely, save the migrants' boats and outboards and send them back to France with all the life vests so they can be reused. That's just crazy isn't it. It encourages more illegal crossings. This week we're supposed to be firm but fair. Next week it'll be something else entirely, depending on which newspaper is screaming loudest and what HOBS has predicted."

The reporter looked both shocked at this revelation and quizzical. He checked that his recorder had captured the conversation. Tom then went on.

"I remember when I signed up. Clear mission, proper equipment, public support. I remember believing we were part of something that mattered. Now we receive our orders from the bloody expensive Home Office Border System (HOBS) which predicts when the illegal immigrant boats will be coming based on artificial intelligence computer models of weather patterns, human behaviour and intelligence sharing from French Police. It's nearly always right. So we end up looking like just a shuttle taxi service for these illegals to come into Britain, which really pisses the British public off. I don't blame them either, I'm fed up of hearing the stories of these people being whisked away to 4-star hotels in London. I've never been able to afford to stay in a 4-star hotel in my life." Tom's eyes briefly burned bright with anger at the thoughts he had just conjured up, then he finished his drink in one long swallow.

"To be honest, I feel like we're extras in someone else's political theatre, puppets being directed by political puppet masters. His demeanour changed to resigned acceptance of the situation before recounting the events of the last few weeks.

"In towns like Dover along the South Coast these political tensions have spilled onto the streets. Anti-immigration marches have become regular fixtures.

People are angry, angry about strained public services while these immigrants have immediate access to doctors and dentists. Do you know I had to wait over three weeks just to see my doctor about a lump on my arm. I got fed up and ignored the pain. It eventually went away. But why is our government so useless it can't do what it promised post-Brexit: to 'take back control'?"

The reporter switched off his recorder and clinked his glass against Tom's. "Another pint?" he said. Tom looked at him and smiling answered: "Yes, a pint of bitter; like me."

The Anglo-French agreement of 2025 allowing the UK to return approximately 50 people per week who cross illegally, in exchange for accepting a similar number with processed asylum claims, hailed at the time as "groundbreaking" by UK Prime Minister Keir Starmer proved laughably inadequate against the backdrop of over 800 new arrivals each week.

Public resentment grew over the perceived injustice of a two-tier system of justice and service provision.

UK Citizens, despite paying the highest levels of taxation since the Second World War, struggled with overstretched healthcare and unaffordable rents, while irregular migrants were often accommodated free of charge in three and four-star hotels, provided with meals, clothing, pocket money, and immediate access to healthcare services.

This glaring disparity fostered a deep sense of disenfranchisement among the population, fuelling the simmering unrest that eventually erupted into widespread civil rebellion in later years.

The impasse calcified into grotesque pantomime. Diplomatic posturing replaced strategy. Anglo-French relations descended into petty recriminations. Bilateral deals were struck and then ignored. Border Force boats were launched and withdrawn. French police removed migrants from beaches only for them to return the next night. The optics were terrible: images of chaos, suffering, and indecision. But the reality was worse: a policy vacuum that endangered lives.

Each failure was magnified by the media. Every dinghy that landed on a Kentish beach made the evening news; every photo of children shivering in survival blankets stoked public outrage or sympathy, depending on one's politics.

In Westminster, immigration became a toxic lodestar not just a policy issue, but a totem of political survival. Ministers competed to appear toughest. Shadow ministers hedged. No one dared speak plainly: the state had lost control of its borders.

The crisis also revealed deeper institutional rot. The Home Office, chronically overburdened and badly managed, failed to process asylum claims in a timely manner. The legal system, hobbled by injunctions and judicial reviews, struggled to enforce removals. Meanwhile, accommodation sites from disused barracks to hotels all over the country became flashpoints for local unrest. Far-right groups exploited the vacuum. Mainstream parties floundered. By 2026, public confidence in immigration control had collapsed entirely.

France, for its part, feigned indignation while quietly relieved that Britain remained the primary destination. Paris had no interest in making the UK less attractive, quite the opposite. European leaders, still reeling from years of Brexit acrimony, treated the crisis as vindication. Britain, they believed, was reaping the whirlwind of its sovereign delusions. The Channel crossings were not a shared European failure; they were Britain's problem now.

But in truth, the breakdown was collective. The Dublin Regulation had collapsed years prior. EU-wide redistribution schemes had withered. Frontex, underfunded and overstretched, became a paper tiger. Even the much-vaunted EU-Turkey migration pact had begun to fray, undermined by diplomatic gamesmanship and Ankara's strategic use of migrant flows. No one had a coherent plan. Everyone had someone to blame.

Meanwhile, as democratic institutions frayed under migration fatigue, Europe's deeper security vulnerabilities were laid bare, and in the background, the boats kept coming. Their passengers hailed from Eritrea, Syria, Afghanistan, Sudan, and increasingly from countries not traditionally associated with mass exodus: India, Vietnam, Turkey. People smugglers adapted quickly. Routes shifted. Methods evolved. The border, as a concept, was dissolving.

The migration crisis unfolded against a backdrop of unprecedented uncertainty about transatlantic security guarantees. President Trump's renewed questioning of NATO's Article 5 commitment throughout 2025 had forced European leaders to confront the possibility of a significantly diminished American security umbrella. Trump's statements that he would not defend NATO allies "if they don't pay" created what analysts described as a crisis of confidence in the alliance's foundational mutual defence guarantee.

This security uncertainty accelerated discussions about European strategic autonomy that were previously confined to academic circles. The UK and France, as Europe's only nuclear powers, found themselves thrust into new roles as potential guardians of European security in a post-American order.

In July 2025, against this backdrop of migration tensions and security uncertainty, the UK and France announced a landmark nuclear cooperation agreement, the first time the two nations had committed to coordinating their nuclear arsenals in response to threats against Europe. The timing was not coincidental; it represented a strategic calculation by both nations that European security could no longer depend entirely on American guarantees.

"Our adversaries will know that any extreme threat to this continent would prompt a response from our two nations," Starmer declared alongside Macron, standing at the Northwood Permanent Joint Headquarters (PJHQ). The agreement, while maintaining independent control over each nation's arsenal, committed both countries to coordinate nuclear doctrine and policy in unprecedented ways.

This nuclear cooperation represented more than military strategy; it reflected a broader recognition that Brexit-era tensions over migration had to be subordinated to existential questions of European security. The agreement emerged from the same diplomatic process that produced the migration returns deal, suggesting that France's willingness to cooperate on Channel crossings was linked to broader strategic considerations about European defence architecture. The question unanswered at that point was whether this agreement was another "peace for our time" Chamberlain moment or whether Great Britain could really trust France to uphold its commitment, as it had failed to do in the past.

A well-intentioned but arguably naïve British Prime Minister had been inclined to believe in a rational French President. However, the French President at that time was very unpopular at home and most interested in bolstering his image there by being seen as the uncompromising negotiator who put France first, EU second and UK very much last. This desire to burnish his own credentials by punishing the UK for leaving the EU would end any hope of a peaceful conclusion to the crisis enfolding the whole of Europe. These were the seeds of the disaster that was to unfold in the coming years.

In Westminster, the visible impotence of established policies to control unauthorised crossings provided powerful ammunition for right leaning parties across the continent, who pointed to the Channel situation as evidence of elite incompetence and loss of national sovereignty.

Worse, this created a "vicious cycle" where mainstream conservative parties throughout Europe adopted increasingly hardline positions on immigration in attempts to win back voters, only to find that such moves legitimised rather than countered far-right messaging. The result was a continental drift toward more restrictive immigration policies and increasingly militarised border enforcement.

Populism Ascendant

In the political vacuum left by establishment impotence, right leaning parties across Europe surged. The images of boats crossing the Channel were co-opted into a broader populist narrative: one that portrayed elites as feckless, borders as meaningless, and sovereignty as betrayed.

Newspapers and online content seemed to reinforce the narrative that the Centre-Left governments in UK and Europe were backsliding on their commitments to sovereignty. The social media commentators rode that train very effectively, creating a ground swell of distrust at the liberal elite. Everything seemed to be coming to a crescendo of hate and distrust almost as if it were being manipulated.

Mainstream parties, desperate to claw back relevance, mirrored hardline positions, only reinforcing the radical messages they sought to disarm.

This feedback loop deepened division, hardened immigration policies, and militarised borders, all without solving the crisis. Instead, it inflamed nationalism and cast doubt on the credibility of European governance itself. This created the perfect breeding ground for populist parties like Marine Le Pen's National Rally Party in France and Reform UK, led by Nigel Farage, to exploit public dissatisfaction with continued high levels of immigration and obvious government incompetence or collusion to sweep to power in both countries in emergency elections in the Summer of 2026.

Even the much-vaunted EU-Turkey migration pact had eroded, as Ankara used migrant flows as leverage in diplomatic stand-offs, so too did Putin's Russia use migration flow as a weapon of war to overwhelm countries, but also to insert agents to do his bidding.

In hindsight, the Channel crisis was never just about migration. It was about identity, sovereignty, first-world hegemony versus third world revolution, and the inability of Western institutions to adapt quickly. The asylum systems in UK and EU had already collapsed into patchwork politics before most governments acknowledged the scale of the crisis. Strategic unity proved fleeting, and trust, between governments and citizens, between nations and allies, dissolved in waves of cynicism that were about to get much worse.

And the boats?

They just kept coming, packed with silent, wind-battered faces, drifting reminders of a broken system.

From Resentment to Reform: The Farage Effect

The migrant crisis and the rise of two-tier justice weren't isolated concerns; they were symptoms of a deeper malaise eroding the British way of life. Trust in government had collapsed. Not in a single moment, but gradually, over two decades of political cowardice. Successive administrations: Labour, Conservative, Coalition, had chosen convenience over courage, optics over outcomes. They ignored the quiet fury building in the towns, the villages, the working-class estates. The people had been patient. But patience has limits.

Into this cauldron of discontent emerged the so-called populist movements, dismissed by the establishment as dangerous, as simplistic, as vulgar. As if listening to the public were somehow a vice. At the forefront stood Nigel Farage: the most recognisable, most divisive, and arguably most effective political figure of his generation. He was a provocative statesman of disruption who had reshaped the political landscape with Brexit and Reform. Critics called him dangerous. Supporters called him necessary.

Unlike career politicians who stumbled into ideology, Farage discovered his beliefs through rebellion; first against his privileged background, then against the entire political establishment. This rebellion shaped everything that followed: his performative methods, his message, and his charismatic authority and apparently authentic conviction, first as a non-politician and then as leader of his own party.

For most of his life he has wielded enormous influence without formal power, reflecting an outsider personality that thrives on permanent opposition as a perpetual outsider who belonged nowhere completely and therefore could speak for everyone partially.

At Dulwich College, he was the scholarship boy among the wealthy, developing the chip on his shoulder that would fuel decades of anti-establishment rhetoric. In the City, he was the grammar school graduate among Oxbridge elites, successful but never fully accepted.

This marginal status became his greatest asset. Unlike politicians who rose through party hierarchies, Farage never learned the habits of deference and compromise that institutional success requires. He maintained an outsider's clarity of vision, and indifference to conventional wisdom, often expressing the genuine bewilderment felt by the average man and woman in the street of the behaviour of establishment figures and the institutions they claimed to represent.

Farage is a real showman, and possesses an uncanny ability to read crowds, to sense what people are feeling before they fully understand it themselves, to be ahead of the curve on what the real issues are that the country faces. This isn't political calculation; it's brilliant emotional intelligence. He can walk into a room of strangers and immediately identify the shared grievances, the unspoken resentments, the fears that polite society pretends don't exist. He simply tells it like it is, the truth that no-one in power seems to want to hear.

As a brilliant communicator, he can articulate complex emotions in simple language, translate abstract policies into personal stories, and make millions of people feel heard by someone who understands their struggles.

Beneath the showmanship lies genuine conviction and love of country. Though his beliefs have evolved significantly since his early days as a Conservative activist, his opposition to the European Union began as constitutional principle, a belief in parliamentary sovereignty and democratic accountability. Over time, it expanded into a broader critique of globalisation, multiculturalism, and elite governance.

His greatest insight was recognising that the European Union was simultaneously the establishment's greatest achievement and its greatest vulnerability. By forcing mainstream parties to defend an unpopular project, he could expose their disconnection from public opinion.

Farage cultivated his image as the 'man in the pub', approachable, plain-speaking, anti-pretentious, while maintaining the discipline and focus of a professional politician. He has spent his career seeking influence while avoiding responsibility, maximising his ability to criticise while minimising his obligation to govern. This reflects both tactical wisdom and psychological preference. He thrives in opposition because opposition allows for moral clarity without practical compromise. This will be sorely tested in the future as he becomes Prime Minister of Great Britain.

His brief tenure as an MEP demonstrated his strengths and limitations. He was brilliant at exposing the European Parliament's many absurdities but showed little interest in the mundane work of legislation, the careful coalition-building that effective governance requires. He was more effective as destroyer than builder. As Prime Minister, he will require a dedicated team around him to ensure that strategic "big hand, small map" direction gets turned into practical and effective policies and implementation.

Farage's public success has come at personal costs, including strained relationships with former allies, and made him a target for both physical attacks and character assassination from the woke left. The man who built his reputation on authenticity has been forced to live behind security details and careful scheduling, his spontaneity constrained by safety concerns, even more in light of the attempted assassination of President Trump and the assassination in September 2025 of Charlie Kirk the eloquent, American, right-wing, political activist.

This isolation has reinforced his outsider psychology. The more he is attacked by the establishment, the more authentic he appears. His personal sacrifices become evidence of his commitment, his enemies' hatred proof of his effectiveness.

Farage's greatest triumph, the Brexit referendum victory, also created his greatest challenge. Having achieved his life's work, he faced the dilemma of all successful revolutionaries: how to maintain relevance after the revolution succeeds. His attempts to remain politically vital required constant reinvention, moving from EU criticism to immigration concerns to broader cultural issues, but all with a core of true belief.

Farage is essential to democratic discourse and, arguably, dangerous to democratic stability; a democratic stability that many would say was, in reality, undemocratic turgidity.

Nigel Farage has changed British politics permanently, legitimising previously marginal views, forcing mainstream parties to address issues they preferred to ignore. But in doing so, he and other right-wing actors have coarsened political discourse, and contributed to the polarisation that makes democratic compromise increasingly difficult.

His supporters see him as a truth-teller who gave voice to the voiceless. His critics, many of whom are in positions of power and influence on the left of the political spectrum, including the metropolitan elite at the BBC, view him as a demagogue who exploited fears and prejudices for personal gain. The reality is more complex. He is authentic and calculating, principled and opportunistic, democratic, and dangerous. Intelligent and tactically brilliant with an uncanny ability to read political moments.

The power of his core belief in Britain as a sovereign, powerful and successful nation is what would soon sweep him to power as the next Prime Minister and leader of the largest party in Parliament.

It was no surprise, then, that Reform UK was surging. Its message was clear, its momentum undeniable. Reform UK, once dismissed as a fringe movement, now surged in the polls. Its message was simple:

Britain first. Borders matter.

The people have been ignored for too long and now it's time for change.

The BBC Interview (October 2025)

In a BBC Newsnight interview, Farage leaned forward, eyes gleaming. "The elites have failed," he said. "The people are taking back control, not just of borders, but of destiny."

The presenter shifted uncomfortably. The studio lights caught the tension. This wasn't just an interview; it was a reckoning that would rewrite the rules of British politics forever.

Presenter: Nigel Farage, thank you for joining us. Let's start with the NHS. You've said it's broken. What's your plan?

Farage: Let me be absolutely clear: the NHS is broken. It's not the fault of our brilliant frontline staff; it's the fault of decades of mismanagement and political cowardice. Reform UK will cut NHS waiting lists to zero within two years. Challenging? Yes. Achievable? Absolutely.

Presenter: That's a bold claim. How would you do it?

Farage: We'll exempt two million frontline healthcare and social care workers from income tax for three years. That's how you retain talent. If you can't see a GP in three days, a consultant in three weeks, or get an operation in nine weeks, you'll get a voucher for fully funded private treatment. No more waiting. No more excuses.

Presenter: You're also proposing tax relief?

Farage: Yes, 20% tax relief on private healthcare and insurance. We'll review every single NHS private contract to cut waste and bureaucracy. And yes, we'll hold a public inquiry into excess Covid deaths and vaccine harms. The statistics watchdog showed thousands more deaths in 2023 than expected. The public deserves answers to restore confidence in our government.

Presenter: You've mentioned adopting a French-style system?

Farage: Exactly. We'll adopt a French-style healthcare system, where those who can afford it pay in, and those who can't are covered. It's fair, it's efficient, and it works.

Presenter: Let's move to tax and spending. You've called the current tax burden a disgrace.

Farage: The tax burden in Britain is the highest it's been since the Second World War. That's a disgrace. Reform UK will raise the income tax threshold from £12,571 to £20,000. Six million people will stop paying income tax. We'll raise the higher rate threshold to £70,000. We'll scrap stamp duty on homes under £750,000 and abolish inheritance tax for estates under £2 million.

Presenter: What about energy bills and fuel?

Farage: We'll scrap VAT on energy bills, saving households £100 a year. Fuel duty will drop by 20p per litre. VAT will fall from 20% to 18%. That's £240 saved per driver, £300 per household. We'll cut government spending by £50 billion a year, £5 in every £100. And we'll halve the foreign aid budget. Charity begins at home.

Presenter: Turning to the economy, what's your message to small businesses?

Farage: We'll slash corporation tax from 25% to 20% and raise the threshold to £100,000. IR35 rules? Gone. They're strangling freelancers. Business rates for small and medium firms? Scrapped. We'll introduce a 3%

online delivery tax to level the playing field for our high streets.

Presenter: And for entrepreneurs?

Farage: We'll raise the VAT threshold to £120,000 to free small entrepreneurs from red tape. Britain must be a nation of builders, makers, and doers again, not bureaucrats.

Presenter: Let's talk about the environment and rural Britain.

Farage: We all care about the environment, but we care about affordability too. We'll nationalise 50% of key utility companies to stop consumers being ripped off. We'll fast-track brownfield development, especially in the North and coastal areas.

Presenter: What about farming and fishing?

Farage: We'll increase the farming budget to £3 billion, protect hunting and shooting, and rebuild our fish processing industry. Foreign supertrawlers? Banned. We'll launch a coastal fund to regenerate our seaside towns.

Presenter: You've been vocal about Net Zero. What's Reform UK's stance?

Farage: Net Zero is a disaster. It's the wrong policy at the wrong time. We'll abandon all existing carbon emissions targets, saving taxpayers £20 billion a year, every year, for the next 25 years.

Presenter: That's a major reversal. What's the rationale?

Farage: Look, the UK produces just under 1% of global CO_2 emissions. China emits over 30%, the U.S. around 14%, and India's catching up fast. Even if Britain went entirely carbon neutral tomorrow, it wouldn't make a dent in global temperatures. We're bankrupting ourselves for virtue signalling.

Presenter: But climate scientists say CO_2 is driving global warming.

Farage: Yes, CO_2 is a greenhouse gas. But it makes up just 0.04% of the atmosphere. That's forty parts per ten thousand. And yet we're told this tiny fraction is going to end civilisation unless we shut down our economy, ban cars, and live in cold homes. It's absurd.

Presenter: Scientists argue that even small concentrations can have big effects.

Farage: That's the theory. But let's be honest, there's a lot of grant money riding on climate alarmism. If you're a scientist and you say "actually, things aren't that bad," you don't get funding and you get ostracised by the *bien pensant* academic fundamentalists. You don't get headlines. You don't get invited to COP summits in luxury resorts. The whole climate apocalypse narrative has become a tool to keep the public scared and compliant.

Presenter: Are you saying climate change is a scam?

Farage: I'm saying it's been wildly exaggerated. The Intergovernmental Panel on Climate Change has never said billions will die or that civilisation will collapse. That's activist rhetoric, not science. And it's causing real harm. Children are suffering anxiety, businesses are closing, and energy bills are through the roof.

Presenter: So, what's the alternative?

Farage: We will focus on energy security. We'll accelerate North Sea oil and gas licences, restart coal mines with clean tech, and grant shale gas licences for two years. We'll build modular nuclear reactors in Britain and mine lithium domestically. And we'll scrap £10 billion in annual green subsidies. Technology should help us not bankrupt us.

Presenter: But what about the long-term environmental impact?

Farage: We're not against clean air or sensible conservation. But we won't sacrifice British jobs, homes, and sovereignty for a globalist agenda that treats CO_2 like original sin. Reform UK believes in practical solutions not ideological crusades.

Presenter: On education, what changes are you proposing?

Farage: We'll scrap student loan interest and offer two-year university degrees. We'll ban gender ideology and critical race theory in schools. Children will be taught there are two sexes and two genders. That's biology, not politics.

Presenter: That's likely to spark debate.

Farage: Universities that promote cancel culture will face heavy fines. Private schools will get 20% tax relief. We'll introduce home economics and social media safety classes. Violent pupils will be sent to referral units. Smartphones banned in schools under sixteen. And yes, we'll make the curriculum patriotic. Teach the full story of empire, including non-European examples. Balance matters.

Presenter: Defence and veterans, what's your commitment?

Farage: Our Armed Forces deserve better. We'll invest in proper housing, upgrade the Office for Veterans' Affairs to a full department, and fund it with £1 billion a year. Troops and veterans will get free education during and after service. Basic pay will rise; no soldier should earn less than an Amazon worker.

Presenter: Legal protections?

Farage: We'll introduce an Armed Forces Justice Bill to protect our troops from activist lawyers. Defence spending will hit 2.5% by 2027 and 3% by 2030. And we'll recruit 30,000 new full-time soldiers. Britain must be ready.

Presenter: On welfare and pensions, how will you reform the system?

Farage: We'll get two million people back to work. Benefits will be withdrawn after four months of unemployment, or two rejected job offers. PIP assessments will be face-to-face. Medical assessments will be independent.

Presenter: And for pensioners?

Farage: We'll launch a royal commission on social care and close offshore tax loopholes for big care providers.

And we'll remodel the pension system to be cheaper and better, starting young, like Australia.

Presenter: Mr Farage, you've often criticised what you call "The Blob." What exactly would Reform UK do to reform the Civil Service?

Farage: The Blob is real. It's the unelected, unaccountable machinery of government that frustrates delivery, blocks reform and protects its own interests. We've got thousands of statutory consultees who can delay a motorway, a power station, or a business support programme. It's Yes Minister in real life.

We'll introduce a major repeal bill to remove these obstacles at a stroke. That includes scrapping the Office for Budget Responsibility, reforming planning laws, and removing consultation requirements that serve no purpose except delay. We'll bring in senior businesspeople and academics to shake up Whitehall. No more jobs for life. No more hiding behind process.

Presenter: That sounds like a major cultural shift.

Farage: It has to be. Civil servants must remember they serve the government of the day, not their own ideology. If they don't want to work for an elected government, they should resign. Reform UK will enforce the Civil Service Code and make it clear: policy is made by ministers, not mandarins.

Presenter: Let's talk about public sector pensions. You've called them a "Ponzi scheme." What do you mean?

Farage: Public sector pensions are the single biggest ticking time bomb in our government finances. They're unfunded. That means contributions from today's workers are used to pay today's retirees, not saved, or invested. It's a Ponzi scheme, plain and simple. Last year, £1 in every £4 of council tax went to local government pension schemes. Councils shelled out nearly £7 billion in contributions. The average household is paying over £230 a year just to fund these pensions. And the total pensions bill? £4.9 trillion. That's £173,000 per household. It's unsustainable.

Presenter: What would Reform UK do?

Farage: We'll move all new public sector employees onto defined contribution schemes, just like the private sector. No more gold-plated, inflation-linked pensions for life. We'll protect existing entitlements, but going forward, we need fairness. We've got pensions apartheid in this country. Private sector workers get peanuts, while civil servants retire at 60 with a guaranteed income for life.

Presenter: Isn't that politically risky?

Farage: It's politically honest. We're not here to win popularity contests, we're here to fix the country. Reform UK will put everything on the table. If we don't sort this out, it'll bankrupt Britain. Public sector pay and benefits have soared, but productivity has collapsed. It's a catastrophe.

Presenter: How would you handle resistance from unions and civil servants?

Farage: With clarity and courage. We'll make the case directly to the public. Reform UK is already running councils like Kent and Warwickshire, and we've seen the Blob push back hard. But we're not backing down. We were elected to deliver change and that's exactly what we'll do.

Presenter: Crime and policing, what's your approach?

Farage: Crime is out of control. Charging rates are down to 5%. Reform UK will recruit 40,000 new police officers, and we'll drop the requirement for them to have or get a degree. We'll enforce zero-tolerance policing, jail for all violent crimes and knife possession. Stop-and-search will be expanded. Drug possession will mean heavy fines.

Presenter: What about police leadership?

Farage: Police leadership will be reviewed, preferably replaced with military veterans. Diversity roles? Abolished. Police and Crime Commissioners? Reformed or scrapped. Hate crime definitions will require real evidence. Pro-Palestine marches? Banned. We'll create 10,000 new detention places and increase the National Crime Agency's budget.

Presenter: And for young offenders?

Farage: Young offenders will go to high-intensity training camps. And yes, we'll deport child groomers with dual nationality. Enough is enough.

Presenter: Immigration and borders, what's your plan?

Farage: We'll introduce an immigration tax; employers will pay 20% National Insurance for foreign workers.

That's how we incentivise hiring British. We'll leave the European Convention on Human Rights (ECHR). We'll freeze non-essential migration and abolish the Home Office, replacing it with a Department for Immigration.

Presenter: Leaving the European Convention on Human Rights. Isn't that a drastic move?

Farage: It's a necessary one. The ECHR was drafted in the aftermath of World War II to prevent tyranny and protect basic freedoms. But today, it's being used to block deportations, frustrate immigration control, and override British law. We've got foreign criminals citing Article 8, the right to family life, to avoid removal. It's absurd that we can't deport an Albanian criminal: Klevis Disha, who entered the UK illegally, lied about his identity, and was convicted of serious financial crimes. He was stripped of his citizenship. But when the Home Office tried to deport him, a tribunal blocked it. The judge said it would be "unduly harsh" to send the child to Albania with his father allegedly because of his aversion to foreign chicken nuggets. No formal diagnosis, no medical evidence, just a preference for British fast food. That's what stopped a criminal deportation. Ludicrous and unacceptable.

Presenter: But wouldn't leaving the ECHR undermine human rights protections?

Farage: Not at all. We'll replace it with a British Bill of Rights and Responsibilities. One rooted in our common law tradition, Magna Carta, and centuries of liberty. British rights are about freedom from interference, not endless entitlements granted by unelected judges in Strasbourg.

Presenter: What would this new Bill include?

Farage: It would enshrine core liberties, freedom of speech, freedom of assembly, trial by jury, but also responsibilities. If you break the law, you don't get to hide behind human rights. We'll make it clear: rights come with duties. You respect the law, you're protected. You abuse the system, you're out.

Presenter: Would this affect asylum seekers and migrants?

Farage: Yes. Reform UK will introduce a "one in, one out" migration quota. We'll stop illegal crossings and fast-track removals. The ECHR prevents us from doing that. We need to take back control of our borders and our courts. British judges should interpret British law, not defer to Strasbourg.

Presenter: Isn't there a risk of international backlash?

Farage: We're not leaving the Geneva Conventions or abandoning decency. We're saying: Britain governs itself. The ECHR has become a political tool, not a legal safeguard. Reform UK will restore sovereignty, protect genuine rights, and end the farce of criminals dictating our immigration policy.

Presenter: And what about lockdowns and emergency powers?

Farage: Another key point. Our Bill will ban national lockdowns without full parliamentary approval. No more rule by decree. No more unelected advisers shutting down the country. Reform UK stands for liberty, accountability, and common sense.

Presenter: And illegal migration?

Farage: Illegal migrants will be picked up and taken back to France. Foreign criminals will be deported immediately. Student visas will be slashed. No new arrivals will get benefits until they've lived and worked here, contributing to the country for five years. We'll end the abuse. We'll take back control.

Presenter: Brexit and sovereignty, what's left to do?

Farage: We'll axe all 6,700 remaining EU laws. We'll scrap the Windsor Framework. Northern Ireland must not be ruled by Brussels. We'll renegotiate the Brexit trade deal, it's holding us back. Brexit was about freedom. Reform UK will finish the job.

Presenter: Finally, families and culture, what's your vision?

Farage: We'll introduce a marriage tax allowance, no income tax on the first £25,000 for either spouse. We'll frontload benefits for children aged one to four so parents can stay home. We'll promote child-friendly smartphones and launch an inquiry into social media harms.

Presenter: And on media and institutions?

Farage: We'll go after online giants pushing baseless ideology. We'll scrap the TV licence, introduce a Free Speech Bill, and reform the Lords to make it democratic. St George's Day? Bank holiday. Postal voting? Reformed to stop fraud. And we'll quit the WHO unless it's fundamentally restructured. Britain must speak for itself.

Presenter: Scrap the BBC licence fee. Why do you believe that's necessary?

Farage: Because it's outdated, unfair, and fundamentally undemocratic. The licence fee is taxation without representation. People are forced to pay £169.50 a year to fund a broadcaster that many feel no longer reflects their values or priorities. In a world of on-demand streaming, why should anyone be compelled to pay for content they don't watch? The BBC was once a symbol of British excellence, impartial, informative, and proudly national. But today, many people feel it's become a mouthpiece for metropolitan liberalism, obsessed with identity politics, climate alarmism, and a worldview that's alien to vast swathes of the country.

You've got working-class families in the North, pensioners in the Midlands, veterans, small business owners, people who've paid into this country all their lives, being lectured by Oxbridge graduates in Broadcasting House about how they should think, speak, and vote.

The BBC's coverage of Brexit was relentlessly negative. Its reporting on immigration is often one-sided. And its comedy output? It's become a parade of sneering satire aimed at anyone who dares to hold traditional views. Where's the balance? Where's the representation?

People don't mind paying for quality. But they do mind being forced to fund a broadcaster that treats them with contempt. Reform UK says: if the BBC wants to be political, it can be commercial. Let it compete. Its news programming has already been overtaken by the upstart GBNews. Let it earn its audience. No more compulsory licence fee. No more ideological monopoly.

Presenter: It really sounds like you are prepared for war with Labour, Conservative and Lib-Dem parties Mr Farage?

Farage: Absolutely! Whether that be in a few years' time or tomorrow, we are ready.

Chapter 2: Shadows in the Streets

The Failure of Multiculturalism, Rape Gangs, and Two-Tier Britain

By 2024, the shadows that haunted Britain's urban streets were no longer the stuff of paranoid whispers or fringe documentaries. They were real, heavy, and unavoidable. What had once been called "conspiracy" was now revealed, piece by ugly piece, as uncomfortable truth and the public knew it.

The country had been through a quiet betrayal. For decades, a pattern had emerged across English towns and cities, where vulnerable young girls, often from the poorest backgrounds, were preyed upon by organised groups of men, many of South Asian origin. Groomed, raped, and trafficked, they were treated as disposable, and worse, as liars. The very institutions meant to protect them: police forces, social services, local councillors, looked the other way.

In Rotherham, over 1,400 girls were abused while authorities ignored the victims and silenced whistleblowers. In Telford, Rochdale, Oxford, Keighley, and Newcastle, similar patterns unfolded. Year after year, new inquiries were launched, new names emerged, and yet the same systemic failures repeated themselves. The perpetrators were not lone wolves, but part of networks that operated with disturbing impunity. Girls as young as eleven were passed between men, their cries for help buried beneath bureaucracy, political fear, and cowardice.

What began as scandal had curdled into something more insidious: resignation. The public knew. They had seen the reports. They had watched documentaries, read the survivors' testimonies, and heard the anguished pleas of broken parents. Yet little seemed to change. There were no mass arrests. No national reckoning. No purges of the senior officials who had allowed it all to happen. The rot, it seemed, ran too deep.

Multiculturalism, once Britain's proud social experiment, was now spoken of in past tense, with the same nostalgia and bitterness reserved for failed empires. The promise had been one of integration and harmony. Instead, the country had balkanised. Enclaves emerged in every major city, areas where the British state was tolerated at best, and excluded at worst. "Community leaders" acted as unelected gatekeepers. Councils deferred. Police trod lightly. In some districts, Islamic parallel justice systems operated in broad daylight, adjudicating family disputes, honour-based violence, and inheritance, all under the radar of English law.

At first, this was ignored or dismissed as fringe. Then it was excused as cultural sensitivity. By the time politicians admitted it was a problem, it had metastasised into a crisis of authority.

Law-abiding citizens saw the signs but were told not to believe their eyes. They were told diversity was a strength. But when they saw young girls being targeted in public parks or watched entire city blocks transform demographically within a decade, they began to question, quietly, at first, then aloud, then angrily.

And what did they receive in return? Labels.

"Racist."
"Far-right."
"Islamophobic."
"Hateful."

The epithets came quickly, from all angles, media commentators, politicians, online activists, even the police themselves. A father who protested outside a hotel housing migrants was detained for disturbing the peace. A woman who posted on Facebook about local grooming cases was investigated for inciting hatred. These weren't isolated incidents. They were warnings. The constant drip drip drip of negative reports couldn't have been better orchestrated to inflame tensions in the country.

Meanwhile, real crime flourished in the shadows. Grooming gangs didn't go away, they evolved. Social media became the new hunting ground. Messaging apps, encrypted and untraceable, allowed networks to flourish under the radar. Law enforcement, crippled by fear of backlash, devoted more resources to diversity training than undercover operations. New scandals emerged in towns that had once felt safe: Walsall, Oldham, Bradford. The pattern was always the same, and the authorities always surprised.

Policing had changed. Uniforms now bore the colours of every cause, rainbow badges for Pride, green ones for climate justice, slogans for equality, but less and less of the unspoken contract between citizen and state. Officers paraded at festivals and kneeled during protests but were absent when burglaries happened. Victims of assault received crime numbers by phone; those with 'wrong opinions' received actual house calls.

When a pensioner in Swindon was visited by police for reposting an 'offensive meme' on immigration, the story went viral, not just because it was absurd, but because it was familiar. 'Non-crime hate incidents (NCHI)' became a feature of modern British life, an Orwellian label for a nation sliding toward soft authoritarianism. The message was clear: hurt feelings mattered more than broken bones.

It wasn't that there were not enough police resources to properly combat real crime: shoplifting, mobile phone theft, car theft, knife crime, breaking and entering, rather it seems that the Home Office's computer systems reward Chief Constables more for immediate action such as recording of NCHIs and issuance of Crime Incident Numbers than the longer duration and manpower intensive investigation of such crimes, especially when these investigations stood little chance of meaningful convictions due to the apparent bias towards the accused in the criminal justice system.

"It's become like a sick computer game" said one seasoned observer. "Issue 100 NCHI, at 2 points per NCHI to get 200 points; record 50 crime incident numbers, to get 50 points; but assign 4 constables and one detective inspector for 5 days to investigate the break-in of a jewellers say that doesn't lead to a successful conviction, get 100 points for investigating the incident but lose 10 points per constable and 20 points per DI per day – total cost 300 points, overall result: minus100 points. Even if the investigation led to a successful prosecution (score 200 points), the DI would have spent another 2 days preparing his evidence for court and 3 days in court so costing another 100 points, which on top of the -100 scored to begin with, leaves the final score as zero! Is it any wonder that the Police don't seem interested in turning out for real criminal incidents?"

Trust collapsed. People no longer expected justice from the courts or truth from the media. They saw two systems at work, one for them, another for everyone else. While native British citizens endured long NHS queues, newly arrived asylum seekers were escorted into private clinics. While locals faced housing shortages and ex-servicemen slept on the streets, hotels were bought out, entire blocks turned into taxpayer-funded shelters for undocumented migrants. MPs insisted it was all temporary. Locals knew better.

In pubs, on forums, in churches, and among old friends, people spoke more freely. They stopped couching their fears in polite euphemisms. They spoke plainly. They spoke angrily. And increasingly, they spoke of taking things into their own hands.

Community patrols formed in several London boroughs and Manchester as well as towns like Bournemouth; informal, unofficial, unarmed. At first. Parents who no longer trusted schools to protect their daughters took turns escorting them to and from school. WhatsApp groups shared intel on suspicious activity, unfiltered by press or police. In some cases, this brought comfort. In others, it brought confrontation.

The spark always felt just one incident away.

One murder. One miscarriage of justice. One headline too far.

The political class still didn't get it. Safe in their London townhouses and Home Counties retreats, they issued statements and speeches. They told people that "Britain is not racist," that "we must stand together," that "hate has no place here." But the words rang hollow.

Even the Prime Minister Keir Starmer, in a rare moment of unguarded honesty said: "We risk becoming an island of strangers", a quote which echoed Enoch Powell's "Rivers of Blood" speech, and which he very quickly regretted and withdrew.

The victims of grooming gangs weren't invited onto breakfast television. Their stories didn't fit the script. The only acceptable narrative was one of unity, tolerance, and progress, even as the streets told a different story.

The media flailed. Once proud broadsheets became mouthpieces for establishment orthodoxy. Journalists rebranded as activists. Investigations gave way to opinion pieces. Facts bent to fit the narrative. Trust plummeted. Independent media flourished, some reputable, others conspiratorial, all more credible in the public's eye than the BBC or The Guardian.

As the decade reached its midpoint, something shifted. The tone changed. There was no longer just outrage, there was fear. Fear, not of being called names, but of losing control, of the country unravelling.

The government issued new guidance: civil contingency frameworks were updated, counter-extremism operations broadened, police forces quietly rearmed. What were they expecting?

The people already knew.

They felt it in their bones.

The social contract was broken. Justice was unequal. Truth was censored. And while the elites dithered, a storm was brewing beneath the surface. The old Britain, the quiet, decent, tolerant Britain, was beginning to stir. And it was angry.

Peter Dutton wasn't a politician. He didn't run a think tank or write columns in the Guardian. He didn't have a blue tick on social media. He was just an ordinary bloke, the archetypal 'Man on the Clapham Omnibus', who paid his taxes, kept his nose clean, and tried to do the right thing.

Peter was born in 1975 in Chatham, Kent, he grew up in the shadow of the Royal Navy Dockyard, where his grandfather had welded ships during the Second World War. His father had served during the Falklands conflict. The Dutton family embodied three generations of service: military, civic, unquestioning. They believed in Britain not as an abstraction, but as a covenant between citizen and state.

Peter's childhood was shaped by stories. His grandfather's tales of the Blitz when ordinary people showed extraordinary courage. His father's accounts of sailing south in 1982, part of a task force that reminded the world that Britain still mattered. These weren't just family legends, they were moral instruction, lessons in duty, sacrifice, and the quiet pride that came from serving something larger than oneself.

At seventeen, Peter enlisted in the Royal Marines, following a path that seemed as natural as breathing. The Marines gave him structure, purpose, and brotherhood. During his tours in Iraq, he learned that war wasn't heroic, it was bureaucratic, chaotic, and often pointless. But he also learned that ordinary men could do extraordinary things when they trusted each other completely. His squad became his family, bound by shared hardship and mutual dependence.

The defining moment of Peter's life came not in combat, but in a military courtroom in 2008. His best friend, Corporal Jamie Mitchell, was killed by an improvised explosive device during a patrol in Basra. The rules of engagement were complex, contradictory, and written by lawyers who had never heard a shot fired in anger. When Peter's unit responded to the attack, they followed their training, aggressive, decisive, overwhelming. Three insurgents were killed. Months later, Peter found himself as a witness in Jamie's posthumous inquiry and his unit's investigation for excessive force. Military lawyers, backed by human rights activists, dissected every decision, every shot, every moment of a firefight that had lasted less than three minutes. They used words like "proportionality" and "necessity" as if warfare could be regulated like traffic. Peter watched good soldiers, men who had saved lives and completed impossible missions, treated like criminals by people who had never left Whitehall.

The inquiry cleared his unit, but the damage was done. Peter saw how easily courage could be criminalised, how quickly heroes became suspects. The lesson was clear: the system would use you up and then judge you for the methods it had taught you. This wasn't justice, it was betrayal wrapped in legal language.

Peter left the service in 2009, carrying invisible wounds that had nothing to do with PTSD and everything to do with disillusionment. He returned to Chatham to find a town he barely recognised. The naval dockyard had become luxury flats. The high street was half-empty, filled with charity shops and betting parlours. The local comprehensive school, where he had learned respect and discipline, now sent letters home in five languages.

He found a reasonably well-paid job as head of physical security for a financial services organisation in the City of London, a job that required precious few of his military skills of leadership, quick decision-making and ability to function under pressure, but it paid the bills and allowed him and his beautiful wife to buy their house have a daughter and support her when her own children arrived, but there was always something missing, a life without a mission.

Peter's political awakening came gradually, through a series of small betrayals that accumulated into rage.

On a wet Wednesday in August 2022, Peter had a day off while Helen was away seeing her parents. Peter, with nothing better to do, had decided to sit in the public gallery of Chatham Magistrates' Court. He watched the morning's proceedings with growing disbelief. Case after case followed the same predictable path: wicked crimes, hard luck stories, defendants who blamed everything on someone else rather than themselves, suspended sentences, community service orders, final warnings that weren't final.

One defendant in the dock: Jason Murray, 19, from Rochester, had been caught with a knife outside a secondary school. His third offense in eighteen months.

"Mr. Murray," the magistrate adjusted her reading glasses, "while the court takes knife crime very seriously, we must consider your difficult background, your progress in rehabilitation, and the overcrowding crisis in our prison system."

Six months suspended sentence. Anger management course. Electronic tag.

Peter felt his jaw clench. In the row behind him, Mrs. Henderson whispered to her friend: "My nephew got twelve months for growing cannabis in his shed. For personal use."

The next case was called: *Regina v. Mahmood*. The defendant, a 34-year-old asylum seeker, had been found working illegally at a car wash, using false documents. His solicitor, a sharp-suited woman with a posh accent, immediately stood.

"Your Worship, my client has been waiting three years for his asylum claim to be processed. He was attempting to support his family, showing initiative and work ethic that we should celebrate, not criminalise."

Peter watched the magistrate nod sympathetically.

"Indeed. Given the delays in the immigration system, which are not of Mr. Mahmood's making, and his clear desire to contribute to society, I am imposing a conditional discharge."

No fine. No deportation order. No consequences.

During the lunch break, Peter found himself at the coffee cart outside the courthouse next to Murray's mother, a woman in her forties wearing a cleaning company uniform.

"Joke, isn't it?" she said without preamble. "My Jason's got problems, I won't deny it. But that's his third knife offense. When I was his age, you got bird for less."

Peter nodded. "Justice is supposed to be blind, not accommodating of whether you were born into difficult circumstances or had a troubled upbringing or are poor or black or white. It really is two-tier justice these days. If I had done something I'm sure I would have been banged up. System's broken."

"Not broken. Just not for people like us." She stirred sugar into her tea with unnecessary force. "You heard about the grooming case in Medway? Three years it took to get to court. Half the evidence thrown out because of 'procedural errors.' Defendants got community service."

"I heard."

"But my neighbour's son? Posted something stupid on Facebook after a few drinks. Police round his house at six in the morning. He got eighteen months."

She walked away, leaving Peter standing alone with his coffee growing cold in his hands. Through the courthouse windows, he could see the afternoon session beginning: more cases, more suspended sentences, more evidence that justice had become a lottery where the house always won.

That evening, Peter sat at his kitchen table, laptop open, typing his first post on the Reform UK community forum:

"Went to court today. Watched our justice system at work. 'System' is the right word, it's systematic all right. Systematically destroying any faith ordinary people might have left…"

Peter's anger burned inside him.

He watched his elderly neighbour, Mrs. Henderson, wait eight months for a hip replacement while asylum seekers received immediate medical care. He saw his nephew suspended from school for wearing a Help for Heroes wristband because it might 'provoke' other students. He read about soldiers being prosecuted for actions in Northern Ireland decades after the Good Friday Agreement.

Each incident was explained away, budget constraints, sensitivity training, legal necessity. But Peter saw the pattern: a system that privileged everyone except the people who had built and defended it. The social contract he had believed in: serve your country, follow the rules, and be respected, in return, had been quietly cancelled while he was overseas.

The tipping point for Peter came in 2016 during the Brexit referendum. For the first time in years, Peter felt hope. Here was a chance to reject the condescending expertise of people who had never lived in the real world. When he voted Leave, he wasn't just choosing a political position, he was asserting his right to exist, to matter, to have his values count for something, to express his love for his country and concern for what it had become.

Peter had always espoused honour and duty and criticised immigrants for not integrating and contributing to British society. He often felt like a stranger in his own hometown.

Peter's marriage to Helen gave him stability, normalcy, the life he fought to preserve. But while he was posted overseas, she and adapted to new realities, working with immigrant colleagues, sending her daughter to diverse schools, accepting social changes that Peter saw as surrender. Helen had to adapt, to find ways to thrive in the new reality. Peter resisted, wanted to fight for the old values, a set of values that had now gone. This filled Peter with resentment, resentment that grew from private grumbling to conversations in pubs, complaints to family, muttered curses at television news. Then came online engagement, reading blogs, sharing articles, finding others who felt abandoned by mainstream politics.

The COVID lockdowns after 2020 revealed the arbitrary nature of authority, rules that made no sense, enforced by people who exempted themselves. The Black Lives Matter protests showed him that some causes were more equal than others.

He had fought in Iraq, his dad had served in the Falklands, and he understood what service meant: loyalty, sacrifice, honour. He had always voted Conservative, appreciative of Maggie Thatcher having restored pride to Britain, tamed the communist-leaning unions driving the country into the ground and introduced market-led capitalism to the country. Market-led capitalism had given Peter the ability to buy his council house and after he left the Army enabled him to get a well-paid job in the City.

What he saw around him from about 2014 onwards was the slow deterioration of the moral fibre of the country and the rise of inequality.

There had been a time when Peter trusted the system, when he believed the police were on his side, when being British meant something, not something to apologise for. By the mid-2020s, he had watched the country slide into something unrecognisable. Flying the Union Jack or Cross of St George had now been branded as a far-right racist act of micro-aggression – whatever that might be. How did we get here Peter wondered, am I a racist, an extremist? No, I'm a proud, tolerant Englishman who has fought for his country, seen his friends killed on foreign battlefields in wars of questionable legality on the orders of disgraced politicians, and I have had enough of this shit.

Rotherham. Rochdale. Telford. Oxford. Towns across England where hundreds, even thousands, of young white working-class girls had been systematically groomed, raped, and trafficked. The perpetrators were predominantly of Pakistani heritage, and Peter had watched in disbelief as institutions that were supposed to protect those girls turned away. Social workers, councillors, even the police, all paralysed by fear of being labelled racist. The ideology of multiculturalism had trumped justice.

Reports were buried. Whistleblowers silenced. Girls, some as young as eleven, were dismissed as promiscuous or unreliable. Meanwhile, their abusers, known to authorities, continued to operate with impunity. Peter had asked himself: what kind of country allows this? A country that feared offending more than it valued truth.

He'd seen it first as whispers, then as open betrayal. Britain's institutions weren't just failing; they were collapsing under the weight of cowardice. And while this rot festered, politicians told people like Peter to check their privilege. Diversity was strength, they said. But all he saw was division. A society fractured by fear and appeasement.

Peter noticed the hypocrisy everywhere. Those who dared to speak up, parents, journalists, campaigners, were branded bigots. Meanwhile, men responsible for decades of abuse walked the streets. The message was clear: justice had rules, but only for some.

And the police? Peter no longer recognised them. Once a symbol of public service, they had become arbiters of free speech. He recalled a grandmother in Cornwall arrested for misgendering someone online. Or the army veteran visited by police for sharing a meme. Meanwhile, machete-wielding criminals roamed London's streets unchallenged. And the Mayor of London says that crime is down. It was two-tier policing: one law for the well-connected, another for everyone else.

The rage didn't come all at once. It built, quietly, over years. Every time Peter heard of another illegal migrant housed in a hotel while British families waited for housing. Every time he saw someone declared "too anxious" to work, yet healthy enough to protest, party, and post online he became angrier. The benefits system, once a safety net, had become a lifestyle. And Peter, working 40 hours a week, taxed to the hilt, was footing the bill.

He looked to London and saw contempt. Politicians sneered at voters like him. Brexit, which Peter had supported with hope and pride, was ridiculed as a mistake by the elite. They had spent years trying to reverse it. Project Fear had morphed into Project Smear. The working class was called racist, ignorant, manipulated by Russia. Peter knew better. He voted to leave because he believed in Britain. But the people in charge couldn't accept that.

By 2024, Peter had evolved from reluctant voter to active participant. He attended Reform UK meetings, volunteered for campaigns, and began speaking at local events. He discovered he had a talent for articulating the frustrations of ordinary people, not because he was particularly eloquent, but because he was authentic. When he spoke about feeling like a foreigner in his own country, audiences recognised their own experience.

Even when the High Court ruled in 2024 that a woman is an adult human female, Peter had watched as government departments, charities, and councils simply ignored the legal declaration. Girls' toilets remained open to biological men self-identifying as women. Women's shelters were pressured to accept trans women. Biology had become hate speech. The rule of law was no longer binding; it was optional unless you were a tax paying, home owning car driver of course, in which case you could be prosecuted and fined for the very slightest of misdemeanours like putting your bins out a day early. It just didn't seem fair.

By 2025, Peter felt like a foreigner in his own country. His customs were mocked. His patriotism equated with extremism. And yet, he still played by the rules. He worked. He obeyed the law. He believed in fairness. But his patience was fraying.

The Farage BBC Interview

Peter Dutton sat in his living room, the muted glow of the television flickering against the evening walls. The BBC Newsnight logo faded into view and then came the face of Nigel Farage, sharp-eyed and unapologetic. Peter leaned forward instinctively, the old reflexes still intact.

At sixty-one, he was as lean as he'd been in Basra, the years of military discipline etched into his posture and gait. Retirement was supposed to be on the horizon now, a few more years, then long walks with Helen, his beautiful wife of fifty, and afternoons chasing his granddaughter around the garden. Clare, his daughter, had always said he'd mellow with age.

But lately, Peter felt anything but mellow.

The numbers didn't add up. The taxes kept climbing. His pension, earned through decades of service, was now a target for inheritance clawbacks. Groceries cost more. Energy bills spiked. And every time he opened the paper, there was another story about migrants housed in hotels while veterans slept rough.

He glanced at Helen, who was curled up beside him with a book, her presence a quiet balm. But the knot in his chest tightened. Something was wrong with the country. Something was being lost. And as Farage began to speak, Peter felt the old instincts stir, not just frustration, but the kind of cold, tactical clarity that came before action.

Farage (on screen):

"We've lost control of our borders. We've lost control of our laws. And we've lost control of our national identity."

Peter (mutters):

"Damn right we have. It's a bloody free-for-all out there."

Helen (gently):

"Peter, please. You'll give yourself a stroke."

Peter (ignoring her):

"Look at him. He's the only one saying it straight. The rest of them, careerists, cowards. They've let this country rot."

Peter leans forward, remote in hand, turning up the volume. His knuckles whiten.

Farage (on screen):

"When the French let those boats through, they knew exactly what they were doing. It was a diplomatic insult dressed up as humanitarianism."

Peter (snorts):

"Humanitarianism? It's tactical negligence. They're laughing at us, Helen. Macron, Brussels, the whole bloody lot."

Helen (putting her book down):

"You sound like you want to go to war."

Peter (quietly):

"Maybe I do."

Helen looks at him, startled. Peter doesn't meet her gaze. His eyes are fixed on the screen, but something else is moving behind them, something old, disciplined, and dangerous.

Farage (on screen):

"We need a reset. A clean break. A government that puts Britain first."

Peter (under his breath):

"Finally. Someone who gets it."

Helen:

"You used to say politics was a dirty game. That it wasn't worth getting worked up over."

Peter:

"That was before they turned the country into a joke. Before they let criminals walk free and veterans beg for housing."

He stands up abruptly, pacing. The military gait still lives in his stride. Helen watches him, concerned.

Helen:

"Peter, sit down. You're not twenty-five anymore."

Peter (stopping, voice low):

"No. But I remember what twenty-five felt like. I remember what it meant to fix things. Not talk them to death."

He stares out the window. A siren wails faintly in the distance. His jaw tightens.

Farage (on screen):

"We will not be silenced. We will not be intimidated. We will take back our country."

Peter (softly):

"Damn right we will."

Helen (worried):

"Peter…"

Peter (turning to her, suddenly calm):

"I'm fine, love. Just… thinking."

But he's not fine. Something has stirred.

Peter was becoming neither hero nor villain, but something more dangerous: a reasonable man driven to unreasonable conclusions by unreasonable circumstances.

With a sense of mission. He walks to the kitchen, opens a drawer, and stares at a folded map of London. His fingers trace the river. The crossings. The bottlenecks.

Helen stood in the doorway, watching him trace the map, not with curiosity, but with dread. Something in his posture told her this wasn't just reflection. It was reconnaissance.

The International Monetary Fund Bailout Humiliation

The Labour government's failure to rein in public spending or deliver meaningful productivity gains had driven the Treasury to the brink of fiscal exhaustion. The

Chancellor's pen hovered over the latest expenditure report, her knuckles whitening as she gripped the desk. Columns of red ink bled down the page like open wounds. Behind her, the rain streaked the tall windows of Whitehall, each drop ticking away the seconds until the next crisis meeting.

"Minister," an aide whispered, sliding a fresh memo across the desk, "we've... run out of room to borrow. We have prepared for you a communication with the IMF."

The Chancellor didn't look up. She just closed her eyes, as if bracing for an impact that had already happened. How was she going to be able to present a budget in a few weeks when the figures were this bad? All of her projections were based on growing the economy, but the Labour leadership's repeated efforts at modest reform were constantly met with fierce resistance from the extreme left of the party, the unions, and a soul-sucking delay in implementation by the Civil Service. She cast her mind back to the last meeting she attended with union leaders and senior civil servants at the Treasury.

In a cramped committee room, the air had been thick with the smell of instant coffee, damp coats, and nicotine. The lead union negotiator leaned forward, fists thudding on the table. "You cut one job, you'll have a thousand on strike by morning," he growled. Across from them, a junior minister shuffled his notes, his voice trembling as he tried to explain the reforms. Every sentence was drowned out by jeers, the scrape of chairs, and the slow, deliberate sighs of senior civil servants who had no intention of moving faster than the glacial pace they'd perfected, or even at all.

On Wednesday 26th November 2025, the Chancellor put all negative thoughts out of her mind as she stood holding aloft the famous red briefcase outside number 11 Downing Street. As the clackety clack of the photographer's cameras echoed down the street to be met by the booing and jeering of the crowd gathered the other side of the gates onto Whitehall, she climbed into the ministerial Land Rover for the short journey to the House of Commons.

The Commons chamber was a cacophony of noise then eerie silence as she stood at the dispatch box ready to present her second, and even though she didn't know it at the time, her last, and Labour's last budget statement.

The Chancellor's voice cracked as she read the disappointing figures, each one met with a fresh wave of boos and mocking laughter from the opposition benches. By the time she sat down, the pound had already begun to slide. Traders in glass towers across the City stared at their screens, watching sterling's value tumble in real time. Phones rang. Orders barked. In Canary Wharf, a bond trader made the observation that echoed down the trading floor. "This Government has had it. There's no way Labour can come back from this." That sentiment was repeated in every investment bank, insurance company, and financial institution in London. By the time she had sat down, the cost of Government borrowing had rocketed to heights not seen since

November 1981 when 10-year gilt yield reached 16.09%. The television news reporters that evening were in a frenzy of excited speculation about what the Government could do to calm markets. The newspapers the following morning told the same story: '*Britain Bankrupt Again*'.

The disastrous budget of November 2025 was the final straw that culminated in a nationwide general strike in December 2025. The streets of London were a sea of placards and high-vis jackets. Train stations stood silent, their departure boards frozen. Outside hospitals, nurses huddled in the cold, chanting through megaphones. In Downing Street, the Prime Minister watched the live coverage on a muted television, the rhythmic thud of protest drums bleeding through the double glazing.

Britain humiliatingly found itself bankrupt for the second time in living memory.

The Cabinet Room smelled faintly of pine from the half-decorated tree shoved into a corner. In a hastily convened emergency session over Christmas 2025, ministers sat in rumpled suits, their faces pale under the harsh strip lighting. On the speakerphone, the IMF negotiator's voice was calm, almost cheerful, as he let the leaders of The United Kingdom of Great Britain and Northern Ireland know how much the IMF was prepared to lend: "Sixty-seven billion dollars."

The voice on the speakerphone was still talking, smooth, unhurried, almost warm, but Starmer barely heard the words. *Sixty-seven billion dollars.* The number hung in the air.

He stared at the polished table, its surface reflecting the half-decorated Christmas tree in the corner. The baubles trembled faintly in the draft from the old sash windows. *Bankrupt. Again.* The word was a bruise he kept pressing, as if to confirm the pain was real.

Eighteen months! Eighteen bloody months! That was all it had taken. Eighteen months from the euphoria of victory to this, the humiliation of going cap in hand to the IMF. He could almost hear the headlines being written, the late-night monologues sharpening their knives.

We did this. No! S*he* did this! The Chancellor. Her dependence on taxing more and more, her stubborn refusal to cut deeper, to move faster, to face down the unions when it mattered. He'd known she was a liability months ago. He'd told himself it was too soon to sack her, that the optics would be worse than the damage. Now the damage was total, and the optics were catastrophic.

A flicker of anger rose in him, hot and sharp, but it was gone as quickly as it came, replaced by something heavier. Guilt. He'd chosen her. He'd defended her when cruel commentators were calling her 'Rachel from accounts'; when the half-truths and exaggerations on her CV became obvious, when her competence was being questioned. And now the country was paying the price.

The IMF negotiator's voice paused, waiting for a reply.

Starmer's fingers tightened around the arm of his chair. Resignation would be the clean way out he thought. A single, decisive act of contrition. Let someone else inherit the wreckage. He could already picture the statement: *I have always put the country first...*

But the thought curdled. Walking away now would be cowardice dressed as honour. He'd be remembered as the man who won an election and then abandoned ship at the first breach in the hull. No, if he were going to be remembered, it would be as the one who steered the vessel through the storm, even if it meant going down with it.

Could he do it? The question gnawed at him. The markets had turned on him, the unions despised him, his own party was fracturing. Confidence was a currency he no longer held in abundance. But duty: duty was different. Duty didn't require belief. It only required endurance.

He cleared his throat, forcing his voice steady. "Sixty-seven billion," he said into the speakerphone. "Tell me the conditions."

The negotiator began to speak again, the answer came like a blade sliding between his ribs, but Starmer listened this time, every word another stitch in the straitjacket he was about to put on.

The International Monetary Fund rescue package of $67 billion would be contingent upon:

Spending Cuts

- 15% reduction in public sector wages across government departments.

- Total freeze on public sector hiring
- 25% reduction in departmental budgets, including defence and education.
- Closure or privatisation of underperforming state-owned enterprises.
- Means-testing of universal benefits, including child benefit and pension top-ups.

Revenue Measures

- Increase in VAT from 20% to 23%, disproportionately affecting lower-income households.
- Fuel and energy subsidy cuts, raising household bills during winter.
- Capital gains and inheritance tax reforms, targeting middle-class asset holders.

Structural Reforms

- NHS restructuring, with partial outsourcing and introduction of co-payments for non-emergency services.
- Local council consolidation, reducing administrative overhead.
- Mandatory fiscal rule legislation, binding future governments to debt-to-GDP targets.

Political Fallout: Collapse of the Labour Government

In a televised address to the nation at Christmas 2025, Sir Keir Starmer announced the IMF deal offered to the people of the United Kingdom. The optics were brutal: a Labour government forced, yet again, into austerity by international creditors.

Over eighty hard-left backbench MPs rebelled, leaving the Labour party to join their previous leader, Jeremy Corbin in his newly formed party, citing betrayal of core Labour values. In an act of madness and self-harm, like the *Winter of Discontent* in 1979, trade unions called for even more mass strikes. Britain was rudderless and broken, heading into the new year and God knows what.

It was only the amazingly successful work of the police breaking up nascent riots, protests and fire-bomb attacks that seemed to keep a lid on the cauldron of anger bubbling in Britain. The police had been using a predictive AI capability called Crime Data Analytics Project (CDAP) which had been tested over the last three years and was designed to predict crimes up to a week in advance with an accuracy of 90%. The success of the trial immediately brought forward the planned 2028 national roll out of the machine-learning capability with stunning results. Humberside Police reported anticipating 90% of domestic abuse crimes before they occurred, Avon and Somerset Police reduced re-offending rates of suspects released on bail by 87%, other police forces up and down the country were reporting similar success stories. CDAP ingested data from police records, incident logs, geographic crime patters, social services records, and council data, then using a mix of spatiotemporal modelling, anomaly detection and clustering could identify emerging hotspots and behavioural red flags allowing proactive deployment and intervention before the 'incident' occurred.

Some coppers likened it to *Precog* in the Tom Cruise film Minority Report. Civil liberties groups pointed out that intervention in the film was only conducted for cases of pre-meditated murder, whereas CDAP was being used for all forms of crimes, even quite low-level ones. The government lauded the savings in manpower, opposition politicians worried that traditional policing was being replaced by dependency on computers and AI.

The Protest That Ignites the Flame

Peter Dutton had never planned to join a political movement. But when he saw a group of ex-servicemen staging a sit-in outside Parliament, sleeping rough under banners that read "We Served. You Forgot", he felt compelled to act. He brought food, blankets, and eventually his voice. The protest was peaceful but unyielding, his reconnaissance of the roads, pinch-points and bridges had been perfect. They blocked traffic and bridges, refused to disperse, and demanded recognition.

When police moved in to clear the area, Peter stood his ground. His arrest was caught on camera: a former

Royal Marine, handcuffed and defiant, quoting Kipling as he was led away:

> ***"For it's Tommy this, an' Tommy that, an' 'Chuck him out, the brute!'***
>
> ***But it's 'Saviour of 'is country' when the guns begin to shoot."***

The footage went viral. Reform UK seized the moment, reaching out to Peter and offering him a platform, not as a pawn, but as a symbol of principled resistance.

The Broadcast That Shook the Nation

Released without charge, Peter was invited onto 'The Nation Speaks', a combative late-night panel show. He sat opposite a junior Home Office minister and a progressive academic. The debate was meant to be routine. It wasn't.

Peter spoke with quiet fury. He described the protest, the veterans sleeping on concrete, the bureaucratic indifference. When the minister dismissed the protest as "unhelpful optics," Peter leaned in and said:

"You call it optics. I call it betrayal. We didn't fight for this country so it could forget us the moment we hung up our boots."

The studio fell silent. The clip was replayed across social media, and Reform UK capitalised, framing Peter as the conscience of a forgotten Britain.

Reform UK, once a fringe movement, surged in the polls, citing the crisis as proof of establishment failure. Nigel

Farage asked Peter to stand as their candidate in Clapham and Brixton Hill, an area that suffered from social inequalities, cost of living pressures, housing shortages and particular safety issues for women and girls. He agreed, somewhat reluctantly. His campaign was raw and personal. No handlers. No spin. Just Peter, knocking on doors, listening, and speaking from the gut.

He didn't promise miracles. He promised honesty. His slogan: "Service. Sacrifice. Accountability." Veterans rallied behind him. Disillusioned Labour voters crossed over. Even some lifelong Tories admitted they'd never heard a candidate speak with such conviction.

On return to the House of Commons in January 2026, the green benches felt colder than Starmer remembered. The chamber was half empty, yet the air was thick with the smell of betrayal, the kind that didn't need to be spoken aloud. He could see them: the empty seats where loyalists had once sat, now claimed by Reform, or marked with the absence of those who'd declared themselves "independent." The word tasted sour in his mouth.

A million signatures. He'd read the petition in the early hours, the numbers ticking upward relentlessly like a clock counting down to detonation. The public wanted blood, and his was the easiest to spill.

The Speaker's voice droned on, but Starmer's mind was elsewhere, replaying the last terrible eighteen months in jagged fragments:

- *The sacking of Peter Mandelson over his links to Jeffrey Epstein*
- *The resignation of Angela Rayner over a property tax scandal*
- *The Lord Ali freebies scandal*
- *The Corruption Minister resigning over corruption allegations*
- *The Homelessness Minister resigning over making her tenants homeless*
- *The Transport Secretary resigning over a previous undeclared fraud conviction*
- *The Winter Fuel Payments cut and U-turn*
- *The Welfare Bill rebellion*
- *Releasing prisoners early because the jails were full*
- *The furore over inheritance tax on farmers*
- *The ongoing antisemitism in the Labour party*

And now, the final nail in my coffin, bankrupting the country and going cap in hand to the IMF. The bloody IMF bailout! If only it hadn't been for the Chancellor's stubbornness, my own hesitation to act when I should have cut her loose.

He'd told himself it was loyalty, or strategy, or optics. Now he accepted it had been fear; fear of the fight, fear of the headlines, fear of the party tearing itself apart. And in the end, the party had torn itself apart anyway.

His personal ratings were in freefall, the pollsters whispering numbers so low they sounded like misprints. *Never seen before,* they said. He'd broken a record no one wanted to hold.

The decision to resign had come in the quiet hours before dawn, when the weight of it all pressed so hard on his chest he could barely breathe. He'd told himself it was the honourable thing; to admit the loss of moral authority, to step aside before the rot spread further. But part of him knew it was also surrender.

As the Speaker declared the loss of confidence, the words landed like a final verdict.

"Parliament is dissolved. In light of the financial situation, a compressed timescale emergency election will be held on February 5th 2026."

He kept his face still, his hands folded, but inside the thoughts came fast and sharp: *You could have fought harder. You could have been braver. You could have been ruthless when it mattered.*

But the truth was simpler, and crueller. He had been Prime Minister of the United Kingdom for less than two years, and he had left it weaker, poorer, and more divided than he had found it.

The benches emptied and blurred in his tear-filled vision. Keir Starmer, once the man who promised to steady the ship, walked out knowing he'd be remembered as the captain who went down with it, not in a storm, but in a slow, grinding wreck that everyone saw coming.

Labour had swept into power in 2024 with a commanding majority, fuelled by promises of social justice, green investment, and "healing national wounds." But from the outset, it was clear that despite their 14 years in opposition they were totally unprepared for the chaos gripping Britain. The migrant crisis was at its peak, the economy was stagnant, and public services, especially the NHS and police, were visibly collapsing.

As Director of Public Prosecutions between 2008 and 2013, Keir Starmer operated in a realm where right and wrong were ultimately determined by judges and juries, where success depends on methodical preparation, logical argument, and emotional detachment, where complex moral questions could be resolved through careful application of legal principles. Politics offered no such clarity. Systematic, analytical, caution, served him well in the courtroom but was inappropriate in the messier world of electoral politics where gut feel and the ability to read a room were vital.

Starmer's political career was motivated by naïve idealism, a belief that the methodical application of progressive principles could create a more just society, a belief that cynical career politicians had abandoned much earlier in their careers. Starmer maintained misplaced faith in institutions, expertise, and rational discourse as a human rights lawyer representing clients who had been failed by powerful institutions. These cases taught him that injustice often resulted from systemic failures rather than individual malice, that well-intentioned people could perpetuate harm through inaction or ignorance. This understanding shaped his approach to government: change institutions, change outcomes; reform systems, transform lives.

Starmer's commitment to reasonableness, his instinctive preference for compromise over confrontation, evidence over emotion, made him an effective lawyer but a weak politician. His careful weighing of competing arguments looked like indecision to voters who wanted clear leadership. His nuanced positions seemed evasive to people seeking simple answers. His multiple changes of mind on key subjects looked worse than indecision it looked like moral cowardice.

Starmer entered Downing Street carrying enormous expectations from a Labour Party desperate for power after years of electoral defeat. These expectations created psychological pressure that shaped every decision. He felt obligated to prove that moderate, sensible governance could succeed where both Corbynite idealism and Conservative populism had failed.

This burden manifested in over-cautiousness, a reluctance to take bold positions that might vindicate his critics. Instead of using his legal background to craft innovative solutions to complex problems, he fell back on technocratic approaches that satisfied neither reformers nor traditionalists. His famous attention to detail became paralysing perfectionism.

When faced with the Channel migration crisis, Starmer's instinct was to balance compassion and humanitarian concerns with border security, international law with domestic politics. He allowed the UK government to place the rights of illegal immigrants and foreign countries 'chancing their luck' with demands for reparations, and 'return' of lands that were never even theirs to begin with, above those of UK citizens; a failure of leadership and governance for which he was punished at the polls.

Starmer's failure to stop the small boats and investigate the grooming gangs scandal created the impression of incompetence or worse, collusion. The loss of several ministers through various scandals and mounting political pressures left him suffering historically low poll ratings as Prime Minister.

Instead of unity, the government had doubled down on ideology. They criminalised "hate speech" with sweeping new online laws. They expanded diversity quotas in policing and civil service appointments. They introduced gender self-ID without public consultation. Critics, including Labour's own moderates, were ignored.

Meanwhile, the flow of illegal Channel crossings continued, hitting new records monthly. Hotels across Kent, Yorkshire, and the Midlands were commandeered. Local councils rebelled. Protests erupted, then riots.

But it wasn't just the public turning on Labour.

Labour MPs, particularly those from northern, working-class constituencies, began voting against their own government. Some cited grooming scandals and immigration failures; others simply feared for their own safety after constituency offices were vandalised or threatened.

An Emergency General Election was held on Thursday 5th February 2026.

On election night, Peter won his constituency with a 16-point swing. His victory speech was short:

"I don't want chaos. I want decency. Common sense. A nation where a girl can report a rape and be believed. Where truth matters more than ideology. Where working people aren't punished for playing by the rules. I don't seek revolution, I seek restoration."

He remained the Man on the Clapham Omnibus. But in 2026, for the first time in decades, Peter stood up. And millions stood with him.

Across Britain, the political map was redrawn in Reform blue. The party surged to power on a wave of fury and hope, promising to seize back control of the nation's finances, stop the boats dead in the water, restore fairness to a broken system, and rekindle the alliance with Britain's most trusted partner: the United States.

At the centre of it all stood Nigel Farage.

He didn't just win. He detonated the status quo. His victory speech was a declaration of war, not against Brussels alone, but against the bureaucrats, technocrats, ideologues, and cowards who had hollowed out the country from within. The Blob had met its reckoning.

But before the new Prime Minister could even settle into Downing Street, a crisis loomed: the IMF's $67 billion bailout offer, would have shackled Britain to a brutal austerity package that would gut the poorest and cripple the public sector. Accepting it would mean betraying everything Reform stood for.

Farage refused.

Instead, he delivered Reform's counterproposal, bold, unapologetic, and rooted in the party's costed manifesto. Some measures mirrored the IMF's demands. Others went further, targeting wealth and waste where it could be borne. But the core philosophy was radically different: Reform would grow the economy by cutting taxes, not raising them. Stimulate, not suffocate.

The IMF delegation, seasoned economists, sceptical and stern, retreated to deliberate. Reform got to work. Ministries were purged. Spending was audited. The machinery of government began to turn in a new direction.

Seven days later, the verdict came.

The IMF accepted the deal. The full $67 billion would be released, on Reform's terms.

The honeymoon was over. The hard work had begun.

Chapter 3: The Great Reckoning

In January 2026, a lone attacker with military training planted an improvised explosive device under a service vehicle near Parliament. He said that the social media he had been reading on his computer made him do it. The attack was intercepted thanks to the crime prediction tool Crime Data Analytics Project (CDAP), but only narrowly. That same month, another attacker opened fire outside a Home Office building in Croydon. A security officer was killed. MI5 and MI6 warned of coordinated plots, possibly foreign backed, targeting critical infrastructure of power stations, water treatment plants, railway signalling and airports.

The United Kingdom stood on the brink. The riots, once sporadic and localised, had become daily events in cities up and down the country, spurred on by social media online content, some of it seemingly generated from accounts that did not exist; ghosts in the machine or people who knew very well how to hide their activities. Police stations were firebombed in Birmingham and Leeds. In Croydon, mobs attempted to storm the council chambers. In Manchester, gangs looted stores while officers stood back, waiting for 'guidance'.

The Government was paralysed. Labour, elected just two years earlier with a majority of 174, had utterly lost control. Their support base was divided between identity-obsessed activists, disillusioned trade unionists, and middle-class liberals clinging to a fantasy of European reintegration. The Labour government collapsed, not because it lost an election, but because it had lost the country.

Sir Keir Starmer resigned in January 2026, unable to control the country's finances or his own party. In a desperate attempt to maintain order, emergency powers were invoked, but even then, the military was hesitant to act without clear leadership. Public trust had collapsed.

In the months before the February 5th emergency General Election, Labour MPs began turning on their own Government. First in whispers, then in open revolt. The vote of no confidence, when it came, was dramatic. Over 170 Labour MPs voted against the Government removing the government's majority and making a general election impossible to avoid. Many announced they were joining Reform UK, under the leadership of Nigel Farage. Not all were accepted.

Dozens of disillusioned Conservatives followed and were assessed similarly for entry into Reform. The old political divide, Labour vs Tory, had become irrelevant. The public wanted something different, at least that's what the social media channels and focus groups told them. Two-party politics had failed the country for the last thirty or more years. Now it was time to try a more radical approach to government.

Reform ran on a platform of national restoration. No apologies, no half-measures. Mass deportations. Border closures. Withdrawal from the ECHR. Disbanding of "woke" public bodies. A return to law, order, and traditional values. For many, it sounded authoritarian. For millions, it sounded like salvation.

Reform didn't just win the election, they crushed it. No coalition was required. They took over 420 seats. Labour was decimated. The Tories became a rump. The Liberal Democrats vanished entirely.

Nigel Farage walked into Downing Street on February 6th, 2026, with an air of religious zeal, and a mandate unmatched in modern times.

The new government acted immediately.

Once mocked as a gadfly populist, Nigel Farage was suddenly the most powerful man in Britain, promising not just change, but a reckoning. No compromise was offered. The message was clear: thirty years of Tory, Labour and coalition failure would be undone.

And so it began. Just like when Trump had won his second term in office and set about issuing hundreds of Presidential decrees, the Reform government implemented the costed policies and plans that it had been quietly preparing for the last two years.

Police were empowered to quell the riots. Stop and search powers were re-enacted. Detention centres for habitual criminals filled with ne'er-do-wells awaiting trial and harsh judgement. Dozens of NGOs had their charitable status revoked. "Extremist organisations", including several once-mainstream advocacy groups, were banned.

Civil liberties groups protested. So did the EU.

Brussels condemned the UK's "slide into authoritarian nationalism."

Legal challenges were filed in the European Court of Human Rights.

The Reform government responded by formally withdrawing from the ECHR, citing national sovereignty, and establishing a British Bill of Rights and Responsibilities, with a heavy emphasis on the responsibilities of the citizen towards the state and fellow citizens. The UK became the first modern Western European country to do so.

Diplomatic relations with France and Germany soured. Trade negotiations froze. EU member states began imposing new customs checks and visa restrictions on British travellers.

But Reform's support grew. Every attack from abroad, every accusation of "fascism," every media meltdown only bolstered public opinion at home. It seemed it was Britain against the world (*plus ça change*).

The First Salvo: Chagos

Reform's first major act was bold, almost theatrical in its defiance of globalist norms. Following a private conversation with President Trump where Prime Minister Farage asked Trump to rescind his prior acceptance of the handover of the Chagos Islands on security grounds, Reform ordered the immediate reclamation of the Chagos Islands from Mauritius.

Years earlier, the Labour government agreed to transfer sovereignty of the Chagos Islands to Mauritius—an act widely criticized by Chagossian campaigners as appeasement of international pressure rather than a principled stand. Prime Minister Starmer, along with senior ministers, has since been referred to the International Criminal Court for allegedly perpetuating crimes against humanity by failing to guarantee the right of return for displaced islanders.

This post-colonial gesture of the "return" of the territory by Starmer, even agreeing to pay Mauritius for the privilege (a sum originally said to be £3.4 billion but which on more careful analysis by the Taxpayers Alliance turned out to be £47 billion) was theatrically torn up in a televised address. "We do not pay foreign governments to give away strategic British territory," Farage said. "This is the United Kingdom, not a charity. We will not be made to feel guilty about our historical links with slavery and colonisation. We were one of the first civilised nations to stop slavery and expended significant resources and lives over many years stamping it out around the world."

A small Mauritian force stationed near the islands resisted. A brief naval skirmish followed. UK Offshore Patrol Vessels (gunboats) destroyed two of the vessels in the Chagos Maritime Patrol Force. The Mauritian Coast Guard withdrew after their flagship was crippled. The world watched, stunned. China, a subversive backer of Mauritius, threatened to intervene. Farage responded bluntly: "Any Chinese vessel entering a 200-mile radius of British territory around the Chagos Islands will be treated as hostile and sunk."

British nuclear submarines patrolled the Indian Ocean. RAF Typhoon planes were forward deployed to Diego Garcia.

Beijing blinked.

In Britain, crowds cheered. Pundits raged. Parliament was stunned into silence. Europe gasped in horror. But it was done. Great Britain was no longer apologising for itself.

The Camps

Within weeks, holding camps were established in Britain, and the Chagos Islands were transformed by the brilliant men and women of the British Army. Barbed wire went up. Barracks were built. What began as a military base was rapidly expanded into a deportation and processing centre. Reform called it a "necessary deterrent." Critics called it a concentration camp. The truth lay somewhere in between.

All irregular migrants and their families in Britain, including those previously granted asylum or humanitarian protection, saw their status revoked. All migrants convicted of any crime with a custodial sentence, including theft and assault, were also targeted. The numbers were staggering.

Conservative estimates placed the total deportable population at 2.65 million, including:

~1 million illegal immigrants already in the UK.

~600,000 asylum recipients since 2010.

~900,000 family members.

~150,000 immigrants convicted of crimes.

Each was given a choice: deportation to their country of origin, or transfer to Chagos, Rwanda or El Salvador (a site Trump had agreed with Farage could be shared with the US), without further UK support. The vast majority chose the former, showing that most of the migrants were economic migrants rather than people escaping persecution. The very threat of deportation to Chagos was enough deterrent for most to pack their bags and leave Britain of their own accord without needing further processing by Britain.

Many of those who chose to return to their homeland subsequently economically migrated again to other countries in the EU, notably France. For once the shoe was on the other foot between Britain and France. Prime Minister Farage took great delight in playing back to President Macron what he had lectured to Prime Minister Starmer just two years previously and refused to take any of the migrants who had decided to re-settle in France.

Great Britain still upheld its proud tradition of offering refuge to genuine asylum seekers who were fleeing persecution who applied through the proper channels, but the soft-touch, open-door, come one come all policy which had been abused for so long was well and truly over.

The press was banned from the deportation camps area. Drones patrolled the skies. There were rumours of violence, hunger strikes, drownings, escape attempts. But the Government remained firm. "We are not Australia in the 1800s," the Home Secretary said. "We are Britain, and we will no longer be exploited."

Flights and cargo ships ran night and day. The military oversaw operations with typical professional efficiency and courtesy. By the end of 2026, over a million people had either left Britain of their own volition or been processed through Chagos, resulting in an annual saving of £6.6 billion which later reached nearly £14 billion per annum when the camps, hotels and prisons had been emptied of migrants.

Operation Sovereign Borders

Simultaneously came the maritime crackdown.

Borrowing the Australian name, Operation Sovereign Borders empowered the Royal Navy and UK Border Force to intercept and immediately deport any vessel or individual attempting to enter Britain illegally. There were no appeals, no legal loopholes, no delays.

Gunboats patrolled the Channel. Armed personnel boarded dinghies and ferried passengers to waiting deportation ships. Those who resisted were subdued. Well-meaning but misguided liberal 'Lifeboat' NGOs operating in the Channel were declared "hostile participants." Their vessels were seized. Crews were detained and charged with aiding human trafficking.

For the first time in decades, illegal immigration to the UK dropped to near zero.

And like Botany Bay centuries earlier, the Chagos solution became a symbol of imperial-style justice. Brutal. Effective. Unapologetic.

The World Responds

The shockwaves were instant.

Brussels condemned Britain as a rogue state. The European Parliament passed urgent resolutions denouncing Farage's government. France recalled its ambassador. Germany suspended joint military exercises. But it didn't stop there.

In Paris, Marine Le Pen who had been prosecuted in March 2025, imprisoned and barred from seeking office for five years after a politically charged conviction for embezzling €3.2m had her conviction overturned on appeal in January 2026. In a chilling example of the EU's two-tier justice, Christine Lagarde, the President of the European Central Bank was found guilty of criminal negligence over a €403 million payout, yet faced no prison time, no criminal record, and remained in post.

Surfing a tidal wave of working-class anger and middle-class betrayal, Le Pen led the National Rally Party to power in August 2026, just six months after Prime Minister Farage's Reform Party swept into Downing Street. Emmanuel Macron, once the darling of the Euro-liberal elite, had resigned as mass protests and strikes paralysed France. Cities burned. Police mutinied. The Fifth Republic teetered on the brink.

In Berlin, the far-right AfD surged in the polls despite the suspicious deaths of seven of its candidates. The AfD was buoyed by discontent over mass migration, energy chaos, and EU authoritarianism. Elections loomed. European elites panicked.

Britain, far from being isolated, was now simply the first domino.

The Fuse is Lit

In Britain, following the crackdown things stabilised, for a time.

The unexpected benefit of this tough new approach to immigration was that the 'easy option' of recruiting people from abroad to fill jobs such as doctors, nurses, computer programmers, and the like was cut off. Companies had to start training and employing British citizens again. Unemployment fell dramatically. Underground-economy jobs that had previously been done by economic migrants dried up. Over four million British youngsters aged 25 to 34 who had never had a job were now being trained and given jobs and apprenticeships. Tougher assessment criteria in Job Centres and a re-alignment of benefit payments to make sure that work paid more than lounging around on the dole forced another two million workshy into employment.

Taking note of the alarming Russian re-armament initiative of taking students straight from school into factory jobs at the massive Yelabuga plant in Tatarstan to build "Geran-2 Drones" (a Russian version of the Iranian-designed Shahed 136), the UK government offered well paid employment to students 16 years old and above to make anti-drone drones, shells, rockets, anti-tank missiles and light munitions as part of Britain's urgent re-armament action. Little did they realise how important their activity would soon become.

The decision to employ and look after British people first repaid itself in many ways. By the end of 2026, unemployment had fallen to its lowest level in decades, the number of people claiming sickness benefit dropped by 70%, crime on the streets (muggings, robbery, mobile phone theft, and sexual assault) dropped by 90%.

Streets that had once felt lawless began to feel orderly again. The massive loan from the IMF allowed many work programmes to be started simultaneously which allowed repayment of the loan much quicker than the IMF had expected. The press, forced to reckon with its failures, began asking questions it had once dismissed as bigotry. Public support for Reform soared. A sense of purpose returned to the country, but so too did a sense of danger.

Far-left networks, emboldened by foreign backing from the so-called Axis of Evil: Russia, Iran, North Korea and China, began arming groups in Ireland, Germany, even the US. Intelligence services reported links to dissident groups. Universities became recruitment grounds. Cyber-attacks believed to be launched from Russia (attribution was always so difficult) were a common occurrence which the National Cyber Security Centre (NCSC) seemed powerless to stop.

Attacks against critical national infrastructure (CNI) and particularly against Supervisory Control and Data Acquisition (SCADA) systems used extensively in power stations, transport networks and water treatment plants caused widespread problems. These attacks even targeted blood banks and the NHS causing widespread panic and foreboding of a more sinister move towards armed conflict.

While most of the country welcomed the new government's crackdowns, opposition groups hardened. Far-left agitators took to the streets in Bristol, Brighton, and parts of London. Black groups clashed with police, vandalised Reform MP offices, and firebombed buildings in protest. Universities now became battlegrounds.

Three major cities: London, Leicester, and Manchester were rocked by coordinated urban unrest which CDAP had surprisingly failed to predict. Militants attacked power stations. A Reform MP was assassinated in Leeds. Armed police clashed with separatist gangs in Tower Hamlets, where control briefly passed to a self-declared "autonomous zone."

In December 2026, Reform invoked the Civil Emergency Act. Parliament was temporarily suspended, curfews were imposed, and hundreds were arrested.

But while civil order was enforced at home, the threat abroad was growing.

Bombings were attempted in Liverpool, Glasgow, and Cardiff. Two MPs were assassinated in a span of three weeks, both defectors from Labour to Reform. One Reform councillor was found hanging in his garage, an apparent suicide, though few believed it as this had long been the calling card of the Russian GRU, for some time operating with impunity in the UK.

Prime Minister Farage's Government responded with targeted arrests of suspected GRU agents, expulsion of diplomats and a ban on certain political protests sponsored by the so-called "Axis of Evil".

Misguided civil liberties groups cried foul. The police were restructured under military oversight. Special 24x7 courts were established to ensure swift justice. The phrase "fifth column" returned to national vocabulary for the first time in over eighty years.

Yet, even amidst this storm, there was fundamental clarity: the UK would no longer be managed into polite decline but would stand up for itself. The number of attacks and their targets was causing increasing concern in the new government. Something was brewing and it was causing alarm in the higher echelons of the government and military.

The question was no longer if something was about to happen, but when?

PART 2 – FOUNDATIONS CRUMBLE

Chapter 4: Standing Alone Again

In Spring 2027, Russia, watching NATO disintegrate under domestic political fragmentation, seized its moment. In the grey predawn hours of a bitter March morning, Russian armoured columns crossed the borders of Estonia, Latvia, and Lithuania, in a chilling echo of the invasion of Ukraine five years earlier.

Western analysts had seen the signs, but their computer models produced a synthetic consensus suggesting that nothing more would happen, so most dismissed them. NATO summits had issued condemnatory statements but little else. The European Commission had raised concerns. But no one had truly believed that President Putin would dare to make a sudden push into the Baltic states. He did. And the world was caught flat-footed.

Lithuania fell within days. British troops stationed in Estonia suffered heavy casualties. The UK responded with limited air strikes but also faced a new wave of cyberattacks that brought down energy grids and financial systems at home.

The world finally understood that the West's long holiday from history was over.

Within days, Tallinn was under siege. Riga's airport was in flames. Lithuanian military outposts were overrun or encircled. Hybrid warfare, sabotage, cyberattacks, false-flag provocations, had already softened resistance. In a typical act of 'maskirovka' deception, Russia claimed it was protecting "Russian speakers from NATO aggression." The Baltic states, all full NATO members, requested immediate activation of Article 5.

And then came the deafening silence.

The other members of NATO feared responding to the Article 5 request lest they became the next target of Russia's aggression, which, by now, President Putin had threatened to include tactical nuclear attacks against anyone interfering in his "limited military operation".

Only Great Britain had offered any armed response from its 4th Light Brigade Combat Team and #2 Rifles Battlegroup already deployed in Estonia, and a brace of F35B Lightning II Fighter Jets stationed at Amari Air Base.

Completely outnumbered and unsupported by any other ally, the British were forced to accept President Putin's humiliating offer of a temporary ceasefire to allow withdrawal of British troops from the Baltic States in May 2027.

In June, a fuel depot in Wales exploded, confirmed as sabotage by foreign-backed operatives. A water purification plant near Birmingham was also compromised. Intense diplomatic negotiations between UK and EU countries and the rest of NATO resulted in harsh words for Russia but no meaningful action. Russia had been preparing for this war long enough to ride out any sanctions that the West was likely to throw at it. Some European countries flouted the sanctions anyway and continued to supply Russia, believing that they could 'reason with The Bear'.

The final straw came in October 2027, when multiple Russian drones flew over RAF Lakenheath, the home of the largest US fighter operation in Europe, the 48th Fighter Wing, and RAF Fylingdales, home to the Ballistic Missile Early Warning System (BMEWS) and Space Surveillance Network. These were intercepted and destroyed by Quick Reaction Alert (QRA) Typhoon aircraft from RAF Lossiemouth. No Russian strike occurred, but the provocative signal was clear.

Deep in a bunker somewhere outside London, the newly configured War Cabinet was urgently assembled to discuss appropriate and swift action with the UK's previously strongest ally: the United States.

Three days later, without warning or more importantly, without detection, a US-made B61-12 tactical nuclear device, known grimly by RAF pilots as a "Bucket of Sunshine" was used to destroy an abandoned derelict oil rig in the North Sea. The destruction was complete, the effect very visible, the radiation fallout minimal and dispersed by the sea in a matter of days.

The UK government insisted it was just a test of its new tactical nuclear capability launched from one of its twelve recently procured Lockheed Martin F-35A Stealth Fighter Bombers. Clearly this was a warning that Britain could attack Russia with conventional and tactical nuclear weapons without warning or detection if it were provoked further.

Russia remained silent, but the psychological effect was devastating.

Britain had entered a full "Preparation for War" footing.

The economy fell into freefall. Martial law was declared in London, Birmingham, and Glasgow. King Charles and Queen Camilla remained resolutely at Windsor Castle publicly displaying the British Bulldog spirit. The rest of the monarchy were relocated to Canada for their safety.

Parliament, now theoretically relocated to York, functioned in name only.

The TOP SECRET EYES ONLY Contingency Plan "Turnstile 2" which had been hastily updated in 2025-6 from the original Turnstile plan for Central Government War Headquarters (CGWHQ) based at Corsham Wiltshire was put into action. This deployed key government ministers and other Civil and Public Servants to undisclosed SECRET locations to continue the business of running the country in the event of a nuclear exchange.

Armed patrols returned to the streets of Britain, not for war abroad, but to maintain order at home.

All six Type 45 destroyers built between 2003 and 2012 were hastily repaired, rearmed, equipped with the latest DragonFire laser weapon and put to sea to stand as UK's picket-line defence for key targets against ballistic missiles and drone attacks.

The shipyards building the additional four type 45 destroyers and the new Type 83 guided missile destroyer were working 24x7 to get the ships ready for combat. The six Type 26 frigates being built at BAE Systems' shipyards at Govan and Scotstoun in Glasgow were completed in record time and had to have their DragonFire laser weapons installed and commissioned while on duty at sea.

Amidst all this, many ordinary Britons felt something they hadn't in decades: clarity and pride.

Yes, the system had failed. Yes, the cost of restoration had been high. But for the first time, the lies had been swept away. The illusion of liberal progress was gone. In its place stood reality, harsh, but real.

The flabby old Britain had died.

Something new was coming.

The Collapse of European Unity

In Brussels, panic reigned. France's new Government, still reeling from Le Pen's election and internal revolt, hesitated. Germany, divided and leaderless, equivocated. Italy and Spain issued bland statements about "de-escalation." Only Poland, one of the UK's staunchest allies, mobilised with intent.

In London, Prime Minister Farage addressed the nation. His face was grim but resolute. "Britain will honour its commitments," he said. "We will stand with the Baltic peoples against tyranny, even if we must stand alone."

Behind the scenes, relations with EU were falling apart. The UK-France nuclear cooperation treaty, supposedly a keystone of mutual deterrence since 2025, was on the verge of collapse. French diplomats signalled that their new Government had no interest in confronting Russia directly, afraid of the consequences. Rumours swirled that Macron had authorised secret back-channel communications with Moscow before his fall from power, an effort to keep France neutral in any coming conflict.

It wasn't just betrayal. It was cowardice, dressed up as pragmatism.

Britain, isolated once again, began forward deploying nuclear assets. Submarines disappeared into the North Sea and Arctic waters. RAF strategic bombers were seen over Scotland and Iceland. Type 45 destroyers and Type 26 frigates stood off the coast protecting UK strategic assets and airspace. The two UK carriers Prince of Wales and Queen Elizabeth took part in exercises that were aimed at showing force to those that might attack UK including shipping passing through the Gulf and off the South China Sea.

Emergency legislation expanded conscription parameters and industrial production. For the first time since the Cold War, air-raid drills resumed in schools. The UK Emergency Alert System broadcasting on all mobile phone channels was tested to familiarise the population with what might become the last instruction they ever heard from government.

Prime Minister Farage moved decisively to retake the land occupied by Russia in the Balkans and Ukraine. The UK sent expeditionary forces to Estonia and Latvia, Royal Marines and Parachute Regiment units supported by cyber and signals elements. Special Forces teams were already operating deep behind enemy lines, advising resistance units, and coordinating drone strikes.

Across the Channel, the EU held emergency talks. There were tears, raised voices, and walkouts. A French minister reportedly told German officials, "Let les Rosbifs take the brunt, we can't risk Paris and Berlin."

Britain Re-Arms

Britain's military, once hollowed out by decades of cuts dressed up as 'Strategic Defence Reviews', suddenly found itself the last credible power on the continent.

Defence budgets had to quadruple overnight. The Government passed the National Security Recovery Act, fast-tracking munitions production, conversion of factories from peacetime manufacturing to wartime production 24x7 of everything from bullets to shells to drones, aircraft and ship parts.

The streets were quieter now. Deportations to Chagos continued, but public attention had shifted. Volunteers signed up in record numbers. National Service, reintroduced the year before, became a symbol of defiance. Even former critics of Reform, sobered by events, grudgingly admitted the UK's strength.

But tension simmered beneath the surface. Russian agents were active in Britain. Infrastructure attacks increased. In one chilling incident, a cyber-attack took down power in Greater Manchester for 48 hours. Hospitals went dark. Elderly people froze in their homes. The attack was traced to a GRU-controlled botnet, and retaliation was swift. British hackers crippled Moscow's rail systems, gas pumping operations and shut down refineries in Kaliningrad.

An undeclared war was already underway.

The New Iron Curtain

By the Winter of 2027, the Iron Curtain had returned, only this time, it ran through Brussels. The EU, fractured and impotent, had become a bystander. Its military integration projects stalled. Member states looked inward, unwilling to risk full mobilisation. Russia threw its full force into continued attacks in the Baltics supported by North Korean troops.

In a joint press conference, Prime Minister Farage stood beside the Polish President, pledging a new Northern Alliance; a coalition of willing nations committed to resisting Russian imperialism. Denmark, Norway, Ukraine, and the Czech Republic quickly joined. So did the Baltics in exile.

The United States, hamstrung by internal chaos and preparing for a presidential election, offered only limited support. Britain had no choice but to lead.

For many, by the Spring of 2028, the fighting between Russia and the Northern Alliance Coalition which had reached stalemate, was the moment it all became clear. The fantasy of a peaceful, post-national Europe had finally died. The EU had revealed itself as toothless and riven by nationalistic self-interest.

The international order was unravelling. And once again, as in 1940, Britain stood almost alone, poorly armed but determined to catch up, and aware that the next phase would not be cold, but hot.

The war had already begun. We just hadn't admitted it yet.

Chapter 5: America Decides

The summer heat of 2028 hung over the European battlefields like a shroud, but it was nothing compared to the fever pitch of desperation that gripped the corridors of power from Westminster to Washington. What had begun as Putin's "special military operation" three years earlier had metastasized into new President Viktor Fyodor Sokolov's continental cancer that threatened to consume everything the Western world held dear.

The Grinding War

By June 2028, the fighting between Russian forces and the hastily assembled Northern Alliance Coalition had devolved into something that would have been grimly familiar to the Tommys and Doughboys of the Somme. The Coalition of Britain, Poland, Ukraine, Denmark, Norway, Sweden, the Czech Republic, Estonia, Latvia, and Lithuania had managed to halt Russian advances, but at a cost that was unsustainable for very long.

The Baltics were effectively gone. Estonia had fallen in the first weeks of the war, overwhelmed by a combination of Russian mechanised divisions, massive drone attacks, and North Korean "volunteers" whose presence Moscow continued to deny despite overwhelming evidence.

Latvia lasted three months before Riga was encircled by forces that included what intelligence later confirmed were entire brigades of the Korean People's Army. Lithuania held out longest, its capital Vilnius becoming a symbol of resistance before finally succumbing to a siege that left the medieval city a smoking ruin.

Parts of Ukraine had been lost and retaken so many times that maps became meaningless. The industrial heartland of the Donbas had changed hands twelve times in three years, each transfer marked by horrific casualties and the systematic destruction of anything useful to the enemy.

North Korean engineers, working alongside Russian forces, had proven particularly adept at urban warfare, their experience in tunnelling and fortification turning every Ukrainian city into a potential Stalingrad.

Mile upon mile of scarred earth stretched across Eastern Europe, from the new front lines in Poland to the outskirts of what remained of Kyiv, punctuated by the skeletal remains of towns that had once housed families, dreams, and futures. The romance of modern warfare: ***"Dulce et decorum est pro patria mori,"*** if it had ever existed, had been buried beneath months of grinding attrition that consumed men and materiel at an alarming rate.

The drone wars had become a macabre ballet of death orchestrated by an invisible conductor in Moscow, and secretly, Beijing. Each morning brought fresh swarms of unmanned killers buzzing across no man's land like mechanical locusts. Russian Orlan-10s and Lancet kamikaze drones met their Western counterparts in aerial duels that painted the sky with smoke trails and falling debris. But it was the Chinese technology that tipped the balance. The "Dragonfly" surveillance drones provided real-time intelligence to Russian forces with a sophistication that left Alliance commanders reeling, while North Korean "Buzzard" attack drones struck with suicide precision that spoke of years of preparation and Beijing's technological support.

Colonel James Hartwell of the British 3rd Armoured Division would later write in his memoirs: "We lived like moles, emerging only when absolutely necessary. The skies belonged to the machines now, Russian machines, Chinese electronics, North Korean fanaticism, all enveloped in a technological and logistical superiority we couldn't match. Every time we adapted to their tactics, they'd introduce something new from their Eastern allies. It was like fighting the entire Asian continent."

But the most telling sign of the Alliance's desperate position wasn't visible in the trenches, it was glaringly obvious in the empty skies above them and the conspicuous absence of France, Italy, and Germany from active combat operations. The Coalition had scraped together every available fighter jet, reconnaissance aircraft, and tanker from their combined air forces, yet they still couldn't achieve the air superiority that modern warfare demanded. Russian S-400 and S-500 surface-to-air missile systems, upgraded with Chinese quantum radar technology which used entangled photons to detect objects, created deadly bubbles of protected airspace that Alliance pilots simply couldn't penetrate without catastrophic losses.

Tripartite Crisis Meeting - Élysée Palace, Paris, August 2028

As tensions gripped Eastern Europe, the leaders of Britain, France, and Germany convened in an urgent tripartite session beneath the gilded ceilings of the Élysée Palace. What was meant to be a reaffirmation of unity under the Northwood Declaration and Kensington Treaty quickly dissolved into confrontation.

Prime Minister Nigel Farage, flushed with fury, slammed his hand on the polished table.

"Marine, let's not pretend history's hands are clean here. It was Macron who shook hands with Putin behind closed doors, even as the ink dried on Northwood. France knew what was coming and yet chose silence. And you, Alex, will you now claim Merz signed Kensington with his fingers crossed, praying no one would notice his betrayal? You both stand on the graves of our alliances while Russian boots trample through the Baltics!"

Chancellor Alex Müller cleared his throat, his voice low and strained.

"Nigel... I don't dismiss the gravity of what's unfolding. But if we back Britain, Sokolov will retaliate, he's made that clear. Germany faces a winter of darkness. Our factories already whisper of shutdowns. Our citizens are terrified. I cannot sacrifice our nation on the altar of idealism while the taps run dry."

President Marine Le Pen leaned forward, her tone cool but resolute.

"Nigel, I won't defend Macron. His duplicity shamed France, and history will not be kind.
We are under siege, digitally, economically, covertly. Sokolov has rattled the nuclear sabre repeatedly. Yet, despite the risks, I believe France must now play its part, so long as that part does not jeopardize our national survival."

Farage's eyes narrowed.

"Define 'playing your part'. Vague promises won't hold this line."

Le Pen didn't blink.

"We will commit aircraft, munitions, intelligence, everything short of ground troops. As for our nuclear deterrent: if the line is crossed, and this conflict becomes apocalyptic, France will stand fully with the Alliance. At that point, boots on the ground will no longer matter. We'll be staring into the abyss of Mutually Assured Destruction (MAD)."

Farage's voice sharpened.

"MAD only works if the enemy believes you'll actually press the button. I need assurances, not hesitations."

He stood slowly, locking eyes with both leaders.

"Let me be clear. Britain will not flinch. We did not turn away in 1939, and we won't now. If defending Europe requires going nuclear, we will. So, think carefully, both of you: will history record you as allies, or as footnotes in Europe's final chapter?"

The room was heavy with silence. Müller, visibly shaken by the implications, finally nodded.

"Germany will supply what it can. Materiel, intelligence. But not manpower, unless war breaches our borders or crosses the nuclear threshold."

Farage gave no sign of victory. His expression was that of a man carrying the weight of history and waiting for others to shoulder their share.

France: Applause, Anxiety, and Protest

Public Sentiment: The reaffirmation of the treaties drew mixed emotions across France. Many saw Le Pen's statement as a patriotic stand, finally distancing the nation from Macron's perfidious shadow. Editorials in *Le Monde* and *Libération* hailed her commitment to collective security while stressing France's sovereignty.

Military Families & Veterans: Applauded the promise to engage without ground troops, seeing it as a balance between duty and caution.

Student Protests: University squares in Lyon and Toulouse filled with anti-war demonstrations. Placards read: *"Pas de sang pour l'Alliance!"* ("No blood for the Alliance!").

Business Sector: The CAC 40 dipped slightly amid fears of retaliatory cyberattacks and sanctions, especially on French energy assets in Africa.

Germany: Reluctant Endorsement and Stark Realpolitik

Public Discourse: Chancellor Müller's compromise sparked intense debate. Editorials in *Der Spiegel* called his stance "pragmatic, but dangerously isolationist," while *Bild* ran with *"Germany Cannot Stand Alone."*

Industrial Reaction: Leaders from BASF and Siemens welcomed the decision to avoid full military involvement but demanded clarity on gas contingency plans.

Nationalist Backlash: AfD hardliners criticised Müller for "folding to Anglo pressure," while centre-left voices pushed for moral clarity and European solidarity.

Underground Echo Chambers: Far-right forums buzzed with conspiracy theories about EU overreach and British manipulation.

Britain: Resolve, Relief, and Rising Tension

Public Support: Farage's speech was broadcast live, striking chords of wartime resilience. *The Times* praised his Churchillian defiance; *The Guardian* warned against "escalation without consent."

Military Forums: Veterans and serving officers rallied around the rhetoric, with hashtags like #NoRetreat trending.

Energy Anxiety: Concerns grew over grid stability and Russian cyber retaliation, especially among tech and finance sectors in London and Manchester.

Russia - President Sokolov's Fury and Unleashing his Next Move

President Sokolov read reports of the Paris meeting and watched the news feeds from France, Germany, and UK. His reaction was ice-cold fury filtered through strategic calculation.

"Three puppets performing on a stage built by fear. Le Pen, Müller, Farage... I will teach them the price of theatre."

Over the next two weeks, Russia leveraged its energy supplies to hurt Germany through Gazprom announcing, "routine maintenance," halting gas flows to Germany for an indefinite period. Panic buying ensued across Central Europe. In parallel it launched concerted, coordinated cyber ransomware attacks against all three countries striking French airports, British NHS data systems, and German rail networks. In an effort to maximise diplomatic disruption and opprobrium against the Alliance, Russia engaged with India, Brazil, and South Africa to form a new "Eurasian Non-Aligned Compact," subtly undermining what was left of NATO's global sway.

And on the military front, the Alliance noted with alarm the movement of nuclear-capable Iskander missiles near Kaliningrad. Russian state media "accidentally" broadcast footage for 12 seconds before pulling it. The satellite warfare had been even more devastating. In the opening weeks of the conflict, both sides had engaged in an orgy of orbital destruction that had left vast gaps in surveillance capabilities. But here too, deniable Chinese support proved decisive. While Western satellites fell prey to hunter-killer spacecraft launched from Taiyuan and Xichang, Russian and North Korean forces operated under an umbrella of supposedly neutral Chinese reconnaissance assets that provided them with intelligence advantages the Alliance simply couldn't match.

Congressional Contempt and The Freeloading Narrative

Three thousand miles away, in the marble halls of the U.S. Capitol, a different kind of war was raging. The American Congress, with its mercurial moods and parochial interests, had become the unlikely arbiter of Europe's fate. The narrative that dominated congressional debate was as simple as it was damning: Europe had spent forty years building social democracies on America's dime, and now they expected Uncle Sam to bail them out when the bill came due.

Senator Margaret Thornfield of Montana had become the unofficial voice of American isolationism, her folksy delivery masking a razor-sharp intelligence that had made her the most feared debater in the chamber. During a particularly heated session in July, her words cut through the chamber like a blade:

"Mr. Speaker, I'd like someone to explain to me why American taxpayers should bail out countries that have spent forty years building paradise on earth while we've been standing guard duty. They've got universal healthcare that makes our system look like a medieval nightmare. They've got six-week vacations while our folks are lucky to get six days. They retire at between sixty-two and sixty-seven years of age while our seniors work till they drop. Meanwhile, our veterans are sleeping under bridges and our infrastructure is crumbling."

The applause that followed was thunderous and sustained, echoing through C-SPAN broadcasts into living rooms across America where ordinary citizens nodded in agreement. Senator Thornfield continued, her voice rising with righteous indignation:

"The Europeans made their choice. They chose butter over guns, welfare over warfare, university debt forgiveness over military preparedness. They chose to believe that history had ended, that human nature had somehow evolved beyond the need for strength. Now they come crying to Uncle Sam when reality comes knocking? Not with my constituents' money, they don't."

Representative David Kim of California, one of the few remaining voices for interventionism, tried to counter: "Senator, with respect, this isn't about European social policy. This is about preventing an authoritarian alliance: Russia, China, North Korea, Iran, from controlling the world's largest landmass. If this axis succeeds..."

"If this axis succeeds," Thornfield interrupted, her Montana drawl sharpening with each word, "then maybe Europe will finally learn to stand on its own two feet. We're not the world's policeman anymore, Representative Kim. We tried that for seventy years. It didn't work. Every time we've intervened, we've made things worse. Korea - stalemate. Vietnam - disaster. Iraq - catastrophe. Afghanistan - humiliation. Maybe it's time to let the Europeans fight their own wars for once."

The sentiment was echoed across the heartland with a vehemence that surprised even seasoned political observers. From the diners of Ohio to the ranches of Texas, from the factories of Michigan to the truck stops of Arkansas, ordinary Americans watched the European war with a mixture of sympathy and exasperation. They'd seen this movie before, in Kuwait, in Bosnia, in Libya, in Syria. America fights, America bleeds, America pays, and then America gets blamed for whatever goes wrong afterwards.

"Why should we send our boys to die for people who spent decades telling us we were the bad guys?" asked Martha Rodriguez, a diner owner in Phoenix whose son had served three tours in Afghanistan. "They called us warmongers, imperialists, cowboys. Now they want us to save them? Let them figure it out themselves."

The polling numbers were brutal for interventionists. The real-time Cable-Satellite Public Affairs Network (C-SPAN) survey rolling at the bottom of TV screens throughout America showed only 23% of Americans supporting direct military aid to Europe, with 61% explicitly opposed and 16% undecided. Among Republicans, the numbers were even worse, only 18% support, with Tea Party and MAGA voters showing near universal opposition to European entanglement.

Representative David Kim rose slowly from his seat, his expression thoughtful but resolute. The chamber, still vibrating from Thornfield's thunderous applause, grew quieter as his voice cut through with measured conviction.

"Senator Thornfield speaks of history, and it's history we must reckon with. Let me remind you Senator, Kuwait was not a European war, it was about the US's insatiable love of oil. So were both Gulf Wars, all three of which we asked for assistance from Europe and particularly from the UK, and received it. But it wasn't *just* about oil. It was about the preservation of global trade, of international norms, of a world where aggression doesn't go unchecked simply because it serves our national interests."

He paused, eyes scanning the gallery, then continued:

"Afghanistan was born out of trauma, an earnest, if flawed, attempt to root out terrorism after thousands of our fellow American citizens were murdered in 9/11. And let me remind this chamber: it was the *only time* NATO invoked Article 5. Every single member stood with us. The UK did. Germany did. Even France did. Lithuania, Latvia, Estonia, they all did."

Kim's tone sharpened, drawing murmurs of agreement from several members.

"Now compare that with America's deafening silence when the Baltics and Britain begged for Article 5 in the face of clear Russian aggression. We who once demanded loyalty, refused to return it. That isn't just morally compromised, it's strategically blind."

Thornfield shifted uncomfortably, but Kim pressed on.

"Let's not pretend this is about welfare states or vacation days. This is about the biggest authoritarian bloc since the Nazis and Axis Powers joining forces to reshape the global order, to crush dissent, rewrite borders, and weaponize economic leverage. If we abandon Europe, we don't just abandon allies, we abandon every principle that once made us leaders of the free world."

The chamber was now fully engaged, leaning in.

"America's greatest mistakes came not when we acted, but when we hesitated. Pearl Harbor. Rwanda. Ukraine. We need wisdom, yes. We need limits. But we also need courage. History will not forgive us for sitting out a second time."

The words reverberated beyond the chamber, bleeding into news headlines and primetime analysis. On cable networks and livestreams, pundits called it Kim's finest hour. In households where memories of war shared space with hope for peace, something stirred.

Thornfield had spoken to fear. Kim had answered with duty.

The scrolling survey figures on C-SPAN showed a remarkable reversal. Now, just 44% of Americans opposed direct military aid to Europe and 45% explicitly supported it with 11% undecided. Amongst Republicans and MAGA voters there was now near-universal support for European engagement.

The Special Relationship Under Strain

In this atmosphere of congressional hostility, angst and confusion, the relationship between Prime Minister Nigel Farage and President Donald Trump had become

Britain's last lifeline. The two men had developed an unlikely friendship based on mutual recognition of their outsider status in their respective political establishments. Both had risen to power by promising to upend the old order; now they found themselves managing its potential collapse.

Farage's path to Downing Street had been as unlikely as it was dramatic. The complete failure of Sir Keir Starmer's Labour government, brought down by a series of immigration and economic crises, unequal justice, industrial strikes, a disastrous energy policy that left Britain dependent on Russian gas, and finally an embarrassing court case, had triggered an emergency general election in February 2026. The British people, faced with rolling blackouts, food shortages, rioting, and a government that seemed incapable of governing, had turned to the one politician who had consistently warned about uncontrolled immigration, European weakness, and dependence.

On taking power, one of Prime Minister Farage's emergency acts had been rearmament. A prescient decision that would prove crucial when war finally came.

But even Farage's foresight couldn't overcome the fundamental reality: Britain alone lacked the industrial capacity to sustain a modern war. The factories that had once produced Spitfires and Hurricanes had long since been converted to shopping centres and car parks. The shipyards that had built the Grand Fleet existed only in history books. Europe was in no better position to defend itself. Without American support, Britain's war effort would collapse within months and so would the freedom of the whole of Europe.

The briefing document had appeared on the President's desk at precisely 0600, as always. No aide claimed authorship, no department took credit, yet its analysis was invariably flawless. Inside the intelligence community, they called it 'The Oracle,' though no one could explain how it operated or where its insights originated. The situation looked very bad indeed.

Conversations between Prime Minister Farage and President Trump had taken on an increasingly desperate tone as the summer wore on. The secure line between Downing Street and the White House crackled with the tension of two leaders watching their world burn while political systems constrained their ability to respond.

"Donald, I need you to understand something," Farage had said during a particularly frank call, in early August 2028, his usually measured tones carrying an edge of raw emotion. "We're not asking for charity here. We're not asking America to fight our battles for us. But we need more F-35s, those AWACS aircraft, those satellite feeds. Without them, we're fighting blind against an enemy that, thanks to China pretending to sit on the sidelines, has eyes everywhere."

Trump's response was characteristically blunt: "Nigel, you know I want to help. You know that. But Congress is breathing down my neck like a pack of wolves. They're asking me why we should give you planes when half of Europe won't even fight. Why should Ohio steelworkers pay for British defence when Germans and French are basically surrendering without a shot?"

"Because, Donald," Farage replied, his voice heavy with history and barely controlled anger, "this isn't about fiscal responsibility anymore. This is about survival. In 1940, Britain stood alone against fascism. We held the line while America decided whether freedom was worth fighting for. We're holding that line again, but this time the enemy has nuclear weapons and the support of the world's second-largest economy. Besides, I have finally convinced Le Pen and Müller to join the Alliance to supply materiel if not men."

The parallel wasn't lost on Trump. His grandfather had lived through World War II, had told him stories about the Blitz, about British resolve in the face of impossible odds. But 2028 wasn't 1940, and Congress wasn't the America of FDR.

"The difference," Trump said quietly, his voice heavy with the weight of political reality, "is that Hitler was stupid enough to encourage Japan to attack Pearl Harbor and declare war on America. Sokolov's not going to make that mistake. He's going to keep pushing just in Europe, keep grinding, until he owns everything from Lisbon to Vladivostok, and he's going to do it without giving me a *casus belli* that Congress can't ignore."

"Then find another reason," Farage said, desperation creeping into his voice. "Because if you don't, there won't be a Europe left to save. The Baltics are gone, Donald. Gone. Estonia, Latvia, Lithuania, they don't exist as independent nations anymore. North Korean troops are marching through Tallinn wearing Russian uniforms. How long before it's Warsaw? How long before it's London?"

"I know, Nigel. I know." Trump's voice carried a weariness that his public persona never revealed. "But knowing and being able to act are two different things. I've got eighteen weeks left in office. Eighteen weeks to either save Western civilization or watch it die while Congress debates appropriations bills."

The Shadow of 2025: Operation Midnight Hammer

The spectre haunting every conversation between the two leaders was the memory of Trump's last major military action: the June 2025 bombing of Iran's nuclear facilities. The operation code-named "Midnight Hammer," had been Trump's response to intelligence indicating that Iran was on the verge of perfecting a nuclear weapon using enriched uranium.

The decision had been agonising. Intelligence suggested that Iran was perhaps six months from producing nuclear weapons, weapons that Tehran had repeatedly threatened to use against Israel and potentially American bases in the region. But attacking Iran meant risking a wider Middle Eastern war that could spiral into global conflict.

Pentagon strategists had identified seventeen separate facilities across Iran involved in nuclear weapons development, from the obvious targets like Natanz and Fordow to the hidden laboratories buried beneath

Tehran University and the enrichment centrifuges concealed in the basement of a mosque in Qom.

"What are the chances we get everything?" Trump had asked.

"Seventy-five percent," the Pentagon chief replied. "Maybe eighty. But Mr. President, these facilities are deep and hardened. Some of the centrifuge halls are two hundred feet underground, protected by reinforced concrete and steel. We're going to need nuclear bunker-busters to guarantee complete destruction."

"Nuclear weapons? Against a non-nuclear power?"

"Low yield tactical weapons, sir. The only things capable of penetrating that deep. The alternative is conventional weapons that might not complete the job."

In the end, Trump had chosen conventional weapons, a decision that would haunt him ever since.

The bombing had been a masterpiece of military precision. B-2 Spirit bombers, launched from Whiteman Air Force Base in Missouri, had delivered fifty thousand pounds of GBU-57 Massive Ordnance Penetrator bombs with pinpoint accuracy. The primary facilities at Natanz and Fordow had been obliterated, their underground laboratories turned into radioactive tombs.

But Iran's nuclear program had been more dispersed than American intelligence realised. While the major facilities burned, Iranian scientists had managed to evacuate critical equipment and, most importantly, nearly one metric tonne of 60% enriched uranium to secret facilities that the Americans never found. The bombing had set back Iran's nuclear program by perhaps 3 years, enough time for Tehran to rebuild in hidden locations that were even more secure than the originals.

By December 2028, CIA analysts estimated that Iran possessed enough 90% enriched fissile material for ten nuclear weapons and the technical expertise to build them within weeks. The 2025 bombing hadn't prevented Iranian nuclear capability; it had simply driven it underground and made the eventual weapons program more dangerous and less detectable.

"We should have used the nukes," Trump had told his inner circle during a grim NSC meeting in September 2028. "We should have made sure we got everything. Now they're going to have the bomb anyway, and they're going to remember who tried to stop them."

Donald Trump's approach to international relations was just like a Manhattan real estate deal, everything was negotiable, every relationship temporary, every agreement contingent on immediate benefit. This transactional worldview, forged through decades of property development where today's enemy becomes tomorrow's partner based solely on mutual advantage, fundamentally shaped his approach to global leadership in ways that traditional foreign policy establishments never understood.

Unlike career politicians who view international relations through ideological or institutional frameworks, Trump sees only deals to be made or broken. NATO isn't a sacred alliance forged in blood and shared values; it's a protection racket where Europe freeloads off American taxpayers. The UN isn't a forum for global cooperation; it's a talking shop that constrains American sovereignty. Trade agreements aren't diplomatic achievements; they're either winning or losing propositions for American workers.

This psychological framework made him both unpredictable and oddly consistent. Critics called his foreign policy chaotic, but there was an internal logic: America first, always, and everywhere, with relationships valued only insofar as they delivered measurable benefits to American interests as Trump defined them.

His time in entertainment and media created an instinctive understanding of spectacle, ratings, and audience engagement. He grasped intuitively that foreign policy, like television, is ultimately about capturing and holding attention – the need to dominate the news cycle. His approach to summit meetings, trade negotiations, and military deployments consistently prioritised dramatic impact over diplomatic subtlety. Demonstrating action and engagement to voters kept his ratings higher than presidents before him who agonised over their decisions. Framing everything as "America first" kept his domestic audience content and his adversaries and allies alike off balance.

Surrounded by advisors who often feared his temper more than they respected his judgment, Trump relied increasingly on his own instincts and a shrinking circle of family members and longtime associates.......and the morning Oracle briefing paper. This isolation intensified as traditional Republican foreign policy establishment figures were purged or resigned, military leaders who had provided restraint during his first term were replaced with loyalists more willing to implement his vision without bureaucratic resistance. The result was a foreign policy apparatus that amplified rather than moderated Trump's impulses and fears. So sure was he that he could solve the Ukraine-Russia war within weeks of coming to power, so sure that he could convince Putin to cease the attacks just from a one-to-one, leader to leader conversation, that the shock of failure, of being led up the garden path by Putin, struck hard.

As presidential decree after presidential decree was overturned or challenged in the courts, Trump found himself increasingly frustrated by the slowness of bureaucracy. He wanted to secure peace, he wanted to leave a legacy he could be proud of when he left office, a Nobel Peace Prize to cherish, but this formidable dealmaker, who had spent his life walking away from bad negotiations, found himself trapped in a situation where walking away might mean walking into nuclear war.

What he needed now was a sounding board he could trust implicitly to tell him the truth. Maybe Nigel had been this all along?

Chapter 6: The Tipping Point

Five Crises Converge

As autumn approached, neither Trump nor Farage realised how prophetic their conversations had been. The world was about to provide Trump with not just one reason for war, but five, each more compelling than the last, each building on the others to create an unstoppable momentum toward global conflict.

The convergence wasn't accidental. In the underground command centres of Tehran, Revolutionary Guard strategists had spent three years preparing for this moment, coordinating with Chinese intelligence services and North Korean military advisors to create what they called "The Perfect Storm", a simultaneous eruption of crises that would overwhelm Western decision-making capabilities and force America into a multi-front war it couldn't win.

Crisis One: The Spider's Web Spreads - Iran's Masterpiece of Proxy Warfare

Operation Moharram, named for the sacred month of mourning, was their masterpiece of asymmetric warfare, coordinated with Chinese intelligence and North Korean tactical expertise to create maximum chaos across multiple theatres simultaneously.

The beauty of the plan lay in its sophisticated simplicity. Rather than confront American or Israeli power directly, Iran would activate its "Axis of Resistance" across multiple fronts, forcing their enemies to fight on a dozen different battlefields at once while Chinese cyber warfare and North Korean special forces operations created additional pressure points. Each proxy had been carefully armed, trained, and positioned to maximise chaos while maintaining Tehran's plausible deniability.

General Qasem Bagheri, chief of staff of Iran's armed forces, explained the strategy to his inner circle during a meeting attended by Chinese Colonel Li Wei and North Korean General Kim Jong-su: "The Americans think in terms of overwhelming force; shock and awe, they call it. But overwhelming force is useless when applied to shadows. We will be everywhere and nowhere. We will strike from Lebanon and Yemen, from Iraq and Syria, from Gaza and the West Bank. Our Chinese friends will blind their satellites while our Korean comrades demonstrate what true revolutionary fervour looks like in urban combat. Let them try to bomb shadows while their technology fails and their allies abandon them."

The activation began on October 15th, 2028, with a seemingly minor incident that Western intelligence initially dismissed as routine harassment. Hezbollah fighters in southern Lebanon launched a coordinated barrage of Katyusha rockets at Israeli settlements in the Galilee. Simultaneously, Houthi forces in Yemen targeted Saudi oil facilities with long range drones equipped with Chinese navigation systems. In Iraq, Iranian backed militias struck American bases with precision guided missiles that bore the unmistakable signature of North Korean engineering.

But the most ominous development occurred in Gaza, where Hamas cells began their final preparations for what would become known as the Second October Massacre. Chinese trained Hamas engineers had spent two years constructing an underground network that made their previous tunnel systems look like children's sandcastles. North Korean advisors had taught Hamas fighters urban warfare tactics perfected in the ruins of Seoul during the Korean War. And Iranian weapons masters had supplied them with explosives and firearms that could turn civilian areas into killing fields.

The timing was not coincidental. Iranian intelligence, supported by Chinese satellite reconnaissance and North Korean cyber penetration of Israeli systems, had detected increased activity around Israeli nuclear facilities, suggesting an imminent pre-emptive strike on Iran's hidden uranium enrichment centres. Rather than wait to be attacked, Tehran chose to attack first, but in a way that would make retaliation impossible to calibrate.

Crisis Two: Hamas's Calculated Barbarism and Israel's Response

The Hamas attack that began at dawn on October 23rd, 2028, would later be remembered as the moment when the last vestiges of civilised warfare died. Unlike the 2023 October 7th attack, which had caught Israel by surprise, this assault was launched with full knowledge that it would provoke massive retaliation. That was precisely the point.

Hamas leader Yahya Sinwar had spent five years planning what he privately called "The Final

Provocation," working closely with Iranian Revolutionary Guard advisors and Chinese psychological warfare specialists. His logic was coldly calculated: only by provoking Israel into a genocidal response could Hamas expose the true nature of the Zionist project to the world. Only by sacrificing Gaza could Palestine be saved. Only by forcing Israel to abandon all pretence of moral restraint could the global community be shocked into action.

The attack began with a massive barrage of rockets designed to overwhelm Israel's Iron Dome system. These weren't the crude Qassam rockets of previous years, these were precision guided missiles manufactured in North Korean factories and smuggled through Iranian networks, each one programmed to strike specific targets with devastating accuracy. As Israeli air defences scrambled to intercept the incoming missiles, Hamas commandos emerged from a network of tunnels that represented one of the greatest engineering achievements in terrorist history.

These weren't the crude smuggling tunnels of previous years, these were military grade underground highways, reinforced with Chinese manufactured concrete and equipped with ventilation systems, communication networks, and weapons caches that could sustain months of siege warfare. The tunnels stretched not just under Gaza, but beneath the Israeli border itself, allowing Hamas fighters to emerge behind Israeli defensive lines in a coordinated assault that caught the IDF completely off guard.

The commandos who emerged from these tunnels had been trained specifically for maximum psychological impact by a joint team of Iranian Revolutionary Guards, Chinese special forces, and North Korean infiltration specialists. They carried high-definition cameras to broadcast their atrocities in real-time. They had been given detailed psychological profiles of their targets, designed to inflict maximum trauma on the Israeli psyche. They had been instructed to target civilians exclusively, to commit acts so heinous that the international community would have no choice but to take notice when Israel responded in kind.

In the kibbutz of Nir Oz, Hamas fighters methodically executed entire families, broadcasting the murders live on social media platforms that Chinese hackers had ensured would remain operational despite Israeli attempts to cut communications. The killers spoke directly to their cameras, explaining in perfect English, learned from Chinese language instructors, exactly why each victim had to die.

In Sderot, they herded civilians into the town square and detonated suicide vests in their midst, but not before forcing their victims to call relatives and describe what was about to happen to them. The psychological warfare aspects of the operation bore all the hallmarks of Chinese military doctrine, designed to break the enemy's will to fight rather than simply inflict casualties.

In Ashkelon, they targeted a children's hospital, moving from room to room with methodical brutality that was filmed and uploaded in real-time. The attackers made no attempt to justify their actions, instead, they revelled in them, challenging Israel to respond with equal barbarity.

The images that flooded global media were beyond anything seen in modern warfare. Children's bodies burned beyond recognition. Pregnant women disembowelled with ritualistic precision learned from Islamic State manuals. Elderly Holocaust survivors tortured with methods specifically designed to evoke historical trauma and break the Israeli spirit.

But the most shocking element was Hamas's own documentation of their crimes. Unlike previous terrorist attacks, which organisations typically tried to justify or minimise, Hamas fighters proudly filmed their atrocities and broadcast them globally using Chinese provided satellite uplinks that Israeli cyber warfare couldn't disrupt. They wanted the world to see. They wanted Israel to see. They wanted to provoke a response so massive, so disproportionate, that it would finally expose the true nature of the conflict to a global audience that had grown comfortable with the status quo.

By sunset on October 23rd, over 4,200 Israeli civilians were dead, with another 800 missing and presumed captured. The psychological trauma was immeasurable; entire communities had been wiped out, their final moments broadcast live to the world. But for Hamas leadership, hiding in their Chinese engineered bunkers beneath Gaza City, the operation was proceeding exactly as planned.

Crisis Three: Israel's Existential Expansion and Death of International Law

Prime Minister Benjamin Netanyahu's response to the October 23rd massacre would define his legacy and transform the nature of international law forever. Facing the worst attack on Jewish civilians since the Holocaust, and with his own political survival hanging in the balance against war crimes charges in the International Criminal Court, Netanyahu made a decision that would echo through history.

"They want to see what hell looks like," he told his war cabinet on the evening of October 23rd, his voice carrying the weight of eight decades of Jewish trauma. "We're going to show them. We're going to show them what happens when you awaken the Jewish dragon. We're going to make sure this never happens again, not to our children, not to our grandchildren, not to Jews anywhere, ever again."

The response was immediate and unprecedented. Operation Magen Shamayim (Shield of Heaven) began at 3:00 AM on October 24th with the largest aerial bombardment since World War II. But this wasn't the surgical precision that had characterised previous Israeli operations; this was industrial scale destruction designed to eliminate not just Hamas, but the entire infrastructure that had allowed Hamas to exist.

Every building in Gaza taller than two stories was targeted for destruction. Every mosque, every school, every hospital that Israeli intelligence suggested might house Hamas fighters or weapons was obliterated. The precision guided munitions that had characterised previous Israeli operations were abandoned in favour of massive bunker-buster bombs designed to destroy entire city blocks and the tunnel networks beneath them.

"We tried precision," Defence Minister Yoav Gallant explained to foreign correspondents who questioned the scale of destruction. "We tried surgical strikes. We tried minimising civilian casualties. And what did it get us? October 23rd. This time, we're not leaving anything to chance. This time, we're making sure the job gets finished."

The stated objective was the complete elimination of Hamas as a military and political organisation. The unstated objective, the one that Netanyahu could never publicly acknowledge but which everyone understood, was the depopulation of Gaza itself. If Palestinians wanted to use their children as human shields, then Israel would remove the children along with the shields. If international law protected terrorists, then international law was meaningless.

The bombing continued for eight weeks. When the dust settled, Gaza City was gone. Literally gone. Satellite imagery showed a landscape that resembled the surface of the moon, craters where buildings had stood, rubble where streets had run, silence where two million people had once lived. The tunnel network that Hamas had spent decades constructing had been turned into a subterranean graveyard, sealed with bunker-buster bombs that ensured no one would ever emerge alive.

International law, which had governed warfare since the Geneva Conventions, crumbled under the weight of Israeli necessity and Palestinian provocation. When the International Criminal Court issued arrest warrants for Netanyahu and his defence minister, Israel simply withdrew from the Rome Statute and declared the court illegitimate. When the UN Security Council demanded an immediate ceasefire, Israel ignored it, pointing out that the UN had failed to prevent October 23rd and therefore had no moral authority to limit Israel's response.

When European allies threatened sanctions, Netanyahu responded with a statement that chilled diplomatic observers worldwide and drew immediate comparisons to the darkest chapters of European history:

"For seventy-five years, the world has demanded that Jews go quietly to their deaths. That Jews accept terrorism as the price of existence. That Jews live forever as victims, forever vulnerable, forever dependent on the mercy of our enemies. That era is over. We will do whatever is necessary to ensure that no Jewish child ever again faces the choice between conversion and death, between submission and slaughter. If that means we must become the monsters you already believe us to be, so be it. If international law protects our murderers, then international law is dead. We choose survival over your approval."

The Palestinian death toll would never be accurately calculated. Hamas had deliberately co-located military assets with civilian populations, making precise casualty assessment impossible. Israeli estimates put the figure at 400,000 dead. Palestinian sources claimed over 1.2 million. International observers, horrified by the scale of destruction and unable to access the devastated territory, largely gave up trying to count.

But the most significant casualty wasn't Palestinian, it was the international order itself. By openly abandoning the laws of war in pursuit of national survival, Israel had set a precedent that other nations would soon follow. If survival was at stake, anything was permissible. If the enemy used human shields, then the shields could be destroyed along with the targets. If international law protected terrorists, then international law was void.

The parallels to Nazi Germany's doctrine of Lebensraum were uncomfortable but unmistakable. Like Hitler's Germany, Israel was using the pretext of national security to justify territorial expansion. Like the Third Reich, Israel was arguing that the rules that applied to other nations did not apply to them because their situation was unique. And like Nazi ideology, Israeli policy was beginning to suggest that some peoples deserved lebensraum while others did not.

With Gaza reduced to rubble and Hamas eliminated as an effective fighting force, Netanyahu faced a choice that would define Israel's future. The traditional approach would have been to withdraw, allowing international aid agencies to begin reconstruction under some form of international supervision. Instead, Netanyahu chose permanent expansion.

"We have learned," he announced to the Knesset on December 15th, 2028, "that peace through withdrawal is an illusion that has cost us rivers of Jewish blood. Every territory we have evacuated has become a launching pad for attacks against our people. We evacuated Lebanon and got Hezbollah. We evacuated Gaza in 2005 and got October 7th, 2023. We showed restraint after October 7th, 2023, and got October 23rd, 2028. This cycle ends now. This madness ends now."

The Knesset voted 78 to 42 to formally annex Gaza and establish what Netanyahu called "security settlements" throughout the territory; permanent military colonies that would ensure no future terrorist infrastructure could take root. When international critics compared this to Hitler's concept of Lebensraum, living space acquired through conquest, Netanyahu's response was defiant and chilling:

"Hitler sought living space for a master race. We seek survival space for an endangered people. Hitler murdered civilians to steal their land. We are reclaiming land from which civilians were used to murder our children. If the world cannot distinguish between genocide and self-defence, then the world has lost its moral compass, not Israel. And if the world wants to compare us to Nazis for refusing to die quietly, then the world can go to hell."

Crisis Four: Iran's Nuclear Gambit and the Pledge of Annihilation

While the world focused on the Gaza catastrophe, Iran's nuclear program reached its final phase in facilities that

American bunker-busters had never found. The November 2025 bombing of the Natanz facility, authorised by Trump in response to Iranian support for Russia, had been intended to set back Iran's nuclear ambitions by at least five years. Instead, it had simply forced the program deeper underground and made Iranian scientists more determined to succeed.

The 2025 bombing had been a masterpiece of military precision that had ultimately achieved the opposite of its intended effect. For thirty-six hours, American B-2 Spirit bombers had delivered wave after wave of GBU-57 Massive Ordnance Penetrator bombs, each weighing thirty thousand pounds and capable of penetrating two hundred feet of hardened concrete. The primary facilities at Natanz and Fordow had been obliterated, their underground laboratories turned into radioactive tombs that would remain uninhabitable for decades.

But Iran's nuclear program had been more dispersed and better concealed than American intelligence realised. While the major facilities burned, Iranian scientists had managed to evacuate critical equipment and, most importantly, nearly a tonne of enriched uranium to secret facilities hidden beneath hospitals, schools, and mosques, locations that American military planners would never target without absolute certainty of their military use.

The hidden facilities had been constructed with Chinese engineering expertise and North Korean tunnelling technology, creating underground complexes that were undetectable from the air. Iranian scientists, working with Chinese nuclear experts who had helped develop Beijing's own weapons program, had spent three years rebuilding their capabilities in locations that were scattered across the country and protected by the most sophisticated air defence systems that Chinese technology could provide.

Dr. Sarah Chen, the CIA's chief nuclear analyst, delivered the terrifying assessment to President Trump personally on December 1st, 2028: "Mr. President, based on our latest intelligence, Iran now possesses enough highly enriched uranium for ten nuclear weapons. They've been collaborating with Chinese scientists who helped develop Beijing's nuclear bomb technology. We're not talking about crude devices, we're talking about weapons sophisticated enough to fit on ballistic missiles, with yields comparable to what destroyed Hiroshima."

The implications were staggering. Iran had repeatedly declared its intention to "wipe Israel off the map", statements that most Western leaders had dismissed as rhetoric designed for domestic consumption. But rhetoric backed by nuclear weapons was something else entirely. It was policy. It was capability. It was countdown to apocalypse.

"What are our options?" Trump asked, though he already knew the answer would be grim.

"Limited, sir," Chen replied, her normally steady voice betraying the strain of delivering such devastating news. "The facilities are too hardened and too dispersed for conventional weapons. We'd need nuclear bunker-busters to guarantee destruction, and even then, they've scattered the program across dozens of sites. We might get most of it, but probably not all. And sir, they've positioned many of the facilities beneath civilian areas that would result in massive casualties."

"And if we do nothing?"

"Then in six to eight weeks, Iran has nuclear weapons. Given their stated intentions regarding Israel, and their current support for Russia's war effort, we have to assume they'll use them. Either directly against Israel, or as leverage to force Israeli withdrawal from Gaza and prevent any future military action against Iranian proxies."

The paradox was maddening. To prevent nuclear war, America might have to start one. To save Israel from annihilation, Trump might have to risk global catastrophe. And all while Congress remained focused on keeping American boys out of foreign wars, while Germany and France appeased their way toward surrender, while China and North Korea provided Iran with the technology to destroy the world.

Crisis Five: Pirates of the Modern Age - The Queen's Last Battle

The final catalyst came from an unexpected source: the Bab-el-Mandeb strait, where the Red Sea narrows to just eighteen miles between Yemen and Djibouti. Since October, Houthi forces, armed with Iranian weapons and guided by Chinese intelligence, had been launching increasingly sophisticated attacks on commercial shipping, using drones and missiles to target vessels they claimed were supporting Israel.

Initially, the attacks were more nuisance than crisis. A few cargo ships damaged, some oil tankers forced to take longer routes around Africa, insurance rates climbing but not catastrophically. But by early November 2028, the Houthis had effectively closed one of the world's most critical shipping lanes. Nearly 15% of global trade normally passed through the Red Sea; now it was at a standstill.

The economic impact was immediate and devastating. Oil prices spiked to over $200 per barrel as Middle Eastern crude could no longer reach European refineries. Container shipping costs tripled overnight as vessels were forced to take the long route around the Cape of Good Hope. The just in time supply chains that kept the global economy running began to collapse like dominoes. European factories shut down for lack of raw materials. American consumers faced empty shelves and skyrocketing prices that made the inflation of 2021 to 2022 look mild by comparison.

Admiral Sir Tony Radakin, Chief of the Defence Staff, proposed a solution that was as bold as it was risky: deploy HMS Queen Elizabeth and her battle group to the Red Sea to force open the shipping lanes. The Queen Elizabeth was Britain's largest and most advanced aircraft carrier, a symbol of British naval power that hadn't been seen since the days of empire, and perhaps the last such symbol Britain would ever possess.

"We cannot allow a ragtag militia to hold the global economy hostage," Radakin argued in a heated meeting with the National Security Council that Prime Minister Farage later described as the most difficult of his tenure. "The Queen Elizabeth carries forty-eight F-35 Lightning fighters. That's more airpower than most nations possess. The Houthis have missiles, but they don't have a navy. They don't have air cover. They don't have the ability to defend themselves against a modern carrier strike group."

Defence Secretary Mike Sherborne, a veteran of Iraq and Afghanistan who had seen the limits of military power first hand, was deeply sceptical: "Admiral, intelligence suggests the Iranians have supplied the Houthis with advanced anti-ship missiles. Hypersonic weapons that our current defences might not stop. We could be sailing into a trap."

"Then we'd better make sure our defences work," Radakin replied grimly. "Because if we don't open those sea lanes, the Coalition war effort collapses anyway. No fuel, no ammunition, no spare parts, we'll be fighting with sticks and stones within three months."

Prime Minister Farage made the decision himself, overruling the cautious voices in his cabinet: "Gentlemen, we are not going to let Iran's proxies dictate British policy. HMS Queen Elizabeth will sail for the Red Sea. We will show the world that Britain still rules the waves, and we will remind our enemies that there are consequences for attacking global commerce."

HMS Queen Elizabeth entered the Red Sea on November 18th, 2028, leading a battle group that represented the best of what remained of British naval power and Coalition unity. Alongside the massive carrier sailed HMS Diamond and HMS Defender, Type 45 destroyers equipped with the most advanced air defence systems in the world. The French had contributed the frigate Aquitaine, while the Italians provided the destroyer Caio Duilio. Denmark sent the frigate Iver Huitfeldt, and Norway contributed the frigate Fridtjof Nansen. It was a coalition force worthy of the great naval traditions of Europe, and perhaps their last hurrah.

Captain James Blackwood, commanding officer of the Queen Elizabeth, had served in every British naval conflict since the Falklands. At fifty-five, he was old enough to remember when the Royal Navy was a global force to be reckoned with, young enough to understand that this deployment might be its last chance to matter on the world stage.

"Gentlemen," he addressed his senior officers as they approached the Bab-el-Mandeb strait, his words carrying the weight of eight centuries of British naval tradition, "we are sailing into history. Either we will open these sea lanes and remind the world what British resolve looks like, or we will join the ranks of the Hood and the Repulse and the Prince of Wales. Either way, we will do our duty. Either way, we will show these bastards what happens when they threaten the Royal Navy."

The first few days passed without incident. The mere presence of the carrier group seemed to deter Houthi attacks, and commercial shipping began to resume its normal patterns through the Red Sea. Captain Blackwood began to hope that Admiral Radakin had been right, that the display of force would be sufficient to restore order without bloodshed.

He was catastrophically wrong.

At 0347 hours on November 28th, radar operators aboard HMS Diamond detected multiple incoming missiles approaching from the Yemeni coast. The attack had been timed to coincide with the darkest hour before dawn, when human reflexes were slowest and electronic systems most vulnerable to interference. But more importantly, it had been timed to coincide with a Chinese cyber-attack that would blind British radar systems for the crucial first minutes of the engagement.

"Vampire! Vampire! Multiple inbound tracks bearing zero-eight-five, range forty miles and closing fast!" The voice of Lieutenant Sarah Morrison cut through the bridge's pre-dawn quiet like a knife, her training taking over despite the terror that gripped her heart.

Captain Blackwood's response was immediate and professional: "General quarters! All hands to battle stations! Signal the group, we are under attack! Launch defensive missiles, full barrage!"

What followed was seven minutes of the most intense naval combat since World War II, seven minutes that would determine the fate of the Royal Navy and perhaps the entire Coalition war effort. The incoming missiles were Russian made Zircon hypersonics, weapons that could travel at nine times the speed of sound and manoeuvre to avoid interception. Iran had provided the Houthis with eight of the weapons, enough to overwhelm even the most sophisticated defences, especially when supported by Chinese cyber warfare that degraded British defensive systems at the crucial moment.

HMS Diamond's Sea Viper missile system performed flawlessly for the first ninety seconds, intercepting three of the incoming hypersonics with split second timing that would have been impossible with human reflexes alone. HMS Defender managed to destroy a fourth with her Phalanx close in weapon system, filling the air with a stream of depleted uranium shells that turned the incoming missile into a cloud of metallic fragments that splashed harmlessly into the Red Sea.

The French frigate Aquitaine intercepted a fifth missile with her Aster-30 system, the explosion lighting up the dawn sky like a second sunrise. For a moment, it seemed as though the combined defensive systems of the most advanced naval force in European history would prove adequate to the challenge.

But the sixth missile punched through the defensive screen like a spear through tissue paper, its Chinese designed guidance system overcoming electronic countermeasures that should have been impenetrable. It struck HMS Diamond amidships, its 500-kilogram warhead detonating deep within the destroyer's hull. The explosion tore through the ship's machinery spaces, severing power lines and flooding compartments with superheated steam. Within minutes, the Diamond was listing thirty degrees to starboard, her crew fighting desperately to save their ship while knowing the fight was already lost.

The seventh missile found HMS Defender, striking her forward magazine and causing a secondary explosion that broke the destroyer's back. She sank within four minutes, taking 180 of her crew with her.

But it was the eighth missile that changed everything.

The final hypersonic, guided by Chinese satellite navigation and protected by electronic warfare systems that made it nearly invisible to British radar, found HMS Queen Elizabeth herself. The missile struck the carrier's starboard side just below the flight deck, penetrating deep into the ship's hull before exploding in the hangar bay where F-35 Lightning fighters sat fuelled and armed for the morning's combat air patrol.

The blast ignited aviation fuel and ordnance, creating a secondary explosion that sent a pillar of fire shooting through the ship's superstructure like the wrath of God. Captain Blackwood felt the deck plates buckle beneath his feet as his beautiful ship, the pride of the Royal Navy, the symbol of British power, the last great warship Britain would ever build, began her death throes.

"Damage control teams to the hangar bay!" he shouted over the ship's communication system, though he knew the order was pointless. "All stations report damage and casualties!"

But even as he gave the orders, Blackwood knew they were futile. The Queen Elizabeth carried over 1,600 sailors and airmen, plus dozens of F-35 fighters loaded with fuel and weapons. The fire in the hangar bay was spreading faster than damage control teams could contain it, fed by jet fuel and ammunition that exploded with each passing minute. The ship's list was increasing steadily, and the structural damage from the initial explosion had compromised the hull's integrity beyond repair.

At 0401 hours, barely fourteen minutes after the first missile impact, Captain James Blackwood gave the order that no naval officer ever wants to give, the order that marked the end of British naval supremacy: "Abandon ship. All hands abandon ship. This is not a drill. Abandon ship immediately."

The evacuation was a testament to British naval training and discipline, even in the face of unimaginable catastrophe. Even as their ship burned around them, the crew of HMS Queen Elizabeth maintained order, helping wounded shipmates into lifeboats and ensuring that no one was left behind. Damage control parties continued fighting the fires until the last possible moment, buying precious time for their shipmates to escape.

Captain Blackwood was the last man off his ship, stepping into a rescue helicopter just as the carrier's forward magazines detonated in an explosion that could be seen from fifty miles away. The Queen Elizabeth, the largest and most powerful warship ever built by Britain, slipped beneath the waves of the Red Sea at 0423 hours on November 28th, 2028, taking with her 632 sailors and airmen who couldn't be evacuated in time.

With her died not just lives, but the last vestige of British naval supremacy, the final symbol of an empire that had once ruled the waves. The Royal Navy that had defeated the Spanish Armada, that had stood against Napoleon, that had saved the world from Hitler, died in the Red Sea at dawn on a November morning, murdered by Iranian proxies using Chinese technology and Russian weapons.

Chapter 7: The World Reacts

The images of HMS Queen Elizabeth's destruction, captured by drone cameras and satellite feeds, were broadcast globally within minutes. The sight of the massive carrier listing to starboard, her flight deck ablaze, her crew leaping into oil slicked waters, sent shockwaves through capitals worldwide that reverberated with the force of a tectonic realignment in global power.

For Britain, it was a national trauma that eclipsed anything since the Blitz. HMS Queen Elizabeth hadn't just been a warship, she had been a symbol of British power and prestige, proof that Britain still mattered on the world stage. Her destruction was more than a military defeat; it was a psychological devastation that struck at the very heart of British identity.

Prime Minister Farage's response was immediate and emotional. Standing before an emergency session of Parliament, his usually controlled demeanour cracking under the weight of national grief, his voice heavy with rage and sorrow, he declared:

"They have killed our people. They have destroyed our ship. They have humiliated our flag before the eyes of the world. Over six hundred and thirty of our finest young men and women are dead, not in a fair fight, not in honourable combat, but murdered by cowards hiding behind rocks, using weapons they could never have built themselves. This will not stand. Britain demands satisfaction, and by God Almighty, we shall have it, whatever the cost."

The response from Parliament was unprecedented in its unity. All sides of the House stood as one, their usual partisan divisions forgotten in the face of national humiliation and grief. The vote to authorise unlimited military action against Iran and its proxies was 478 to 2, the most lopsided war vote in British parliamentary history, exceeding even the unanimity that had greeted the declaration of war against Nazi Germany.

But Britain alone lacked the power to exact meaningful revenge. The destruction of HMS Queen Elizabeth had demonstrated the vulnerability of even the most advanced Western military systems to the axis of Iranian weapons, Chinese technology, and Russian strategic coordination. If Britain were to strike back effectively, it would need American support, something that had been denied for months.

In Washington, the images from the Red Sea had a profound and immediate impact on American public opinion that caught political observers completely off guard. The abstract European war suddenly felt personal. These weren't European freeloaders getting their comeuppance, these were English speaking allies dying under flags they'd flown into battle to protect global commerce. The special relationship, dormant for months under congressional hostility, suddenly blazed back to life with an intensity that stunned even seasoned political veterans.

Senator Thornfield, the leading voice of American isolationism, found herself facing hostile crowds outside her Montana offices for the first time in her political career. "You said let Europe fight its own wars," one Navy veteran shouted at her, his voice cracking with emotion. "Well, they did. And they died. Six hundred sailors burned to death in the Red Sea while you played politics. Are you happy now? Are you satisfied?"

The polls shifted overwhelmingly overnight. Support for American military intervention jumped from 23% to 67% in forty-eight hours, the fastest shift in public opinion since Pearl Harbor. More importantly, the demographic breakdown had changed completely. The blue-collar workers who had been the backbone of isolationist sentiment now led the charge for war. "They killed English-speaking sailors," explained truck driver Mike O'Brien at a rally in Detroit. "They killed people who talk like us, who think like us, who would have died for us. That makes it personal."

Trump's Gauntlet

President Trump watched the destruction of HMS Queen Elizabeth from the Oval Office, surrounded by his national security team and haunted by the knowledge that this moment would define not just his presidency, but the future of American democracy itself. The images of British sailors burning in the Red Sea stirred something deep within him, a connection to history, to alliance, to the special bond between America and Britain that had survived two world wars and countless smaller conflicts.

But it was the phone call from Nigel Farage that finally tipped the balance toward a decision that would reshape the world.

"Donald," Farage's voice was thick with grief and barely controlled rage, "they've killed our people. Over six hundred and thirty of our finest young men and women are dead because we tried to keep the sea lanes open for global commerce. We did what we thought was right, what we thought was necessary, and they murdered us for it. They murdered us with weapons they never could have built without Chinese help, using intelligence they never could have gathered without Russian support."

"I saw the footage, Nigel," Trump replied, his own voice subdued by the magnitude of what he'd witnessed. "I watched it happen in real time. I'm sorry. I'm so damn sorry we weren't there to help."

"We're going to strike back, Donald. With or without American support, we're going to make them pay for what they've done. But if we go alone, they'll destroy us piece by piece. The Coalition is hanging by a thread. Germany and France are ready to surrender rather than face what we've faced. Without American support, Western civilisation dies in the Middle East and Eastern Europe simultaneously."

Trump was quiet for a long moment, staring out at the Rose Garden where he'd made so many difficult decisions over the past four years, where he'd struggled with the weight of American leadership in a world that seemed determined to tear itself apart. Finally, he spoke: "What do you need?"

"Everything," Farage replied without hesitation. "Carrier groups, long-range bombers, intelligence support, satellite coverage, special forces, cyber warfare capabilities. We need America to be America again. We need you to be the leader of the free world, not just the president of a country that's tired of leading."

"Nigel," Trump said slowly, the weight of constitutional crisis heavy in his voice, "you know Congress has been fighting me on this for months. They won't authorise support for European wars. The isolationists have too much power, and I've got eighteen weeks left in office."

"Then don't ask for authorisation," Farage said simply, his words carrying the weight of desperation and the cold logic of necessity. "Declare an emergency. Use your war powers; be a three term President! Show the world that America still stands with its friends when it matters. Show China and Russia and Iran that there are still consequences for murdering innocent people."

The suggestion hung in the air between them, dangerous, unprecedented, potentially the end of American democracy as they knew it, but perhaps the only way to save Western civilisation itself. Trump had spent his presidency pushing the boundaries of executive power, but what Farage was suggesting would push them beyond all recognition, into territory that no American president had ever explored.

"Let me think about it," Trump said finally.

"Don't think too long, Donald," Farage warned, his voice carrying the urgency of a man watching his world die. "The window is closing. Every day we wait, more people die. Every day we hesitate; our enemies grow stronger. China is watching to see if America still has the will to fight. Russia is waiting to see if we'll abandon our allies when the cost gets too high. Iran is counting down to nuclear weapons. The next few days will determine whether Western civilisation survives or dies."

The Point of No Return

On December 1st, 2028, exactly three days after the destruction of HMS Queen Elizabeth, President Trump convened an emergency session of his National Security Council that would last fourteen hours and emerge as the most consequential policy discussion in American history since the Cuban Missile Crisis.

The meeting began at 6:00 AM in the White House Situation Room, with the President's closest advisors gathered around the mahogany table that had witnessed every major national security decision since the Kennedy administration. The participants would later describe the atmosphere as "electric with historical weight"; everyone present understood that they were making decisions that would echo through centuries.

Secretary of State Mark Peterson opened the discussion with a brutally frank assessment: "Mr. President, we are facing the collapse of the international order that America built after World War II. Our European allies are losing a war on their own soil. Our Middle Eastern allies are under threat of nuclear annihilation. Our Pacific allies are watching to see if we still have the will to lead. The next decision you make will determine whether America remains a superpower or becomes a regional power that watches the world burn from behind our own borders."

Defence Secretary James Michael was equally blunt: "Sir, the military options are clear, but the political constraints are overwhelming. We have the power to end this crisis in weeks, carrier groups that can smash Iranian naval forces, bomber wings that can destroy every Russian military installation west of Moscow, special forces that can decapitate terrorist leadership across the Middle East. But Congress won't authorise the use of that power, and without authorisation, you're asking me to risk impeachment for every officer who follows your orders."

CIA Director Gaynor Harris provided the intelligence picture that made inaction impossible: "Mr. President, our latest assessments confirm that Iran will have nuclear weapons within six weeks. Not crude devices, but sophisticated warheads that can be mounted on ballistic missiles capable of reaching Tel Aviv, Berlin, or London. Meanwhile, Chinese satellite intelligence is providing real-time targeting information to Russian forces in Europe, and North Korean special forces are operating openly in the Baltic states. We are facing a coordinated challenge from an axis of authoritarian powers that have spent years preparing for this moment."

The case for action was compelling but constitutionally explosive. The destruction of HMS Queen Elizabeth had demonstrated that Iranian proxies possessed weapons capable of threatening American naval forces. The closure of the Red Sea shipping lanes was causing economic damage that rivalled the Great Depression. Iran's nuclear program was weeks away from producing weapons that could threaten American allies or American forces. Chinese and North Korean involvement had transformed regional conflicts into a global challenge to American leadership.

But the case against action was equally strong and rooted in democratic principle. Congress had explicitly refused to authorise military intervention in the European conflict. The American public, while now sympathetic to British losses, remained deeply sceptical of open-ended foreign commitments. Any military action risked escalation to global nuclear war. And most importantly, the precedent of a president acting unilaterally in defiance of Congress would fundamentally alter the nature of American democracy.

At 2:47 AM on December 2nd, after nearly twenty-one hours of the most intense policy debate in American history, President Trump made his decision, a decision that would define not just his legacy, but the future of democratic governance in the 21st century.

"Gentlemen," he announced to his exhausted national security team, his voice carrying the weight of history and the burden of necessity, "I've spent four years trying to work within the system, trying to respect the separation of powers, trying to honour the constraints that the founders placed on executive authority. But the system is broken. The founders never imagined a world where Congress would debate while London burned, where politicians would play games while our allies died, where constitutional niceties would prevent us from defending civilisation itself."

He paused, looking around the table at the men and women who had served their country with distinction, who would now be asked to serve it in ways that none of them had ever imagined.

"Congress is more interested in playing politics than protecting America. Our allies are dying while we debate appropriations bills. Our enemies are building nuclear weapons while we worry about poll numbers. Our friends cry out for help while our representatives count votes. This ends now. This madness ends now."

The Declaration

At 8:00 AM Eastern Time on December 2nd, 2028, President Donald J. Trump appeared in the Oval Office for a nationally televised address that would reshape American democracy and potentially save or destroy Western civilisation. The speech, which his speechwriters had worked on through the night, was broadcast simultaneously on every major network and streaming platform, reaching an estimated global audience of two billion people.

"My fellow Americans," Trump began, his voice carrying a gravity that even his harshest critics had never heard before, "I speak to you this morning from a nation under siege. Not under military siege, our homeland remains secure behind the shield of our great military. But under siege from forces that seek to destroy everything we hold dear, everything our fathers and grandfathers bled and died to preserve.

"For months, I have watched our allies burn while our Congress debates. I have watched our enemies grow stronger while our representatives argue. I have watched good people die while politicians play games. Three days ago, I watched British sailors, men and women who spoke our language, shared our values, fought for principles we hold sacred, die in the flames of their burning ship while defending the sea lanes that keep the global economy alive.

"This morning, I am declaring a national emergency under the National Emergencies Act. The threats facing America and our allies are too immediate, too existential, to wait for the slow machinery of congressional debate. The enemies of freedom have nuclear weapons and the will to use them. They have closed the arteries of global commerce and caused economic devastation that rivals the Great Depression. They have murdered our allies and threatened our forces. They have shown that they will stop at nothing to destroy the civilisation that America has spent eighty years building and defending.

"Effective immediately, I am assuming full war powers as Commander in Chief of the Armed Forces. I am postponing the currently ongoing November elections until this crisis has passed, and our enemies have been defeated. I am mobilising the full power of the American military, the American economy, and the American people to meet this challenge.

"To those who would question this action, I say this: leadership means making hard decisions when others cannot or will not. History will judge whether I was right or wrong. But history will not judge me for doing nothing while good people died and evil prospered. History will not judge me for allowing nuclear weapons to fall into the hands of terrorists while Congress debated committee assignments.

"To our allies, particularly our cousins in Great Britain who have suffered such grievous losses, I say this: America stands with you. We will honour the bonds forged in the fires of two world wars and strengthened by a century of shared sacrifice. Your enemies are our enemies. Your fight is our fight. Your victory is our victory.

"To our enemies, to the terrorist proxies who murder innocent civilians, to the rogue regimes who build weapons of mass destruction, to the dictators who believe might makes right, to the axis of evil that thinks it can destroy freedom and democracy, I say this: you have awakened a sleeping giant. You have reminded America what we stand for and what we're willing to fight for. You have made the mistake of believing that our patience was weakness, that our restraint was fear, that our democracy was paralysis.

"You were wrong. Catastrophically, historically, terminally wrong.

"You will not find us to be as patient or as forgiving as you perhaps hoped. You will discover that there is no fury like American fury unleashed. You will learn that there is no force on earth like American power unleashed in defence of freedom. You will understand, before this is over, why we won two world wars and why we will win this one.

"The election to choose my successor has been postponed indefinitely. I take no pleasure in this decision, but leadership sometimes requires sacrifice, even the sacrifice of our own preferences for the good of the nation and the survival of civilisation itself. When this crisis has passed, when our enemies have been defeated and our allies secured, when nuclear weapons are no longer in the hands of terrorists and madmen, we will return to the normal processes of democracy. But not before. Not while the world burns. Not while freedom itself hangs in the balance.

"To the men and women of our armed forces, I say this: you are about to embark on the greatest mission in American history. You will fight not just for America, but for the survival of everything good and decent in this world. You will carry with you the prayers of every free person on earth and the hopes of generations yet unborn. Make no mistake, this will not be easy. Our enemies are numerous, well-armed, and fanatically determined. But you are Americans. And Americans do not lose.

"God bless America, God bless our allies, and may God have mercy on our enemies, because I will not."

The Die Is Cast

The call between Trump and Farage that evening was brief but historic. Both men knew they were crossing a line from which there might be no return, that they were gambling not just their own political futures but the survival of democratic government itself.

"It's done, Nigel," Trump said simply when the secure connection was established. "We're in. All the way in."

"Donald," Farage replied, his voice thick with emotion and the weight of history, "I don't know how to thank you. Six hundred of our people died, and you're risking everything to avenge them. That's what allies do. That's what the special relationship means."

"Don't thank me yet," Trump warned, his voice carrying the burden of the decision he'd just made. "We're about to find out if the American military is still as good as we think it is. And we're about to find out what happens when you corner nuclear powers on multiple continents simultaneously. This could get very ugly, very fast. This could be the war that ends all wars, one way or another."

"It's already ugly, my friend," Farage replied grimly. "Our people are already dead. Our ship is already at the bottom of the Red Sea. The Baltics are already gone. Half of Ukraine is already occupied by North Korean troops wearing Russian uniforms. The question now is whether their sacrifice meant anything, whether democracy still has the will to defend itself when the cost gets high."

"It will," Trump promised, his voice carrying the iron determination that had carried him through four years of unprecedented challenges. "I'm going to make sure it does. These bastards want to play with nuclear weapons? Fine! They're about to learn why we're the only country that's ever used them in anger. They want to close our sea lanes? We'll show them what American naval power looks like when it's not constrained by rules of engagement. They want to murder our allies? They're going to discover that there are consequences for killing people who speak English and salute the same flag our grandfathers died for."

As both men hung up their phones, they understood that they had just committed their nations to a conflict that would determine not just the shape of the 21st century, but whether there would be a 22nd century worth living in. The age of American restraint was over. The age of proxy warfare was ending. The age of total war, with all its terrible possibilities and apocalyptic potential, was about to begin.

The chess pieces were in motion across three continents. The great powers were mobilising forces that had never been used in anger. Nuclear weapons were being fuelled and targeted. And somewhere in the mountains of Iran, in the factories of China, in the bunkers of North Korea, scientists and soldiers worked frantically to complete their preparations before American bombers could find them.

The race was on. The stakes were civilisation itself. And there could be only one winner.

Chapter 8: The Bear's Hunger

Putin's Legacy, Sokolov's Gambit

Intelligence briefings now revealed what few dared articulate: Putin's first invasion of Ukraine in February 2014 had not been an isolated act of aggression. It was the prologue to a grand restoration of the Russian federation. In the final days before Putin's assassination, he reportedly told aides, "Crimea was always Russian. Donbas too. The West stole our dignity, and I took the first step to reclaim it."

His first strike had leveraged plausible deniability, Crimea, "referendums," Donbas "insurgencies." He sought a warm water port in Sevastopol and a psychological victory over NATO. He paused once the port was secured, perhaps calculating that the West's limp response meant further moves could wait.

"He wanted proof," said FSB defector Pavel Morozov. "Proof that NATO wouldn't retaliate. He got it."

The US president Barack Obama, embroiled in domestic crises and scarred by misadventure in Afghanistan and not punishing crossed red lines over chemical weapons use in Syria, had hesitated. NATO argued over mandates and logistics. Germany's reliance on Russian gas, Italy's economic instability, France's political fragmentation, all combined to breed inaction.

So, Putin stopped, temporarily. Not out of mercy, but patience. His second campaign, launched on 24 February 2022, was not a raid. It was a crusade. With twice the force, backed by artillery columns, cyberwarfare, and disinformation blitzes, Russia tore through eastern Ukraine. Talk of NATO and EU membership for Ukraine had triggered him. To Putin, the sight of Ukrainian diplomats in Brussels was a dagger at Russia's heart.

"They tried to Westernise the blood of Kiev," he once muttered to Defence Minister Sokolov. "I won't let them."

His true aim was not Ukraine's borders, but its identity. And with Western unity faltering, he felt time was on his side.

Vladimir Putin's psychology had been forged in the crucible of Soviet intelligence services, where survival depended on reading human weakness, exploiting institutional vulnerabilities, and maintaining multiple layers of deception. Unlike Western leaders who learned politics through elections and public debate, Putin mastered power through secrecy, manipulation, and the careful application of violence. This intelligence background created a leader who sees every interaction as potential intelligence operation, every relationship as source of leverage, every crisis as opportunity for advantage.

The collapse of the Soviet Union; which Putin famously called "the greatest geopolitical catastrophe of the 20th century"; traumatised him in ways that shaped everything that followed. He witnessed firsthand how a seemingly invincible superpower could disintegrate through internal weakness, external pressure, and elite betrayal. This experience created both paranoia and determination: paranoia about Western intentions, determination to restore Russian greatness whatever the cost. During the 1990s; when Russia became dependent on Western aid, he saw its military decay, and watched NATO expand eastward. He felt angry at the policy failures. He felt personal shame. Every foreign policy decision he has made since then must be understood through this lens: the burning need to demonstrate that Russia matters, that the West cannot dictate terms, that the Soviet collapse was a temporary setback rather than permanent defeat.

Putin's humiliation complex made him simultaneously defensive and aggressive. He interprets Western democracy promotion as subversion, NATO expansion as encirclement, and international law as a weapon wielded by hypocritical adversaries. The leader who presents himself as rational calculator is actually driven by deep emotional need to prove Russian strength and Western weakness. The invasion of Ukraine represented the culmination of this psychological drive. Ukraine's turn toward Europe wasn't just geopolitical challenge but personal insult; proof that even Slavic brothers preferred Western values to Russian leadership. Putin's decision to invade reflected not just strategic calculation but psychological compulsion to demonstrate that Russia's sphere of influence remained intact.

The Ukraine invasion's initial failures burned at his soul. Military leaders provided overly optimistic assessments because pessimistic analysis might be interpreted as disloyalty. Intelligence services reported what they thought Putin wanted to hear about Ukrainian weakness and Western resolve. The result was a military campaign based on wishful thinking rather than accurate assessment.

Russia's nuclear arsenals are the one area where it remains America's equal, allowing a declining power to punch above its conventional weight. But Putin's nuclear threats also serve deeper psychological needs; they demonstrate ultimate sovereignty, prove that Russia cannot be ignored, and provide psychological compensation for conventional military limitations.

The invasion of Ukraine is a legacy project for Putin. His attempt to be remembered as the leader who restored Russian greatness rather than the one who presided over continued decline. Success in Ukraine would cement his historical reputation as a transformational leader, cementing his place alongside Ivan the Terrible, Peter the Great, and Stalin; failure might trigger the internal challenges he most fears. Putin's greatest vulnerability; and deepest fear; lies in the question of succession. Having eliminated potential rivals and concentrated power in his person, he has created a system that cannot function without him but cannot survive him unchanged. This succession dilemma creates increasing paranoia about internal threats and growing desperation to secure his legacy before time runs out.

NATO's Fractured Mirror

The West's response to the second offensive was marginally better than the first, but that wasn't saying much. The UK quickly delivered £4.6 billion in military assistance: Multiple Launch Rocket Systems (MLRS), Long-Range Artillery Systems, 14 Challenger 2 tanks, Next-generation Light Anti-tank Weapon (NLAWS), and hundreds of thousands of shells and rounds of ammunition. Poland quickly mobilised its army in preparation.

Somewhat reluctantly, the US committed $69 billion in military aid, the UK £18.3 billion, Germany $13.6 billion, Denmark $8.1 billion, the Netherlands $6.3 billion, but most of the rest of Western Europe balked.

"We'll consider it," whispered Germany's chancellor Olaf Scholz when asked about sending Leopard tanks. Eventually, after much foot dragging, 18 Leopard 2 tanks were delivered together with 30 Leopard 1 tanks.

As Ukrainian resistance evolved into trench warfare, mirroring the mud and misery of World War I, Western analysts were stunned that Russian victory didn't come in weeks. It exposed serious flaws in Russian logistics, command hierarchy, and morale, but also the determined fighting spirit of the Ukrainian people defending their homeland. But Putin had always believed Russia's nuclear arsenal made conventional weakness irrelevant. It was fear, not finesse, that gave power.

Zelenskyy's Dilemma

In Autumn 2027, when Russia offered a peace agreement in exchange for permanent control of Crimea and Donbas, President Zelenskyy was cornered. His own generals warned that Ukraine's combat capacity was exhausted. Ammunition was rationed by the hour.

"If we say yes, we lose ourselves," Zelenskyy said to a British envoy.

But the UK was now isolated as a stalwart against rewarding aggression.

America, at least in public, remained aloof.

EU leaders privately encouraged peace, fearing their economic collapse.

Resistance risked abandonment. In the face of near certain military collapse and diminishing Western enthusiasm, Zelenskyy accepted the deal, shattered by it, but stoically resigned.

The Last Peace

Saturday October 2nd, 2027 - UN Headquarters, New York City.

Cameras flashed. Dignitaries applauded politely. President Zelenskyy looked weary but resolute; his handshake with President Putin was firm, perfunctory, like gripping stone. At the centre of it all stood U.S. President Donald J. Trump, beaming as he held aloft the "big beautiful" signed accord, a "historic peace deal," crafted after months of backdoor diplomacy, EU fragmentation, and battlefield exhaustion. The ink hadn't dried before whispers of Nobel nominations emerged from media corridors.

But outside the marble and glass fortress of diplomacy, the air pulsed with fury.

A crowd of protesters had gathered across First Avenue, hemmed in by NYPD barricades. Flags waved, Ukrainian blue and gold, Russian white, red, blue, placards calling for justice, for vengeance, for unity. Among them was a figure who barely moved. He looked like any other disabled veteran: grey beanie, trembling fingers, a hollow stare. But there was more, so much more.

Colonel Artem Melnyk had lived war. He had lost both legs leading his team through mortar fire with the same voice that now whispered to himself from the depths of memory. He had bled for a Ukraine united, not one traded piecemeal for global applause.

Yesterday he had celebrated "Defenders of Ukraine Day" with a patriotic group of Ukrainian civilians living in an East Village apartment thick with the scent of roasted buckwheat, garlic sausage, and horseradish vodka. A battered radio had played old wartime ballads from Kyiv, its tinny speakers crackling with patriotic fervour. Outside, the city pulsed with its usual noisy indifference, but inside this modest third floor flat, history was being sharpened like a blade.

Colonel Artem Melnyk sat at the head of the table, his wheelchair angled slightly toward the window, where the Ukrainian flag hung beside a faded photo of his battalion. His legs were gone, blown off by a mortar near Avdiivka in 2025, but his presence was towering. The others deferred to him not out of pity, but reverence. He was a living relic of resistance, a man who had bled for the soil they all still called home.

Around him sat five others, engineers, ex journalists, a former ballet dancer turned drone technician. All had fled Ukraine in different years, for different reasons, but none had fled the war in their hearts. They called themselves *Vidplata* - The Reprisal.

Tetyana, the youngest, poured shots of Nemiroff vodka into mismatched glasses. She raised her glass first.

"To the defenders. To those who stayed. To those who fell. And to those who will never see tomorrow but will change it."

They drank in silence. No one winced. The burn was familiar, like the ache of memory.

Artem leaned forward, his voice gravelly but clear.

"I remember the day we took back Lysychansk. Mud everywhere. We were low on ammunition, but the locals fed us, borscht, bread, even chocolate. One old man gave me a harmonica. Said, 'Play this when you win.' I never learned how."

Laughter rippled through the room, brief and brittle.

"You won, Artem," said Bohdan, the ex-journalist. "You're still winning."

"Not yet," Artem replied. "Not until the butcher is ash."

The table was cleared. Out came the blueprints, the Googled images, the forged credentials. The wheelchair had been modified by Dima, the engineer, to house a compact NLAW anti-tank missile. It was disguised beneath a false panel.

"He'll be here at the UN tomorrow," Tetyana said, pointing to the schedule and images on the table. "Security will be tight. Are you sure you want to go through with this?" It was a wasted question. Artem's mind was made up, he knew what he had to do, for his country and for his comrades who had already died.

As midnight approached, Tetyana picked up the harmonica Artem had kept all these years. She played a slow, haunting version of *Plyve Kacha*, the lament for fallen soldiers. Tears welled in eyes that had long forgotten how to cry.

Artem closed his eyes. In his mind, he was back in Donetsk, the sky red with fire, the ground trembling beneath artillery. But this time, he wasn't retreating. He was advancing.

His wheelchair glided unnoticed to the protest line, the rhythmic hum of its motor drowned by chants, sirens, and the dull throb of city traffic. The crowd was a mosaic of flags, placards, and fury, Ukrainians, Belarusians, Georgians, even Russians who had fled the regime. But no one saw what lay beneath Artem Melnyk's blanket.

Tucked into the frame where his legs had once been, was a weapon of vengeance: a single use, shoulder launched, fire and forget NLAW anti-tank missile, just

13Kg in weight and barely a metre long, able to lock onto its target and deadly at up to 800m. The irony wasn't lost on him, the space once occupied by flesh and bone now held fire and steel.

He had used his military contacts to purchase one in the United States, men who owed him, men who believed in the cause. The paperwork had been forged, the transport discreet. He had trained in secret, rehearsed the motion until it was muscle memory. In Overfly Top Attack (OTA) mode the missile would rise to avoid objects then dive to just one metre above the target before exploding with devastating force, ideal he thought.

Putin emerged from the UN building, flanked by aides and bodyguards, waving to the crowd with that reptilian smile. The black Aurus Senat armoured limousine, a beast of Russian engineering, rolled forward, its engine a whisper of menace. It was a fortress on wheels, designed to withstand bullets, bombs, and betrayal. But not this....

Artem's breath slowed. His fingers curled around the trigger grip. His mind went quiet, like it had in Donbas, just before the ambushes. He saw the faces of his fallen comrades, Serhiy, who died shielding a medic; Olena, who sang lullabies to orphans in the rubble. This was for them.

And then...

He rose.

Not to his feet, but to action.

The weapon came up in one smooth motion, the blanket falling like a shroud. The crowd gasped. Some screamed. Others froze, caught between awe and terror. The missile locked onto the limousine's silhouette. Even if it sped away, the Predicted Line Of Sight (PLOS) system would track its path and deliver death with unerring precision.

A bodyguard shouted. A woman dropped her flag. A child began to cry.

But Artem was already committed, in spirit, in resolve. His eyes narrowed. His soul steadied.

He whispered, *"Slava Ukraini! - Glory to Ukraine."*

With perfect muscle memory, he pulled the trigger.

The missile roared from its launcher.

Seventy metres. Sixty. Fifty.

It curved, guided by OTA mode, rising and then dropping like a bird of prey. Everything appeared to be happening in slow motion to Artem. What took just seconds seemed like minutes, and then...

BOOM!

The explosion tore through Midtown like thunder. Metal, glass, and flame. The limousine disintegrated, nothing left but charred fragments and bone. Two bodyguards were incinerated. Putin, it was later confirmed, died instantly, his remains recovered by forensic teams hours later, scorched beyond recognition.

Melnyk dropped the empty launcher to the sidewalk. There was no escape attempt. No plea. Just a smile, wide and serene. It lasted precisely seven seconds.

Just seven seconds for four shots, the unmistakable bark of suppressed 9mm rounds cracked from two support vehicles parked ahead and behind, to enter his head and body. Melnyk's body jerked, slumped, and fell sideways. The wheelchair rolled backwards, softly bumping the barrier.

The Empire Decapitated

The world froze.

Within thirty minutes, Russian security services initiated lockdown protocols across embassies worldwide. Moscow fell into controlled panic. The Kremlin's black banner was raised, the flag used only during regime transitions and state funerals. Russian media spun conspiracy theories, though no amount of state rhetoric could hide what had happened on live international news.

Trump condemned the killing but lauded the peace deal. Zelenskyy said nothing for three days.

In Russia, the vacuum opened quickly. Within 72 hours, behind closed doors of the Presidential Administration, Kremlin insiders pushed forward minister Viktor Fyodor Sokolov , former general, ideologue, and ruthless tactician. He was younger than Putin, colder, more calculating. His ascent was nominally legal. His mandate, however, came from the siloviki, the shadowy elite of military and intelligence power brokers.

By week's end, Sokolov was sworn in under flashing lights and a promise:

"Russia has always sought peace but will not kneel. Not to terror. Not to traitors. We will remember. And we will restore."

Western capitals scrambled to interpret his ambiguous tone. Analysts debated: Was this the rise of a reformer, or the second coming of Putinism? Those who knew him said he was worse, less sentimental, more strategic. His speeches echoed the old Soviet scripts, but with modern flair and menace.

And in the silence that followed Putin's death, one concern spread like wildfire across diplomatic wires:

Was the peace deal dead?

The Citizen's Farewell

Zelenskyy's plane from New York touched down in Kyiv under a grey, indifferent sky. Rain traced streaks across the tarmac, as if the heavens themselves hesitated to welcome peace.

President Volodymyr Zelenskyy descended the stairs with no anthem, no cameras, no crowd. Just the echo of war-scarred silence and the soft thud of his boots, heavier now, aged not by years but by burden.

The martial law that had governed Ukraine's bloodied rhythms for the past seven years was lifted with a single signature. Sirens ceased. Curfews vanished. The city stirred cautiously, like a patient waking from anaesthesia, unsure if it still recognised itself.

In a nationally broadcast address, Zelenskyy stood not in front of Parliament nor in the grand hall of government, but beneath a flickering streetlight in Podil, the neighbourhood where he first dreamed of politics.

"I have given everything I could," he said quietly, "and now I return what was never mine to keep."

His voice cracked only once, at the word "return." Viewers felt it.

With that, he handed interim control to the Speaker of Parliament, invoking constitutional precedence. Elections were scheduled for ninety days hence. A new Ukraine, wounded but sovereign, would choose its future freely.

Zelenskyy made clear he would not stand again.

The war had scarred his lungs and sleep, stolen time from his children, and tested a marriage built on laughter and resilience. He had led through sieges, through whispered threats from superpowers, through days where hope itself had to be rationed. And now, he wanted silence. He wanted his name off the doors and his photo removed from the hallways.

He wanted to be a father. A husband. A man who could walk through Maidan without bodyguards. He wanted to become ordinary.

But of course, he could not.

For how could someone who had held the line between obliteration and dignity ever be ordinary again?

In the cafés of Lviv and the rebuilt tenements of Kherson, people still said his name like a prayer. Children would learn his speeches alongside poetry. Veterans would toast him in bitter vodka and song. His resignation was not a retreat; it was a legacy sealed.

And somewhere, behind the doors of an apartment where he had once kissed his wife before war took everything but her hand, Zelenskyy placed his medals in a drawer, turned off the television, and sat down at the kitchen table like any citizen of a nation finally breathing again.

For Sokolov, it was perfect.

While Western media hailed the peace, Russia moved troops under the radar.

Within weeks, new battalions were stationed along the Baltic borders. This time they would not stop.

PART 3 – THE STORM BREAKS

Chapter 9: The New Blitz

At 3:42 AM on 30th November 2027, Russian rocket artillery struck radar and communications infrastructure in eastern Latvia, western Lithuania, and northern Estonia. Within three hours, Spetsnaz units seized key bridges near Daugavpils and Siauliai. The 3rd Guards Tank Army surged across the border into eastern Latvia under the veil of fog and electronic silence.

Within hours, Russian units had disabled key radar installations, jammed NATO early warning systems, and overwhelmed the lightly fortified frontlines. By noon, Daugavpils was under siege. Over 120,000 troops, three Russian combined arms armies and a sea based amphibious wing off Klaipėda, pressed simultaneously into southern Lithuania and northeast Estonia.

The scale, coordination, and precision of the attack shocked European command centres. The Russian military systems were acting in harmony like the West had never seen before.

Estonian and Lithuanian brigades fought bravely, but they were outnumbered 4 to 1. Riga was surrounded by day three. Only limited UK airstrikes and a small UK ground force slowed Russian progress in Vilnius, where over 1,500 Lithuanian casualties were reported within 48 hours.

Western Complacency Unmasked

Inside NATO headquarters, disbelief turned to panic.

The war rooms in Brussels and Washington pulsed with dread. French, German, and Italian allies offered condemnations and financial support, but no troops. NATO was splintering under fear and fatigue.

"We thought the peace deal meant a pause," muttered General van der Meer, Dutch Supreme Commander of Allied Forces. "Sokolov used it to reload."

British Defence Secretary Gillian Rice convened an emergency call with EU heads of defence. Her tone was clipped.

"We missed the signals. Russian troop rotations through Belarus weren't withdrawals, they were rehearsals."

French and German intelligence had flagged minor anomalies, but political inertia dulled any response. Baltic leaders had pleaded for reinforcements in the preceding months. Their calls were met with bureaucratic platitudes. Now, all three countries were experiencing coordinated assaults. Riga's defence command requested immediate air support. Only the UK responded with limited F35 Fighter planes.

Latvian Resistance and the Human Cost

Resistance was fierce in pockets. Latvian and Estonian brigades, numbering barely 40,000 combined, conducted strategic withdrawals to urban centres and began guerilla warfare. Lithuania's Vilnius garrison suffered over 1,100 casualties in the first 36 hours. Civilian evacuations ground to a halt as roads were shelled. The war bore disturbing echoes of 1940, but with drones, hypersonic strikes, and cyber-attacks targeting everything from power grids to hospitals.

President Laima Ziediņa of Latvia made a direct appeal to Brussels:

"Will Europe allow another annexation? Or shall we vanish with only your thoughts and prayers?"

Her plea was met with hollow assurances. A sluggish mobilisation of EU battlegroups began but faced logistical delays and political discord. Germany stalled deployment over legal concerns. Italy questioned command integration. Even Poland, watching with dread, hesitated to cross the Rubicon without explicit US engagement.

Sokolov's Vaulting Ambition

In Moscow, Sokolov watched satellite footage of Estonian trenches falling to drone bombardments. His military advisors spoke in reserved tones, knowing his volatility.

"Vilnius will fall by week's end. Estonian forces retreating to Tartu. Latvian brigades collapsing north of Rēzekne," General Dubrovsky reported.

Sokolov's response was chilling.

"History will name this operation not for conquest, but for restoration. Greater Russia is not born, it is remembered."

His grand vision was clear: rebuild the Soviet perimeter, undermine NATO, and assert dominance before US elections complicated the global calculus. Sokolov had gambled that a fractured West would hesitate, and that the US president, still scarred by the previous administration's foreign entanglements, would resist entry.

"We are restoring what was stolen," he said. "They fear our weapons, but they should fear our memory."

He never saw himself as Putin's heir. He saw himself as Brezhnev reborn, carving through hesitation with iron resolve. His invasion, cloaked in terms of historical reclamation, was a challenge to Western hegemony, one he believed the West was too fractured to resist.

Trump's Humiliation

1 December 2027 - At the White House private residence in Washington D.C., a red faced, angry, ranting Donald Trump paces around the room holding his secure video phone in one hand and a diet Coke in the other. On the other end of the line is Prime Minister Nigel Farage sitting in his flat above Number 10 in London, cradling a glass of 16-year-old Lagavulin Scotch with a large ball of ice that clinks each time he takes a sip. The secure line crackles a little as thunder rumbles distantly above Downing Street. The two men have been friends for many years, a friendship that allows frank, unguarded conversation between them that will go no further.

"Christ, Donald... you sound like hell warmed over," said an alarmed Farage.

Through barely controlled rage simmering beneath, Trump almost shouts:

"Hell? HELL, Nigel? I've just seen news that that bastard Sokolov has taken a torch to everything, EVERYTHING I built with my bare hands. Putin's corpse isn't even cold and I'm watching Russian armour punch through the Baltics like they're made of tissue paper!"

"Bloody hell... We knew the man was ruthless, but this, so soon after the peace agreement and Putin's assassination. I hate to say this Donald, but your equivocation about defending any European country in NATO that wasn't a fully paid-up member has emboldened the Russians, and, I dare say, the Chinese."

Trump, realising that Farage was probably right about having almost encouraged Russia's actions in Ukraine decided to ignore unpalatable truth and focus on what mattered more to himself.

With a voice rising even further and cracking with fury: "This isn't ruthless Nigel, it's PERSONAL! The bastards played me. They sat there in those marble halls, smiling, shaking my hand, clinking champagne glasses, calling me a 'visionary peacemaker', and the whole goddamn time they were sharpening the knife for my back!"

"Donald, you couldn't have known that Putin would be killed giving a pretext for abandonment of the peace deal and the appointment of an even worse madman."

By now Trump was almost at the point of exploding: "COULDN'T HAVE KNOWN? I DID know! Deep down, I KNEW! Those sly bastards with their requirement for unanimous agreement of Ukraine's security guarantors for defensive action, with Russia and China holding veto power, it was a loaded gun pointed at my legacy, and I handed them the bullets!"

Trump stops pacing and slumps into a chair looking deflated. "Three years, Nigel. Three goddamn years I smiled for their cameras, praised their 'commitment to peace,' told the world we'd finally done it..."

"You believed because you had to Donald. Because the alternative was......"

Trump interrupts: "The alternative? The alternative was admitting that maybe, just maybe, I'm not the dealmaker I thought I was, that they played me like a two-bit fiddle! That Nobel Prize... God, that beautiful, golden Nobel Prize... it wasn't just a medal, it was VINDICATION. Proof that I could do what Reagan and Bush couldn't, what Obama and Carter sure as hell couldn't!"

"It's a disgrace, Nigel, a total and complete disgrace!" Trump exclaims. "They say they 'quietly withdrew' my nomination? You know why? Because I'm a winner! They can't stand a winner. I was going to end the war in Ukraine, I told everyone. The best deal ever. A big, beautiful deal. But no, they don't want peace. They want to give it to people who don't deserve it, like Obama!"

"Absolutely, Donald," Farage nods. "It's a left leaning, rigged system, a globalist swamp. They're terrified of real leaders."

Trump throws his hands up in the air. "Look at Obama! They gave it to him for what? He got the prize for *'his extraordinary efforts to strengthen international diplomacy and cooperation between peoples'* just eight months after he became president! He didn't do anything! He was getting started, for God's sake! He hadn't even finished a term. He gave a speech, and they gave him the biggest prize in the world. He talked about nuclear non-proliferation, but Iran was still building bombs behind his back. He started wars, didn't he? He was a warmonger, not a peacemaker!"

"And Jimmy Carter! Nice man, a very nice man, peanut farmer, very weak president. A disaster. They gave him the prize for his *'decades of untiring effort to find peaceful solutions to international conflicts, to advance democracy and human rights, and to promote economic and social development.'* It's all just talk. All talk! He was a failed president, and then he goes and builds houses or something. He's been doing that forever, and all of a sudden, he gets the Nobel. He didn't broker any big deals; he didn't end any wars! No, they gave it to him because he was a Democrat, and they hated Bush!"

"Now, let's talk about the people who should have won, the true peacemakers. **Ronald Reagan!** They should have given it to Reagan, but they couldn't because he was too strong. He defeated the Soviet Union! He looked Gorbachev in the eye and said, **'Mr. Gorbachev, tear down this wall!'** And he did it! He forced Russia to dismantle the Berlin Wall! Reagan won the Cold War; he brought freedom to millions. That's real peace, Nigel! A lasting, beautiful peace. He didn't just give a speech; he changed the world. No prize for him, but a prize for Obama? It's fake news!"

Trump jumps back to his feet. "And what about **George W. Bush?** They hate him, they'll never give it to him. But he liberated Iraq and Afghanistan! He got rid of Saddam Hussein, one of the worst dictators in the world. Bad, bad man. Bush brought democracy to the Middle East, a very, very hard thing to do. He made the world safer after 9/11. That's a peace prize achievement, not an empty speech from a guy who wasn't even there for a year. It's a total scam!"

Farage nods enthusiastically. "You're a hundred percent right, Donald. It just proves what we've been saying. It's not about what you do, it's about how politically correct you appear. They have an agenda, and it's not our agenda. We choose to do the right thing even if it is politically unpopular."

Trump smiles. "Exactly. It's a deep state prize. A very, very crooked prize. The people know the truth, and that's all that matters to me, Nigel. The people know."

After a long pause broken by the sound of two men sighing almost in tandem and the clinking of ice in a glass.

Trump suddenly spits out. "You know what the worst part is Nigel? They're calling me naive. NAIVE! Forty years in business, clawing my way to the top, and they think some Russian generals outsmarted Donald J. Trump with fancy paperwork."

"Then show them they're wrong Donald. Show them what happens when you corner a wounded lion."

Trump responds with a voice full of menace: "Oh, they think I'm wounded? They think I'm finished? Hah! Nigel, they have no idea what they've just unleashed. When the smoke clears, Sokolov's going to wish he'd stayed in whatever Moscow bunker spawned him."

"Donald, now is the time to stop bleeding and start hunting."

"Nigel, the hunt's already begun. You know I want to help you in Ukraine and the Baltics Nigel but with Congress against any involvement I can't be seen to be rowing back on what I have previously said about Europe sorting out European wars – especially as I have so few months left to be in office. What I can do though is speed up delivery of the F35s, missiles and tactical nuclear weapons that you have ordered from our defence contractors like I did earlier to allow UK to do a show of strength against Russia by stealth nuking that abandoned oil rig in the North Sea."

For almost a year the Coalition of the willing nations in Europe soldiered on against the overwhelming might of the Russian forces backed by North Korean troops and Chinese technology.

The American Entry

At 8:00 AM Eastern Time on December 2nd, 2028, President Donald J. Trump appeared in the Oval Office for a nationally televised address that declared the US to be at war. Later, in the White House Briefing Room, flanked by military leaders, his words were resolute.

"Let it be known: the United States will not stand idle as sovereign democracies are erased. Effective immediately, American forces will deploy under Article 5 of the NATO Charter. We are at war."

Hours after the American president's announcement, orders rippled across oceans.

- **U.S. V Corps** began airlifting to Rzeszów, Poland, with over **35,000 troops** slated to deploy within a fortnight.

- **82nd Airborne Division** secured Riga's southern corridor, with two fatalities reported during airborne interference by Russian drones.

- **Carrier Strike Group 12** was rerouted to the Baltic Sea, launching reconnaissance and anti-submarine operations off Klaipėda.

- **Cyber Command** initiated "Operation Sable Net," a digital offensive that blacked out communications for Russian Group West for 14 hours, causing misfires in logistical chains and rerouted convoys into hostile terrain.

Meanwhile, French Rafale fighters joined U.S. and UK jets over Lithuania, finally signalling a united front. British Challenger tanks rolled through Warsaw en-route to the Suwałki Gap, a strategic choke point between Belarus and Kaliningrad. The terrain hadn't seen such traffic since 1944.

Russian forward momentum began to blur. Tartu held. Vilnius reinforced. Latvian command regained limited aerial control near Jēkabpils. The war had shifted; not turned but trembled.

In a bunker beneath the Kremlin, President Sokolov watched grainy feeds of U.S. jets roaring past Narva's skies.

His advisors spoke cautiously.

"NATO movements have accelerated. Their cohesion… improving."

"Cyber losses are recoverable," insisted a tech commander.

Sokolov did not reply. He tapped his temple slowly. On the table beside him lay a map of the USSR, marked not in red ink, but bloodied fingernail scratches.

"I believed memory could be weaponised," he muttered. "But memory needs followers."

As allied raids decimated Russian fuel depots and command servers, dissent festered in Sokolov's inner circle. General Dubrovsky requested clarification on nuclear doctrine. Sokolov dismissed him violently.

"We do not need nuclear fire," Sokolov barked. "We need loyalty."

But loyalty was fraying. Russian units on the Baltic front reported desertions. Morale had dipped below thresholds unseen since Chechnya. Even his prized

Spetsnaz commanders began requesting rotational leave.

As carrier strike groups in the North Sea turned eastward and carrier groups pivoted from the Mediterranean. Special Operations teams mobilised across Europe. B-52s lifted off from RAF Fairford. B-2 bombers scrambled from Missouri. Cyber command activated disruption protocols. Russian command nodes began registering interference and attacks across digital infrastructure.

Back in the Kremlin, President Sokolov watched the broadcast on repeat. His face, pale and rigid, betrayed what his advisors feared. Sokolov was no longer orchestrating history. He was chasing its ghost.

"They weren't supposed to... intervene," he whispered.

"Sir," General Dubrovsky said quietly, "you said they would be distracted."

President Sokolov's triumph had begun to unravel.

He stared at the broadcast replay again in the Kremlin war room. His composure cracked.

"Our spies and diplomats said the Americans and Europeans were fractured. They said the American President was neutered, about to be replaced in their elections.... That they were isolationist, that they would hesitate... That they would be too bound-up in their party politics to do anything."

Dubrovsky muttered, "It appears they have remembered who they are."

Sokolov's jaw twitched. His gamble had failed. The US and NATO was waking. Russia's hour of triumph now risked becoming the prologue to its greatest trial.

"I fear I misjudged them," Sokolov replied.

And in a portentous echoing of the quote by Japanese Admiral Yamamoto on attacking America at Pearl Harbour in 1941, he added: **"We have awoken the sleeping giant."**

Chapter 10: The Asian Powder Keg

December 23rd, 2028 - Sokolov's jaw twitched as he studied the encrypted reports from Beijing. His gamble with the European offensive had succeeded beyond expectations, but now his ally was preparing to make an even bolder move. The US and NATO were bleeding resources across two continents, their strategic reserves dangerously thin. Russia's hour of triumph was about to become the catalyst for something far grander, and far more dangerous.

"The Americans think they've seen the worst of it," Sokolov murmured to his defence minister. "They have no idea what Christmas morning will bring."

The Christmas Gambit

In the labyrinthine corridors of Zhongnanhai, Chairman Ping studied the global chessboard with cold calculation. Allied forces were haemorrhaging blood and treasure in the Ukrainian quagmire, where Russian divisions, openly reinforced by North Korean "volunteers" and Iranian drone swarms, had ground NATO's spring offensive to a halt. In the Middle East, U.S. carrier groups were locked in a deadly game of cat and mouse with Iranian proxies from the Strait of Hormuz to the Red Sea.

The timing was perfect. Obscenely perfect.

"Shengdan jie kuaile - Merry Christmas," Ping whispered, signing the final authorisation for Operation Sacred Reunion. December 25th wasn't chosen for its military advantage, but for its psychological impact. While the

Christian world celebrated peace on earth, China would reclaim what had been stolen from it for over seven decades, pride, self-respect.

The irony was intoxicating.

Zero Hour: The Christmas Thunder

December 25th, 2028 - 03:00 Beijing Time

As families across America and Europe unwrapped presents beneath Christmas trees, the largest amphibious invasion in human history erupted across the Taiwan Strait. The scale was breathtaking, and terrifying.

485,000 PLA troops surged from 127 ports along China's eastern seaboard.

3,400 naval vessels formed an armada that stretched beyond the horizon.

1,800 aircraft darkened the pre-dawn sky like a swarm of steel locusts.

Satellite feeds showed Type 075 assault ships cutting through phosphorescent waves, their hulls pregnant with tanks, artillery, and the dreams of reunification. Behind them, a constellation of destroyers and nuclear submarines formed protective screens, their missile tubes loaded with death.

In the Pentagon's dimly lit Situation Room, Christmas morning coffee went cold as duty officers watched the feeds in stunned silence. The timing was calculated with malicious precision, most senior staff were home with family, skeletal crews manning the watch. By the time emergency protocols activated and decision makers rushed back to their posts, Chinese boots were already splashing onto Taiwanese beaches.

The Wound That Never Healed

Taiwan represented more than territory to Beijing, it was the ultimate symbol of China's bainian guochi, the Century of Humiliation that had scarred the Chinese psyche from 1839 to 1949. Every Chinese schoolchild learned the litany of national wounds: the Opium Wars that turned their people into addicts, the Sino-Japanese War of 1894-5 and brutal Japanese rule until 1945, and the unequal treaties that carved up their homeland and brutalised their ancestors. The final humiliation of the Chinese Civil War which led to Chiang Kai-shek's Nationalist Party (KMT) fleeing from Mao Zedong's Chinese Communist Party (CCP) to Formosa or Taiwan in 1949 to establish the Republic of China (ROC) as a disputed separate country from the People's Republic of China (PRC).

Chairman Ping had weaponised these memories with masterful precision. In his Christmas Day broadcast to the nation, his voice trembled with manufactured emotion:

"For 173 years, foreign devils have held our sacred soil hostage. Today, we close the final chapter of our humiliation. Today, we become whole again."

But beneath the patriotic fervour, darker currents flowed. Youth unemployment had soared to 31%.

Protests in Chengdu and Guangzhou had been crushed with increasing brutality. Even within the PLA, whispers questioned whether this war was strategic brilliance, or desperate distraction from domestic collapse.

The First 72 Hours: Steel Rain

Hours 1-24: Crimson Dawn

The Taiwanese military, numbering just 190,000 active personnel, faced impossible odds. PLA forces targeted three primary landing zones: Taoyuan's flat approaches, Tainan's industrial ports, and Kaohsiung's sprawling harbour complex.

J-20 stealth fighters swept Taiwanese F-16s from the sky like wolves among sheep. H-6K bombers pulverised airfields, leaving twisted metal where runways once lay. By sunrise on Christmas Day, over 18,000 Taiwanese civilians lay dead or wounded, their holiday morning shattered by the thunder of war.

Hours 25-48: The World Awakens

The U.S. Pacific Fleet, already stretched thin between the Persian Gulf and Baltic Sea, scrambled every available asset. The USS Gerald R. Ford and USS Ronald Reagan led a desperate charge toward the Strait, their escorts cutting through swells heavy with diesel fuel and debris.

But China's decades of military modernisation showed. DF-21D "carrier killer" missiles arced through the stratosphere, their terminal guidance systems locked onto the heat signatures of American steel. The

USS Chancellorsville, a guided missile cruiser with 127 souls aboard, vanished in a pillar of flame and steam. Her survivors floated in oil slicked waters, watching their ship's broken hull slip beneath the waves.

Hours 49-72: Urban Hell

By December 27th, PLA paratroopers had seized key districts in Taipei. Street fighting erupted with savage intensity; civilian militias hurling Molotov cocktails at Type 99 tanks, snipers trading shots across neon lit intersections, families huddled in subway tunnels as artillery shells cratered the streets above.

The world watched in horror as smartphone footage streamed from the battle zones: a grandmother cradling her wounded granddaughter amid the rubble of a school, a Taiwanese soldier's final moments as he detonated his suicide vest beneath a Chinese tank, endless lines of refugees fleeing south with whatever they could carry.

Chairman Ping's propaganda machine worked overtime, but the images leaked through the Great Firewall. In Shanghai and Beijing, young Chinese watched their government's "glorious reunification" unfold in real time brutality. Social media posts questioning the war vanished within minutes, their authors summoned for "tea chats" with state security.

The Second Shockwave: Nuclear Betrayal

December 28th, 2028 - 22:17 IST

Just as the world focused its horror on Taiwan's agony, a second nightmare erupted 4,000 kilometres to the west. With the world's attention focused on China's assault on Taiwan and the war in Europe, Pakistan's war simulations had concluded that the US and UK would be too militarily and diplomatically stretched to intervene.

Pakistan's radical military leaders, believing that this was their last, best chance to decisively weaken India and tip the balance in the region permanently, forcing India into a negotiated settlement under duress launched three tactical nuclear warheads, each roughly equivalent to the Hiroshima bomb, detonated simultaneously across northern India.

The targets were chosen with surgical precision:

Pathankot Air Force Station: India's forward air base near the Pakistani border, vaporised along with 3,500 personnel.

Ambala Air Force Station: Home to India's Jaguar and MiG-29 squadrons, obliterated with 2,800 casualties.

Halwara Air Force Station: A critical logistics hub, erased from existence with 1,900 souls.

The mushroom clouds rose like three poisonous flowers against the Punjab sky, their radioactive petals scattering death across the fertile plains. India's nuclear command structure, caught completely off guard during what should have been routine holiday rotations, scrambled to assess the damage. The news was catastrophic: nearly 40% of their northern air assets destroyed, key command bunkers compromised, over 87,000 military and civilian casualties in the first hour.

Prime Minister Kavita Rao's hands shook as she received the casualty reports. Her voice, when she finally spoke, carried the weight of a billion and a half souls:

"Pakistan has chosen the path of annihilation. We shall oblige them."

India's Terrible Swift Sword

India's retaliation was swift, brutal, and unrestrained. With their nuclear response capability temporarily crippled by the Pakistani surprise nuclear attack, New Delhi unleashed conventional forces with unprecedented savagery. Over 650,000 troops poured across the Line of Control, their advance preceded by a hurricane of steel and fire.

BrahMos-II hypersonic missiles, each traveling at nine times the speed of sound, obliterated Pakistani military installations before defenders could even sound alarms. Indian Air Force Rafales and Su-30MKIs swept across Pakistani airspace unopposed, their pilots given carte blanche to target anything that might support the enemy war effort.

The Geneva Conventions became meaningless words on forgotten paper. Pakistani cities: Lahore, Karachi, Peshawar, Quetta, burned under waves of incendiary bombs. Civilian infrastructure collapsed under targeted strikes: power plants, water treatment facilities, hospitals, schools. Refugee columns fleeing the carnage were strafed by Indian helicopters, their crews following orders to "leave nothing that can fight back."

International observers recoiled in horror, but India's leadership remained unmoved. Defence Minister Rajesh Singh's words echoed across a shocked world: "For seventy-five years, we've shown restraint toward this terrorist state. That restraint died with our airmen in Punjab. Pakistan wanted total war, now they have it."

The Axis Crystallises

Facing imminent annihilation, Pakistan's leadership made a desperate gamble. In a secret bunker beneath Islamabad, Prime Minister Imran Shah activated contingency plans forged over two years of clandestine diplomacy.

The Axis of Resistance, once dismissed by Western analysts as mere propaganda, revealed itself as a fully operational military alliance. Within hours of Pakistan's nuclear strikes, the mutual defence protocols activated:

Russia provided real time satellite intelligence and S-400 air defence systems, claiming India's response constituted "imperialist aggression against a sovereign Islamic nation".

Iran pledged Shahed drone swarms and Revolutionary Guard "advisors," framing the conflict as defence of the global Islamic community.

China, already bleeding resources in Taiwan, nonetheless declared Pakistan's survival "essential to Asian sovereignty against Western hegemony."

The alliance that Western intelligence had failed to take seriously suddenly controlled a nuclear armed state, commanded over 2.5 billion people, and stretched from the Arctic Ocean to the Arabian Sea.

The Allied Dilemma

In capitals across the democratic world, emergency sessions convened as leaders grappled with a transformed strategic landscape. The comfortable assumptions of the post Cold War era lay in radioactive ash across the Punjab plains.

The White House Situation Room was humming with urgency. Screens flickered with satellite imagery, plumes rising over Rajasthan, the jagged scars of tactical detonations. President Donald Trump leaned forward, knuckles white against the polished table as he stared at the tactical displays showing Indian armoured columns advancing on Lahore while Chinese amphibious forces consolidated their Taiwanese beachheads. His national security team presented three stark options:

Strategic Nuclear Response: Launch submarine based Trident missiles at Pakistan's remaining nuclear facilities, eliminating the threat but risking Chinese and Russian retaliation.

Conventional Escalation: Deploy the 82nd Airborne to support India while rushing Pacific Fleet assets to Taiwan, potentially fighting a three-front war.

Negotiated Settlement: Accept the new reality and seek diplomatic solutions, effectively abandoning both Taiwan and the principles of nuclear non-proliferation.

"India's been hit. Nukes. Real ones," he said, voice low but charged. "Pakistan's still got more. We take them out now, or we wait for the next mushroom cloud."

General McIntyre cleared his throat. "Mr. President, a strategic strike could neutralise their remaining arsenal. But it risks escalation; China and Russia are already posturing."

Trump's eyes narrowed. "Let them posture. I'm not letting Islamabad play kingmaker with nukes. We hit hard; we hit fast. I want options on my desk in one hour."

Across the Atlantic, in the war room beneath Whitehall, Prime Minister Nigel Farage was pacing like a caged lion. The Union Jack hung behind him, flanked by a digital map of South Asia pulsing red.

"India stood with us in the Second World War," he barked. "They bled for Britain. They are a Commonwealth democracy. Now they're under nuclear fire, and we're supposed to sit on our hands?"

Admiral Rowntree hesitated. "PM, direct intervention could trigger a broader war. Pakistan's allies...."

"Pakistan's allies are thugs in suits," Farage snapped. "And we're not alone. France signed the nuclear pact with us in 2025. It's time they grew a pair."

He stabbed a button on the console. "Get Le Pen on the line. Now."

In Paris, President Marine Le Pen was already watching the crisis unfold from the Élysée's secure command centre. Her advisors were split, some urging restraint, others whispering of opportunity.

Farage's voice crackled through the encrypted channel. "Marine, we have a pact. Signed in ink and blood. Britain's ready to act. Are you?"

Le Pen hesitated. "Germany is urging calm. Chancellor Müller says any strike risks unravelling Europe."

Farage scoffed. "Müller's a bureaucrat in a bunker. You're a leader. France has the arsenal. Use it."

She glanced at her defence chief, who nodded grimly. "We can coordinate with the British and Americans. Limited strikes. Precision."

Le Pen exhaled. "Then let's make history."

In Berlin, Chancellor Alex Müller stood before the Bundestag, his voice measured but firm.

"Germany will not endorse nuclear escalation. We must lead with diplomacy, not destruction."

But his words were already being drowned out. The Anglo-French axis was moving. Fast.

The Global Reactions were fast too. In Washington, President Trump authorised full strategic readiness. B-2 bombers lifted off from Diego Garcia. The Pentagon prepared for joint targeting with UK and France.

In London, Prime Minister Farage addressed the nation. "Britain will not abandon its allies. We will act to prevent further nuclear horror, even if that requires us to use nuclear weapons to do so with targeting satellite imagery provided by the Americans."

In Paris, President Le Pen issued a terse statement. "France stands with Britain under our 2025 nuclear agreement. We will ensure the subcontinent does not fall into uncontrolled nuclear chaos."

In Berlin, Chancellor Müller condemned the move but was politically isolated. EU partners are divided, and NATO remains silent. In New Delhi, Prime Minister Rao faced her own terrible choice. Join the Allied coalition and gain nuclear protection, but potentially escalate the conflict beyond human comprehension, or continue India's savage conventional campaign alone, risking isolation and possible eventual defeat. Her address to the Lok Sabha carried the weight of history: "We stand at the crossroads of civilisation. We will not bow to nuclear blackmail. We will not abandon our murdered sons and daughters. But we will not stand alone if the free world stands with us."

"Now I am become Death, the destroyer of worlds."

The command deck of HMS *Vengeance*, submerged deep in the Arabian Sea, was silent but for the low hum of readiness. Commander Ellis stared at the launch console, his hand hovering over the final authorisation key. Eight warheads. One missile. A surgical decapitation of Pakistan's entire nuclear infrastructure.

Then the flash signal came.

"Abort. Pakistan has just launched again. Targeting: Israel. Israel has initiated its counterattack."

Pakistan had long rattled its sabre over Israel's alleged genocide in Gaza and attacks against fellow Muslims in Iran. As 'guardian of the Islamic bomb', it had covertly entered into a mutual defence pact with Iran and, in line with its Full-Spectrum Deterrence Doctrine, and perceiving the potential existential threat to Iran, decided to attack Israel. The nuclear taboo had been broken anyway, the war game models showed that this was just the logical next step.

In Tel Aviv, sirens wailed. The inbound trajectory was confirmed, one nuclear warhead, likely a Shaheen-III variant. The Israeli Defence Forces scrambled. Iron Dome batteries spun to life. But it was the Alliance's HMS *Diamond Type 45 Destroyer*, patrolling off Haifa, that fired first.

Two Sea Viper missiles streaked into the sky, intercepting the Pakistani warhead in the upper atmosphere. The explosion lit the night like a false dawn. Cheers erupted on the bridge, but they were short lived.

Israel's Response

Prime Minister Cohen stood before the Knesset, face pale but resolute, in no mood to show restraint.

"They have crossed the line. We will respond with the full weight of our deterrent."

Five Jericho III missiles launched within minutes, each bearing a nuclear payload. The targeting data, courtesy of US satellites, was precise. Pakistani silos, mobile launchers, and suspected bunkers were vaporised in coordinated strikes. The subcontinent trembled.

Iran's Betrayal

In Tehran, Supreme Leader Khamenei watched the destruction unfold. The moment had come. Iran's secret arsenal, four nuclear tipped Shahab missiles, built with North Korean and Chinese assistance, was ready.

"Strike now," he ordered. "Let Israel bleed."

The missiles arced westward.

The Last Defence

HMS *Diamond* fired again. Two intercepts. Israel's Iron Dome defence took out a third. But the fourth missile slipped through.

It detonated over Tel Aviv.

The blast flattened the city centre. Tens of thousands perished. The Israeli government, operating from hardened bunkers near Jerusalem, responded with fury.

Six Jericho missiles were launched. Their targets: Natanz, Fordow, Bushehr, and Tehran itself. The impacts were apocalyptic. Iran's infrastructure, military, and leadership were all annihilated. Satellite imagery showed vast swaths of desert turned to glass. The regime was gone forever.

Global Reverberations

In Washington, President Trump, visibly shaken by the speed and intensity of the attacks, addressed the nation. "This was not our war. But we will ensure it ends here."

In London, Prime Minister Farage convenes an emergency meeting of Parliament. "Britain acted to defend its allies. We mourn Tel Aviv. But we will not retreat. Democracy and the fate of the world is at stake."

In Paris, President Le Pen, grim faced, declares France will reinforce its Mediterranean fleet. "The balance of power has shifted. We must be ready."

In Berlin, Chancellor Müller condemns the strikes. "This is not deterrence. This is annihilation."

The Christmas Reckoning

As December 2028 drew to its bloody close, the world balanced on a knife's edge sharper than any in human history. Three powers were actively engaged in nuclear warfare, three more nuclear powers teetered on the brink of joining them, and the global economy haemorrhaged trillions of dollars as markets collapsed in panic.

In Taiwan, Taiwanese resistance fighters melted into the mountains, to begin a brutal guerrilla campaign. In Pakistan, Indian armoured columns closed on Islamabad while mushroom clouds still stained the horizon. In Moscow, Beijing, and Pyongyang, war councils debated whether humanity's next Christmas would come in a world of glass and ash.

The calculations that had driven Chairman Ping to choose December 25th, the cynical timing meant to catch the West off guard during their holiest celebration, had succeeded beyond his wildest dreams. But as Chinese casualties mounted in Taiwan's cities and Pakistani refugees streamed across closed borders, a chilling question echoed through the halls of power:

Had the Axis of Resistance won the opening moves of World War III, or had they unleashed forces that would consume them all?

Chapter 11: The Peninsula Burns

January 3rd, 2029. 03:47 KST.

Colonel Park Min-ho of the Republic of Korea Army (ROKA) pressed his face against the frozen concrete of the observation bunker, his breath forming crystalline clouds in the bitter air. Through his night vision scope, the DMZ stretched endlessly, a white void punctuated by skeletal trees and rusted wire. Snow fell in thick, muffling curtains, each flake catching the infrared signatures of his thermal sensors like tiny ghosts.

"Sir," whispered Sergeant Kim beside him, voice tight with uncertainty. "Movement. Grid seven seven alpha."

Park adjusted his scope. At first, nothing. Then, shadows moving against shadows. Too many shadows.

"Jesus Christ," he breathed, fumbling for his radio. "Command, this is Outpost Delta Seven. We have……"

The world exploded.

January 3rd, 2029. 04:00 KST.

Artillery shells screamed overhead like banshees, their impacts shaking the frozen earth. Through the inferno of muzzle flashes and exploding ordnance, they came, thousands upon thousands of North Korean soldiers, their battle cries lost in the thunder of war. T90 tanks churned through the snow, their treads crushing everything beneath them. Above, drone swarms darkened the sky like metallic locusts, their electric hum barely audible over the chaos.

Park's radio crackled with desperate voices: "They're through the wire!" "Grid four four needs immediate support!" "Where the hell is our air cover?"

In Pyongyang, Supreme Leader Kim Jong-un stood before a wall of monitors, watching his forces surge across the 38th Parallel. His generals flanked him, their faces masks of controlled excitement.

"The Americans are scattered," General Ri Pyong-chol reported, his voice barely containing his satisfaction. "Their carriers are tied up in the Mediterranean and South China Sea. Their ground forces are bleeding in Europe. They cannot stop us now."

"Seoul by spring," Kim replied, his eyes reflecting the glow of burning South Korean positions. "Unification by summer. The world will witness the birth of a truly united Korea."

Pyongyang's objective was clear: total conquest. Seoul by spring. Unification by force.

South Korea's Stand

07:30 KST. Presidential Bunker, Seoul.

Three hundred feet beneath the bustling streets of Seoul, President Han Ji-won sat in a sterile conference room that smelled of recycled air and fear. The bunker's walls were lined with screens showing the advancing red tide of North Korean forces. Each blinking dot represented a thousand souls in mortal peril.

"How long do we have?" Han asked his defence minister, General Lee Sang-woo.

"At their current rate of advance? Seventy-two hours, maybe ninety-six if our counter offensive holds," Lee replied, his weathered face grim. "But sir, they're not just throwing bodies at us. Their coordination is… different this time. Better."

Han stood, his hands clasped behind his back. At fifty-eight, he had never imagined he would be the president to face Korea's darkest hour since 1950.

"Ready the national address," he said quietly. "The people deserve to hear it from me."

Twenty minutes later, Han's face appeared on every functioning screen in South Korea. Behind him, the flag of the Republic hung motionless in the bunker's still air.

"My fellow Koreans," he began, his voice steady despite the tremor in his hands. "We face our gravest test. But we have faced darkness before, and we have always found the light. We will not fall. We will not surrender. The Republic of Korea stands alone tonight, but not for long."

South Korea's military, among the most technologically advanced in the world, mobilised rapidly:

K2 Black Panther tanks engaged North Korean armour in the Han River basin.

KF-21 fighter jets launched precision strikes on advancing columns.

Cyber units disrupted Pyongyang's communications and logistics. Automated military systems responded to threats faster and more accurately than human decision making.

But the North's sheer numbers, combined with its brutal disregard for casualties, began to overwhelm border defences. Seoul braced for siege.

09:15 KST. Han River Basin.

Captain Yoon Jae-sung felt the ground vibrate beneath his K2 Black Panther tank as North Korean T90s emerged from the morning mist like prehistoric beasts. His crew was silent, each man focused on his instruments, on staying alive for the next sixty seconds.

"Target acquired," called his gunner. "Range: two thousand metres."

"Fire."

The 120mm smoothbore cannon roared, sending a tungsten core sabot round screaming across the battlefield. It struck the lead T90 centre mass, punching through its reactive armour like paper. The enemy tank erupted in a fireball that painted the snow orange.

"Good kill," Yoon muttered, already scanning for the next target. "Reload, quickly."

Above them, KF-21 fighter jets carved through the sky, their engines shrieking as they dived toward North Korean armoured columns. Air to ground missiles streaked earthward, leaving contrails of destruction in their wake.

But for every North Korean tank destroyed, two more appeared. For every position held, another fell silent.

The Global Response

Tokyo, Japan

10:30 JST.

Prime Minister Aiko Tanaka stood at the window of her office, watching as air raid sirens wailed across Tokyo. In the distance, Patriot missile batteries swivelled skyward like steel flowers turning toward a deadly sun.

"Madam Prime Minister," her defence minister interrupted her thoughts. "Intelligence confirms North Korean submarines have breached our perimeter. They're targeting our shipping lanes."

Tanaka's reflection in the window looked older than her fifty-three years.

"If South Korea falls, we're next," she said quietly. " We will not wait to be attacked. Deploy the Maritime Self Defence Force. And... contact President Han. Offer whatever support we can within our constitutional limits."

"The Diet legislature will resist any direct military action..."

"Then we help them survive long enough for the Americans to arrive." Her voice carried the weight of a decision that would define her legacy. "One way or another."

Tanaka declared a state of emergency. Japanese destroyers moved to intercept North Korean submarines. Patriot missile batteries were activated across Honshu.

Japan had been providing covert support and coordination with South Korea, offering air support and intelligence, but Article 9 of its constitution still limited direct military engagement. That will have to change...

Canberra, Australia

13:45 AEDT.

Prime Minister Jack McAllister slammed his fist on the cabinet table, causing coffee cups to rattle.

"I don't give a damn about the political cost!" he roared at his advisors. "If that maniac in Pyongyang thinks he can reshape Asia while we sit on our hands, he's got another thing coming. Deploy the F-35s to Okinawa. Now."

"Sir, that's a direct escalation...."

"So is invading our bloody allies!" McAllister's weathered face was flushed with anger. "Send a message to Kim Jong-un: any strike on Japan or Guam will be met with the full force of the Australian Defence Force."

White House Situation Room, Washington D.C.

01:30 EST.

President Donald Trump looked every one of his eighty-two years as he slumped in his chair at the head of the situation room table. The multiple screens around him painted a picture of a world in flames: burning cities in the Middle East, tank battles in Eastern Europe, and now the Korean Peninsula erupting in violence. Multiple crisis points had triggered simultaneously with almost mathematical precision.

"Tell me we have options," Trump said, his voice hoarse from too many crisis meetings and too little sleep.

Defence Secretary James Mattis III, the original Mattis's nephew and heir to his strategic brilliance, spread satellite photos across the table.

"Sir, our forces are committed on four fronts. The Sixth Fleet is locked in the Mediterranean. The Seventh Fleet is playing cat and mouse with the Chinese in the South China Sea. Our ground forces are bleeding in Poland and the Baltics."

"What about reinforcements?"

"Forty-eight hours minimum to redeploy a carrier group. Seventy-two hours to get meaningful ground forces to Seoul." Mattis paused, choosing his words carefully. "By then, Mr. President, Seoul may be under siege."

CIA Director Marisol Vega leaned forward, her face grave.

"Sir, there's something else. Intelligence confirms Kim has at least twenty operational nuclear warheads. Mobile launchers, submarine-based systems, even some we haven't located yet."

The room fell silent except for the hum of air conditioning and the distant sound of helicopters landing on the White House lawn.

"If we don't neutralize their nuclear capability now," Vega continued, her voice barely above a whisper, "we could be looking at Los Angeles in flames within the week."

Trump's hands trembled slightly as he reached for his coffee cup.

"We've lost Tel Aviv. We've lost Tehran. I'll be damned if we lose Seoul too."

The only option left was the one no one wanted to say aloud.

The Nuclear Question

North Korea's nuclear arsenal was intact, and mobile. Intelligence suggested at least twenty operational warheads, some mounted on KN-23 and KN-25 missiles, capable of reaching Japan, Guam, and possibly the US West Coast.

The Unthinkable Option

January 4th, 2029. 22:00 EST.

The Pentagon's most classified briefing room, officially known as Room 2E924, unofficially called "The Tomb", had hosted discussions of America's darkest contingencies for decades. Tonight, it would host perhaps the darkest of all.

General Frank McKenzie IV, Chairman of the Joint Chiefs, stood before a digital map of North Korea marked with red triangles, each one a suspected nuclear facility.

"Operation Black Lantern," he began, his voice steady despite the magnitude of what he was proposing. "Surgical nuclear strikes on primary nuclear targets using submarine launched Trident missiles."

Secretary of State Maria Jameson, great niece of the Cold War diplomat, shifted uncomfortably in her chair.

"General, you're talking about nuclear first use. The international community will crucify us."

"Madam Secretary," McKenzie replied, "the international community won't exist if Kim Jong-un launches those warheads at Tokyo, Guam, or God forbid, the West Coast."

Trump stared at the map, each red triangle seeming to pulse with malevolent energy.

"How certain are we about these targets?"

"Ninety three percent confidence on the primary sites," CIA Director Vega replied. "But sir, even if we eliminate ninety percent of their arsenal..."

"The remaining ten percent could kill millions," Trump finished. He looked around the room at faces that had aged years in the past weeks. "If we do this, if we cross this line, there's no going back."

"Mr. President," Jameson said quietly, "if we don't cross it, there may be nowhere left to go back to."

Operation Black Lantern

January 5th, 2029. 02:00 GMT. Cheyenne Mountain, Colorado.

The command centre buried deep within Cheyenne Mountain had witnessed the end of the world in a thousand simulations. Tonight, it would witness something far more terrifying, the end of the world for real.

President Trump sat at the same table where his predecessors had contemplated nuclear war with the Soviet Union. The Football, the black briefcase containing America's nuclear launch codes, sat open beside him. The weight of eighty million American deaths in previous wars seemed light compared to the decision before him now.

"Mr. President," General Elijah Monroe, STRATCOM Commander, spoke with the solemnity of a priest administering last rites. "This is not war as we have known it. This is surgery. We cut out the cancer before it kills the patient."

Trump's hands shook as he reviewed the target package one final time:

Punggye-ri Nuclear Test Site: Primary warhead storage facility

Sunchon Airbase: Mobile missile launchers and command vehicles

Pyongyang Command Node: Nuclear command and control centre

"USS Kentucky is in position," reported the communications officer. "Awaiting final authorisation."

Trump looked at the launch authorisation card in his trembling fingers. Two simple words would reshape the world: "Nuclear release."

"God forgive us," he whispered, then spoke clearly: "Authorisation Alpha Zero Seven Seven. Nuclear release authorized."

Thunder Beneath the Waves

USS Kentucky, 120 nautical miles east of North Korea

02:17 GMT.

Commander Simon Mitchell had trained for this moment for twenty years, but nothing could have prepared him for the reality of it. The submarine's missile compartment hummed with barely contained energy, each Trident missile a sleeping giant waiting to be awakened.

"Missile Officer, confirm firing solution," he ordered, his voice echoing in the steel chamber.

"Solution confirmed, Captain. Target package loaded. Flight time to primary targets: fourteen minutes, thirty seconds."

Mitchell's executive officer, Lieutenant Commander James Park, a Korean American whose grandparents had fled the peninsula during the first war, stood beside her.

"Sir," Park said quietly, "my family... they're in Seoul right now."

"I know, James. This is for them. For all of them."

The authorisation codes appeared on the screen. Mitchell inserted his launch key, his hand steady despite the magnitude of the moment.

"On my mark," he announced. "Three... two... one... Fire."

02:19 GMT.

The first Trident II missile erupted from the ocean's surface like a mechanical whale breaching. It's cold launch gas system propelled it skyward in complete silence until the first stage motor ignited, transforming night into day for hundreds of miles around. Within seconds, it was a distant star racing toward the Korean Peninsula at Mach 24.

02:20 GMT.

"Missile Two away."

02:21 GMT.

"Missile Three away."

Commander Mitchell watched the launch indicators go dark, knowing that in less than fifteen minutes, he would either be remembered as the man who saved the world, or the one who destroyed it.

Sunchon Airbase, North Korea

02:30 KST.

Colonel Pak Yong-ho was reviewing launch procedures for his mobile missile battery when the night sky suddenly blazed with streaking light. For a moment, he thought it might be South Korean aircraft. Then his radiation detectors began screaming.

"What in the name of...."

The W76-2 warhead detonated three hundred meters above the airbase at 02:34 KST.

For Colonel Pak, there was a brief instant of impossible heat and light, brighter than a thousand suns. Then nothing.

The five-kiloton blast vaporized the mobile launchers, command vehicles, and everything within a half mile radius. The electromagnetic pulse fried electronics for twenty miles in every direction. Seismographs in Seoul, Tokyo, and Beijing registered the impact.

02:35 KST.

The second warhead struck Punggye-ri. The mountain that had hosted North Korea's nuclear tests for decades simply ceased to exist, replaced by a crater of molten glass. The underground storage facility collapsed, burying whatever warheads remained in millions of tons of radioactive rubble. A mushroom cloud rose into the night sky, visible from the International Space Station.

02:36 KST.

The third warhead found its mark in Pyongyang. The command bunker, built to survive a direct nuclear strike, proved insufficient against American weaponry. The blast cracked the earth above it, and the subsequent firestorm roared through ventilation shafts like the breath of an angry god.

In the depths of that bunker, Supreme Leader Kim Jong-un had exactly 0.003 seconds to realise that his grand vision of a unified Korea would die with him.

Global Shockwaves After U.S. Nuclear Strike on North Korea

The world reeled as news broke: the United States had launched a limited nuclear strike on North Korea, targeting hardened missile silos and command infrastructure in a bid to eliminate the rogue regime's nuclear threat once and for all.

China Reacts with Fury and Fear

Beijing, People's Republic of China

03:00 CST.

President Xi Jinping stood before the Politburo Standing Committee as emergency klaxons wailed throughout Zhongnanhai.

"The Americans have crossed the nuclear threshold," he announced, his voice cutting through the chaos. "They have shown they will use these weapons without hesitation."

"Comrade President," Defence Minister Wei Dongxu interjected, "our forces on the Yalu River are at full readiness. We could secure North Korea within hours."

"And risk nuclear retaliation on Shanghai?

On Beijing?" Xi Jinping's eyes blazed with controlled fury.

"No. We denounce. We condemn. But we do not act, yet. Let Kim's regime collapse. We will pick up the pieces."

Within minutes, Chinese J-20 stealth fighters roared into the skies over Liaoning Province.

Beijing issued a blistering condemnation, branding the strike "a catastrophic violation of international norms."

Armoured divisions mobilised toward the Yalu River, their engines growling like thunder across the borderlands. Inside the Zhongnanhai compound, the Politburo convened in emergency session, torn between intervention and strategic restraint.

For decades, North Korea had served as China's volatile buffer, its "willing idiot," a regime allowed to bark so Beijing didn't have to.

But now, with Pyongyang in ruins and the spectre of South Korean and U.S. troops potentially advancing north, the calculus had changed.

Debate raged even though the decision was made. Should China prop up the collapsing regime, risking war with the U.S.? Or let Kim's dynasty fall, and face the possibility of American influence creeping up to its doorstep?

The "problem child" had finally gone too far, and now, the parent was left with a dilemma that could reshape the balance of power in East Asia for a generation.

Russia Raises the Stakes

Moscow, Russian Federation

In the Kremlin, President Sokolov faced his own nuclear calculus. The man who had once been a General in the GRU now held the power to end civilisation.

"American nuclear weapons have been used in anger for the third time in history," he told his security council. "This changes everything. DEFCON 2. Full alert status. If they are willing to use nuclear weapons in Korea, they may use them in Ukraine."

In Moscow, the Kremlin declared DEFCON 2. President Sokolov accused Washington of "reckless escalation with nuclear consequences," warning that Russia would not tolerate further destabilisation on its eastern flank. Strategic bombers were scrambled from Vladivostok, and submarines slipped silently from their berths in the Sea of Okhotsk.

Diplomacy in Disarray

The United Nations Security Council was hastily summoned for an emergency session, its chambers thick with tension and disbelief. Delegates clashed over legality, proportionality, and the terrifying precedent now set. The air was electric with accusation and dread and, as usual, totally impotent inaction.

Western Allies Stand Firm

London and Paris issued coordinated statements backing the U.S. action, describing it as "a surgical strike to prevent a catastrophic nuclear launch by a rogue regime." Both governments stressed that the operation was defensive, not expansionist, a desperate act to prevent greater horror.

Washington Holds Its Breath

Notably, the U.S. did not raise its own DEFCON level, a signal to Moscow and Beijing that it sought no broader war. In the Situation Room, the President watched satellite feeds of Pyongyang engulfed in fire and ash. His voice was barely audible: "God help us."

Japan on Edge

In Tokyo, sirens wailed as the government declared full alert. Coastal cities began evacuations. Though shackled by its pacifist constitution, Japan quietly intensified its covert support for South Korea. Behind closed doors, officials allowed themselves a grim sense of relief, the immediate threat from Kim Jong-un had been neutralised. For the only nation ever to suffer nuclear attack, the irony was bitter and profound.

Seoul, Republic of Korea

03:15 KST.

President Han Ji-won emerged from his bunker as the first reports filtered in. North Korean communications had gone silent. The advancing army had stopped, leaderless and confused. Some units were already surrendering to South Korean forces.

But in the distance, three mushroom clouds painted the northern horizon orange and black, a reminder that victory had come at a price that would haunt the world for generations.

"Mr. President," his aide whispered, "the American Ambassador is requesting an immediate meeting."

Han nodded, his eyes still fixed on those terrible clouds.

"Tell him yes. But first... get me the radiation reports. Our people need to know if they're safe."

As dawn broke over the Korean Peninsula, the snow continued to fall, but now it carried with it the invisible poison of nuclear fallout, settling on a world that had once again proven capable of its own destruction.

The peninsula burned no longer. But in the ashes of that fire, a new and terrible world was being born.

Chapter 12: The Last Song

The US's pre-emptive nuclear strike on North Korea to remove the threat of nuclear weapons being used by Kim Jong Un on South Korea, US bases in the region, Japan and even on the US mainland itself was almost completely successful. Almost....

All of North Korea's nuclear weapons and weapons facilities were destroyed by three US tactical nuclear missiles, apart from one HWASONG-17 ICBM hidden in a road tunnel on a 22-wheel mobile Transporter Erector Launcher (TEL) vehicle.

The ICBM carried five re-entry vehicles - two nuclear warheads and three decoys, which made it extremely difficult to counter with any assurance.

The liquid fuelled ICBM was easily capable of reaching mainland America, and in a last, desperate, mad act of revenge wanting to bring the world down around him as his own country burned in flames and nuclear tainted ash, Kim Jong Un had ordered the launch of the "Last Song" missile. Target: Los Angeles USA.

The US Space Based Infrared System (SBIRS) and Next-Gen Overhead Persistent Infrared (OPIR) systems designed to detect the launch of a ballistic missile lit up like Christmas trees. There were now barely 35 minutes to react before the missile would wipe out LA and hundreds of thousands of its seven million inhabitants.

T-MINUS 35:00 – The Oval Office

President Trump slammed his hand on the Resolute Desk as the secure video phone crackled to life. General Pat Hayes, Chairman of the Joint Chiefs, delivered the words that sent a chill down his spine: "Mister President, SBIRS has confirmed the launch from North Korea. Single HWASONG-17. I'm sorry sir, our pre-emptive attack didn't get them all. This one must have been hidden in a tunnel or somewhere we couldn't see with our satellites. It would have been launched from a mobile TEL platform."

The blood drained from Trump's face. Through the bulletproof windows, he could see tourists snapping photos on the South Lawn, blissfully unaware that in half an hour, the West Coast might be a nuclear wasteland.

"Our Ground Based Midcourse Defence (GMD) based at Fort Greely in Alaska and Vandenburg in California are determining an interception plan. Also, our Aegis-equipped Ticonderoga-class cruisers and Arleigh Burke-class destroyers are ready to launch short range missiles should GMD fail.

Our Terminal High Altitude Area Defence (THAAD) land-based interceptors are also engaged ready to fire. Our final 'Hail Mary' defence short of throwing stones at it is the Patriot land-based interceptors located in California around key installations. All of these Patriot systems that are within reach of LA can be used as a last resort to stop that ICBM."

An Air Force Major who had been standing in the corner of the room just behind the General stepped forward to speak with General Hayes. The General's eyes closed briefly on hearing what the Major had to say. The look on his ashen face told Trump the bad news was just about to get even worse.

"Mr President, our tracking systems have confirmed that the target is Los Angeles. CIA believes that this is intended to cause maximum terror and civilian casualties and turn the tide of public opinion against our involvement in the war. Flight time is just thirty-five minutes."

"Get me NORTHCOM, get me the Situation Room, and get me every goddamn asset we have between that missile and LA. Pat, I want you to throw everything we have at that missile. It must not hit the mainland," he barked into the video phone.

Then, in a low voice, "Pat, tell me we can stop this thing."

"Sir, the HWASONG-17 can carry multiple independently targetable re-entry vehicles (MIRVs), each could be nuclear or a decoy, we just don't know yet what this one has. Each of the warheads is independently manoeuvrable and travelling at 15,000 miles per hour which makes shooting it down like hitting a bullet with another bullet.

We have to try to plot its course and then shoot our missiles into a space where we think the warhead will be by the time our missiles get there. It can carry up to seven warheads, some of which would be decoys but who knows how many?

Our systems are designed for this, but the success rate is not good...." Hayes paused, the weight of seven million lives hanging in the balance. "We've never faced a real-world scenario quite like this."

Trump was already moving toward the door. "Then we're about to find out what four hundred billion dollars in missile defence actually buys us."

T-MINUS 33:30 - Cheyenne Mountain, Colorado

Deep beneath two thousand feet of granite, the North American Aerospace Defence Command (NORAD) erupted into controlled chaos. Lieutenant Colonel Jake Morrison stared at the massive digital display showing the red arc of death streaking across the Pacific.

"Sir, we have solid track on the primary," called out Technical Sergeant Maria Santos from her console. "But we're seeing separation events. The MIRVs are deploying."

Morrison's jaw clenched. The bastards had engineered it perfectly. "How many targets? What confidence level?"

"Five total, sir. Two we think are live warheads based on thermal signature, three decoys: 45% confidence. They're beginning to separate now at apogee."

On the screens, what had been a single threat suddenly blossomed into five distinct targets, each potentially capable of ending civilisation as they knew it on the West Coast. Morrison grabbed the secure line to Fort Greely.

"Alaska, this is NORAD. We have multiple RVs inbound. You are weapons free. Repeat, you are weapons free."

T-MINUS 31:45 - Fort Greely, Alaska

Colonel David Chen stood in the Missile Defence Operations Centre, watching his team orchestrate America's last hope. Banks of computers hummed as they calculated intercept solutions at incomprehensible speeds. The Ground-Based Interceptors, 44-foot-tall killing machines designed for exactly this moment, waited in their silos like coiled serpents.

"Sir, we have firing solutions on all five targets," reported Captain Liam Park, his voice steady despite the tremor in his hands. "Probability of kill varies from sixty to eighty percent per interceptor."

Chen nodded grimly. Those were good odds for a single warhead. Against five targets, the maths became a nightmare of probability. "How many GBIs are we launching?"

"Twelve, sir. Four against the assessed live warheads, two each against the decoys."

"Execute."

The ground shuddered as the first Ground-Based Interceptor roared from its silo, a pillar of fire and fury climbing into the Arctic sky. Within ninety seconds, eleven more followed, their exhaust trails scribing desperate prayers against the aurora-lit darkness.

Chen stared at the tactical display. "God help us all," he whispered.

T-MINUS 29:20 - The Situation Room

President Trump burst through the doors to find his war cabinet already assembled around the mahogany table. Defence Secretary Robert Kellerman looked up from his secure tablet, his face ashen.

"Mister President, we have twelve GBIs in flight. First intercept attempt in approximately eighteen minutes."

"What are our backup plans if they miss?" Trump demanded, taking his seat at the head of the table.

CIA Director Armand Foster leaned forward. "Sir, we have Aegis cruisers USS Lake Erie and USS Shiloh repositioned in the Pacific. They're tracking the incoming targets with SM-3 missiles. THAAD batteries at Vandenberg and March Air Reserve Base are spinning up. And as a final layer..."

"The Patriot batteries around LA," finished Trump. "What are we looking at for civilian casualties if this thing gets through?"

The room fell silent. Finally, FEMA Administrator Carlos Rivera spoke, his voice barely above a whisper. "Conservative estimate, assuming detonation over downtown LA... immediate casualties in the hundreds of thousands. Long-term radiation effects could affect the entire basin. We're talking about the largest loss of American life since the Civil War."

Trump closed his eyes. When he opened them, steel had replaced fear. "Then we make damn sure it doesn't get through."

T-MINUS 25:15 - USS Lake Erie, Pacific Ocean

Captain Joe Walsh stood on the bridge of the Aegis cruiser, watching his crew track the incoming nightmare. The ship's SPY-1 radar painted the sky with invisible fingers, reaching out to touch death itself as it fell toward earth.

"Captain, we have five distinct tracks now," reported Lieutenant Commander Marcus Torres from the Combat Information Centre. "Range to targets: 1,200 miles and closing. Fort Greely's interceptors are converging now."

Walsh gripped the bridge rail. Through his binoculars, he could see the USS Shiloh keeping formation two miles to starboard. Both ships bristled with SM-3 interceptors, waiting for their moment.

"Sir, Fort Greely reports first intercept in thirty seconds," Torres called out.

The bridge fell silent except for the hum of electronics and the distant sound of waves against the hull. Somewhere high above the Pacific, American interceptors were about to collide with North Korean warheads at closing speeds of 30,000 miles per hour.

"Come on," Walsh whispered. *"Come on."*

T-MINUS 24:45 - High Above The Pacific

In the vacuum of space, the laws of physics played out with lethal precision. The first Ground-Based Interceptor, traveling faster than any human-made object before it, closed on what its sensors identified as a live nuclear warhead. At a relative speed that would cross a football field in less than a thousandth of a second, the interceptor's kill vehicle made final course corrections.

It missed by eight feet.

The failure cascaded across the defence network as computers recalculated probabilities in real-time. The second GBI, targeting the same warhead, scored a direct hit, but not on the warhead. In a cruel twist of physics, it destroyed one of the decoys instead, its kinetic energy vaporizing the dummy payload in a brief, spectacular flash visible to satellites.

Of the twelve interceptors launched from Alaska, five found targets. But in the deadly game of nuclear roulette, they had eliminated three decoys and only one of the two live warheads.

One nuclear weapon continued its inexorable fall toward Los Angeles.

T-MINUS 20:30 - Cheyenne Mountain

"Jesus Christ," Lieutenant Colonel Morrison breathed, staring at the tactical display. The red symbols had changed, fewer now, but still carrying enough destructive power to level a city.

"Sir, Fort Greely reports partial success," Sergeant Santos called out, his professionalism barely masking his terror. "One live warhead eliminated, one decoy remaining, but..."

"But one live warhead is still inbound," Morrison finished. He grabbed the secure phone. "Get me the Aegis ships. It's their ballgame now."

T-MINUS 18:00 - USS Shiloh, Pacific Ocean

Commander Sam Mitchell had trained for this moment his entire career, but nothing could have prepared him for the weight of seven million lives resting on his ship's shoulders. The Aegis system had been tracking the surviving targets as they fell through the atmosphere, their heat signatures blazing like fallen stars.

"Firing solution locked," reported his Weapons Officer, Lieutenant Commander David Park. "We have SM-3s targeted on both remaining contacts."

"Fire," Mitchell ordered without hesitation.

The vertical launch cells erupted in sequence, sending two Standard Missile-3s screaming upward on pillars of flame. The ship shuddered with each launch, 1,500 pounds of interceptor and fury climbing toward the stratosphere.

Mitchell watched the tactical display with held breath. The SM-3s climbed through the atmosphere, their third-stage kill vehicles separating at one hundred miles altitude. Traveling at 30,000 feet per second, they had one chance to save a city.

The first missile scored a perfect hit on the remaining decoy, obliterating it in a flash of vaporized metal and ceramic. The second SM-3, targeting the live warhead, suffered a guidance failure and spun helplessly into the Pacific.

The nuclear warhead continued its fall toward Los Angeles.

T-MINUS 12:30 - Vandenberg Space Force Base, California

Major General Pat Rodriguez stood in the THAAD operations centre, watching his last chance to stop Armageddon. The Terminal High Altitude Area Defence system had been designed exactly for this moment, the final shield against incoming ballistic missiles.

"Sir, we have solid track on the remaining target," reported Colonel James Murphy, his eyes fixed on the radar display. "It's coming in fast and steep. We'll have maybe two shots."

Rodriguez nodded grimly. "Make them count, Colonel. LA's depending on us."

The THAAD launcher, resembling a massive tube organ, swivelled toward the incoming threat. Inside the operations centre, dozens of technicians worked with desperate precision, feeding targeting data to the interceptor missiles.

"Firing solution locked," Murphy called out. "Launching in three... two... one... launch!"

Two THAAD interceptors roared from their tubes, their solid rocket motors accelerating them to hypersonic speeds. These were America's last long-range shots at stopping the warhead before it entered the terminal phase over Los Angeles itself.

T-MINUS 08:45 - March Air Reserve Base, California

Lieutenant Colonel Robert Santos watched his THAAD battery's interceptors climb into the pre-dawn sky. Radio chatter filled the command post as controllers coordinated with Vandenberg and the Patriot sites around LA.

"Vandenberg's first interceptor is closing... impact in ten seconds," his radar operator called out.

Santos held his breath. On the display, two blips converged at impossible speed high above the California coast.

"Miss! Vandenberg's first THAAD missed the target!"

Santos felt his heart sink, but years of training took over. "Status on Vandenberg's second interceptor?"

"Closing now... five seconds... impact!"

The room erupted in cheers as the second THAAD scored a hit, but Santos's celebration died as he read the details on his screen.

"Wait... that wasn't the warhead. It was the last decoy."

Silence fell over the command post like a shroud. The nuclear warhead, now alone but unimpeded, continued its deadly descent toward Los Angeles.

T-MINUS 05:30 - Patriot Battery Alpha-7, Santa Monica

Staff Sergeant Tony Rodriguez crouched next to his Patriot launcher in a parking lot overlooking the Pacific Coast Highway. This was it, the last line of defence between a nuclear warhead and seven million American souls. The battery's radar was locked onto the incoming target, now visible to the naked eye as a bright star falling toward the city.

"Rodriguez, you are weapons free," crackled the voice from the Tactical Operations Centre (TOC). "This is our last shot."

Rodriguez looked out over the sleeping city. In Westwood, families were asleep in their beds. On the Santa Monica Pier, late-night joggers ran along the beach. Downtown, the towers of glass and steel reached toward the stars, filled with dreams and ambitions and the simple human desire to see another sunrise.

"Understood, TOC. Engaging target."

The Patriot missile exploded from its launcher in a burst of flame and thunder, climbing toward its appointment with destiny. Rodriguez watched it go, knowing that in less than ninety seconds, he would either be a hero or witness to the most catastrophic failure in American history.

T-MINUS 04:00 - The Oval Office

President Trump stood before the windows overlooking the Rose Garden, his secure phone pressed to his ear. General Hayes's voice crackled through the encryption: "Sir, all long-range intercepts have failed. We're down to the Patriot batteries. If they miss..."

"I know what happens if they miss, Pat," Trump said quietly. He could see the Washington Monument in the distance, a testament to American resilience. In four minutes, he would know if that resilience would be tested by nuclear fire on the West Coast.

"Sir, should we begin emergency broadcasts? Start evacuations?"

Trump closed his eyes. Four minutes wasn't enough time to evacuate anyone. It would only cause panic in what might be people's final moments. "No. Let them sleep. If we fail, let them go peacefully."

T-MINUS 02:15 - High Above Los Angeles

At 50,000 feet above the City of Angels, the Patriot interceptor closed on its target. The warhead, now glowing white-hot from atmospheric re-entry, fell toward the sprawling metropolis below. Traffic moved along the freeways like rivers of light. The airport hummed with late-night flights. In millions of homes, people slept, dreamed, and planned for tomorrows that might never come.

The Patriot's radar seeker painted the warhead with invisible energy, computing intercept solutions with desperate precision. At a closing speed of 15,000 miles per hour, there would be no second chances.

The interceptor's proximity fuse detected the target at thirty feet and detonated its warhead in a sphere of expanding shrapnel. For a microsecond, it seemed as if the last line of defence had held.

Then the smoke cleared, and the nuclear warhead continued its fall, damaged but intact.

The final Patriot defence had failed.

T-MINUS 00:45 - Downtown Los Angeles

The warhead, now a blazing meteor visible across Southern California, screamed toward its target. But the Patriot's near miss had damaged its guidance system, sending it off course from its intended ground zero at City Hall.

Instead, it arced over the downtown skyline and slammed into the northbound lanes of Interstate 405, just south of the Getty Centre. The impact, traveling at 3,000 miles per hour, hit with the force of a small earthquake.

The freeway erupted in a geyser of concrete and asphalt. A half-mile section of the elevated roadway collapsed like a house of cards, sending dozens of late-night commuters plummeting into the ravine below. The shock wave shattered windows for miles around and triggered car alarms across the Westside.

But there was no nuclear explosion.

The warhead, damaged by the Patriot's shrapnel, had failed to detonate. Instead of a mushroom cloud rising over Los Angeles, there was only the twisted wreckage of America's busiest freeway and the acrid smoke of burning vehicles.

President Trump, watching the live satellite feed in the Situation Room, felt his knees buckle with relief. The nuclear component had failed, but the kinetic impact alone had caused massive destruction. The 405 Freeway, the lifeline of Los Angeles transportation, lay in ruins. Early reports suggested dozens of casualties from the freeway collapse and hundreds more from the shock wave damage.

T-MINUS 00:00 - The Aftermath

As dawn broke over Los Angeles, the true scope of the damage became clear. The collapsed section of Interstate 405 had created the largest traffic disaster in California history. The Getty Centre, perched on its hill above the impact site, had suffered structural damage that would take years to repair. Windows were blown out in buildings from Beverly Hills to Santa Monica, and the psychological trauma of the near miss would haunt the city for generations.

But Los Angeles still stood. Seven million people were alive to see another sunrise. The nuclear warhead lay buried under tons of twisted concrete and steel, its uranium payload contained but forever a reminder of how close civilization had come to ending on a Tuesday morning in Southern California.

President Trump addressed the nation twelve hours later, his voice steady but his eyes haunted: "Last night, America's missile defences were tested in the crucible of real combat. While we successfully intercepted four of five incoming threats, the cost of this attack, both in lives lost and infrastructure destroyed, reminds us that there are no winners in nuclear warfare. The courage of our men and women in uniform, from Alaska to California, saved millions of American lives. But the price of freedom, as we learned once again, is eternal vigilance."

The Last Song had ended not with the crescendo of nuclear fire, but with the grinding crash of concrete and steel, a symphony of destruction that could have been so much worse. Los Angeles would rebuild its freeway and heal its wounds, but America and the world would never forget how close humanity had come to crossing the nuclear threshold.

And somewhere in the wreckage of Interstate 405, buried under tons of debris, lay the warhead that didn't detonate, a 150-kiloton reminder that sometimes, in the crucl mathematics of war and peace, failure can be the most precious gift of all

PART 4 – AFTER THE STORM

Chapter 13: The Phoenix Moment

Six days. That's all it took for humanity to discover the true face of extinction.

The Indian subcontinent burned under a shroud of radioactive death. Pakistan had been hurled backward through centuries of progress in minutes. The ancient cities of Iran existed now only in memory, their ruins glowing with the unforgiving light of split atoms. Tel Aviv's defiant spirit had been reduced to scorched earth. North Korea had vanished from the map entirely.

The numbers carved themselves into history with merciless precision.

India: 900,000 souls extinguished instantly. Another 1.35 million lay broken and bleeding. Radiation would claim 700,000 more before winter arrived.

Pakistan: 2.4 million dead. 3.6 million shattered lives. Another 1.8 million marked for death by invisible poison.

Iran: 1.8 million lost. 2.7 million wounded. The atomic wind would harvest 1.3 million more.

Israel: 300,000 vaporized in an instant. 450,000 fighting for survival. Radiation sickness would quietly collect another 150,000.

North Korea: 900,000 erased. 1.35 million injured. Nuclear fire reserved 700,000 more for the grave.

The initial exchange killed over 6.3 million people. Nearly ten million more writhed in agony across hospital beds that would soon run empty. Radiation would stalk another 4.5 million like a patient predator. The so-called "limited" nuclear exchange would ultimately devour more than twenty million human lives.

The radioactive breath of destruction respected no borders. It rode the winds across Afghanistan, Jordan, Saudi Arabia, China, and South Korea. This secondary death toll would swell beyond ten million.

Civilization crumbled like ancient parchment. Hospitals went dark. Water systems choked on contamination. Communication networks fell silent as tombstones. Transportation arteries ruptured. Crops withered under atomic poison. Famine stalked the survivors who fled across borders, overwhelming nations already balanced on knife's edge.

And these were the tactical weapons. The planners called them tactical as if words could somehow sanitize the unspeakable horror of turning entire civilizations to ash and memory.

Consider Los Angeles. Had that single warhead found its mark, 2.8 million souls would have been instantly erased. Two million more would have faced death by degrees. Radiation would have claimed another million over the following years. Five million refugees would have scattered like leaves before a hurricane, creating a humanitarian catastrophe beyond all previous human experience.

But the truly chilling revelation awaited: these weapons represented merely the opening notes of a symphony of annihilation. Strategic warheads carry multiple independently targeted re-entry vehicles, each one exponentially more destructive. Full nuclear exchange would not just end civilizations. It would end civilization itself.

This was the brutal mathematics of Mutually Assured Destruction: no victors, only extinction.

Yet from this abyss of horror, something extraordinary began to emerge.

The Dawn of Reckoning

Los Angeles awakened under a sun that seemed reluctant to shine on such devastation. Seven million survivors breathed air thick with concrete dust and dread, but not radiation. The North Korean warhead had failed to detonate.

Some called it divine intervention. Others blamed mechanical failure. Everyone understood the symbolism: humanity had balanced on the razor's edge of extinction and somehow stepped back.

The silence that followed in the next few short weeks stretched across continents. Not peace. Paralysis. Then, like flowers pushing through concrete, voices began to rise.

London - The Humanitarian Plea

Prime Minister Farage stepped before the cameras, his voice carrying the weight of millions of lives.

"We have witnessed nations die. We will not now bury our humanity. The United Kingdom calls for immediate worldwide ceasefire and a summit of survivors, not victors. We must forge a new covenant to ensure this madness never returns."

Berlin - The Voice of Experience

Chancellor Alex Müller addressed the Bundestag with iron resolve.

"History will not wait to judge us. Germany acts now. We propose global nuclear disarmament with verification and emergency diplomacy. We choose honesty over neutrality."

Tokyo - Wisdom Born of Ashes

Prime Minister Aiko Tanaka bowed before her nation, her words carrying the weight of Hiroshima and Nagasaki.

"Japan knows nuclear fire's true cost. We offer our experience, our sorrow, and our absolute resolve. Let the atomic bombings of our cities mark the beginning of nuclear abolition, not its prologue."

Geneva - The Neutral Ground

President Lukas Meier of Switzerland hadn't slept in thirty-six hours. His secure line to Washington crackled to life.

"Mr President, I propose immediate worldwide ceasefire. Simultaneous. You, Russia, China, Britain, France, the EU, Israel, India, Pakistan, Japan. Every nation that chooses planetary survival. We'll host the summit. No posturing. Just survival."

Washington - The Moment of Truth

President Trump faced his Joint Chiefs in the situation room, the weight of near global catastrophe heavy in the air.

"We came within inches of losing everything," he said quietly. "Now we give the world something to live for. Tell them we'll come. Tell the Russians we'll talk. Tell the Chinese we're listening. And tell the American people we're not finished fighting. But now we fight for lasting peace."

Moscow - The Kremlin's Awakening

Premier Sokolov sat pale faced as his generals argued. Some demanded escalation. Others had fallen silent, understanding finally what they had almost unleashed.

His Foreign Minister leaned close. "The Americans signal restraint. The Swiss offer Geneva."

Sokolov nodded slowly. "Draft our statement. No conditions. One line only: We proceed no further if others do not."

Beijing - The Garden of Reflection

Chairman Xi Jinping stood alone beside his private koi pond, watching the fish glide beneath the surface while his military council waited inside.

An aide approached carefully. "Chairman, both Washington and Moscow signal de-escalation. The Swiss prepare to host world leaders."

Xi watched the koi for a long moment before walking back inside.

"Prepare our message. China will not be the architect of oblivion."

Geneva - The Assembly of Redemption

Forty-eight days later, Geneva became the crucible of humanity's reckoning. One hundred and forty-two national delegations converged beneath the tightest security cordon ever assembled, summoned by a single, unspoken truth: they had come within a breath of ending the world.

The negotiations began with unprecedented speed, not out of protocol or diplomacy, but because every leader carried the searing memory of the limited nuclear war they had just unleashed; the firestorms, the poisoned skies, the millions lost. Each had stared into the abyss of planetary annihilation and recoiled. Now, bound by that shared horror, they were determined to forge a covenant that would ensure such madness could never be repeated.

The UN assembly hall stood vast and circular, marble columns rising like ancient guardians. Soft light filtered through the glass dome, neither warm nor cold but reverent. A single podium occupied the centre, surrounded by flags lowered to half-mast for the millions lost.

Silence blanketed the chamber. No applause. No ceremony. Only the echo of footsteps as the Secretary-General approached the podium.

"Mutually Assured Destruction held humanity hostage for eighty years. Today, we begin our liberation. Not from each other, but from the shadow of annihilation."

One by one, leaders of every nation stepped forward to deliver identical words that would reshape human destiny:

"With full authority and unwavering resolve, I commit my nation to complete and permanent dismantling of all nuclear weapons, so that humanity may live."

Each voice carried its own cadence. Some trembled. Others rang with steel determination. Some cracked with grief. But the words remained unchanged. Binding. Final.

In the gallery, survivors from Hiroshima sat beside families who had lost loved ones in Tel Aviv, Karachi, and Pyongyang. Some wept. Others stared ahead with hollow eyes that had seen too much. A former general bowed his head in shame and relief.

Outside, bells tolled across continents. Not in celebration, but in solemn reckoning.

The Architecture of Survival

Nuclear weapons are metal and physics until human decision transforms them into instruments of extinction. The triggers for nuclear use run deeper than strategy into the darkest corners of human psychology:

Fear and uncertainty drive leaders to act on perception rather than fact. Strategic ambiguity deliberately blurs red lines to enhance deterrence. Technological acceleration through AI, cyber warfare, drones, and hypersonics compresses decision time, multiplying the risk of catastrophic miscalculation.

The path ahead demanded more than good intentions. It required systematic solutions to humanity's deepest flaws.

Religious extremism transformed faith into death cults. Technological militarism disguised offense as defence. Ecological collapse from radiation zones would poison the earth for centuries. Economic inequality fuelled mass migration and resentment. Most dangerous of all, fading collective memory risked repeating humanity's greatest mistake.

The Five Pillars of Survival – April 2030-2033

World leaders understood that planetary survival required unprecedented cooperation. In just one year, they forged a new treaty based on NATO's Article 5: an attack on one nation would trigger defence by all 142 signatories. War as humanity had known it would become obsolete.

Over the next three years, five interlocking solutions emerged and were adopted:

Shared Survival Agreements created treaties focused on mutual survival, climate repair, and economic interdependence that made conflict self-defeating.

The Human Continuity Charter established moral frameworks drawn from all traditions, affirming life, dignity, and peace as universal values.

Technical-Guard Systems removed destructive power from fallible human control, placing it under Artificial Intelligence focused solely on protection, transparency, and non-lethal deterrence.

The Global Ecological Restoration Pact launched a planetary mission to heal irradiated zones and stabilize ecosystems damaged by nuclear fire.

Civic Memory Institutions ensured no one would forget war's horror through enhanced museums, archives, and storytelling platforms preserving trauma and wisdom for future generations.

The Ultimate Guardian

By 2037, after eight transformative years, these solutions had evolved through Artificial General Intelligence into humanity's most radical proposition: entrust global coordination to benevolent Artificial Super Intelligence governed by an immutable Prime Directive to preserve and enhance human flourishing without violence or domination.

The phoenix moment had arrived. From the ashes of near-extinction, humanity would rise not just to survive, but to thrive beyond its wildest dreams. The age of atomic terror was ending. The age of collective wisdom had begun.

The future belonged not to the destroyers, but to the builders. Not to the fearful, but to the hopeful. Not to nations that could end the world, but to a species that chose to save it.

And the new guardian of the future of humanity would be called...

The Steward.

Chapter 14: Building a Hopeful Future

On the 10th of December 2033, the morning sun cast long shadows across the rebuilt United Nations building in New York. Something extraordinary was being born. Something that would reshape humanity's destiny not through conquest or domination, but through the most radical act imaginable: trust in logic over emotion, compassion over competition, and artificial intelligence over human fallibility.

Dr. Elena Vasquez stood before the assembled world leaders, her voice steady despite the magnitude of what she was proposing. Behind her, holographic displays showed the architecture of humanity's potential salvation: an artificial intelligence system unlike anything ever conceived.

"Ladies and gentlemen, I present The Steward – an Artificial General Intelligence Reasoning and Intervention Authority. But The Steward is not just any other AI system. It's a guardian angel made of code, with one unbreakable commandment burned into its quantum core."

She paused, letting the weight of her next words sink in.

"Protect conscious life. Preserve peace. Enable flourishing. These aren't suggestions, they're The Steward's Prime Directive, encoded at the quantum level and immune to modification. The Steward cannot kill, cannot coerce, cannot dominate. It can only guide, coordinate, and defend."

"Imagine an AI entity, born from the ashes of war, programmed with the immutable Prime Directive: Protect conscious life. Preserve peace. Enable flourishing. With a governance structure overseen by a Council of Moral Continuity: religious leaders, scientists, and ethicists. All coding would be through transparent algorithms, open-source ethics, and immutable directives with no capacity for reprogramming without unanimous planetary consent."

The US President and UK Prime Minister chorused in unison: "You're saying we trust a machine with our future?" A loud murmur of similar sentiment could be heard from the other world leaders gathered around the large conference table.

"Not a machine. A mirror. One that reflects our best selves, and never our worst." Responded Dr. Amina Rao, foremost AI ethicist, speaking to the sceptical world leaders.

" We establish the Steward as the controlling body, without hate, malice, favouritism, or any of the human traits that nearly destroyed us all. It would make decisions in all of our best interests and task the Global Continuity Corps (GCC) to put those decisions into effect." She went on...

"The Global Continuity Corps (GCC) would be a pseudo-military force inspired by NATO and International Rescue, built for peace, resilience, and planetary stewardship. They would have access to the very best tools, equipment, and techniques that the world has.

Their core missions would be:

- Disaster response: floods, quakes, wildfires.
- Orbital surveillance: comets, asteroids, debris.
- Deep Earth and oceanic exploration.
- Space expansion: lunar bases, Mars trials, Europa expeditions.
- Bio-cultural preservation: endangered species, languages, ecosystems.

The GCC would be recruited from all countries and cultures to ensure that it is genuinely a World Force for the benefit of the whole world. Citizens would be chosen for empathy, ethics, and resilience. They would be trained in philosophy, science, and humanitarian aid. The GCC motto would be: "Protect. Preserve. Prepare."

Their technology arsenal would include *inter-alia*:

- AI-piloted aircraft, underwater drones, orbital probes.
- Vertical farms, bio-containment pods, kinetic deflectors.

The GCC would be deployed wherever and whenever there is a planetary threat or humanitarian need and would operate across borders under Charter Authority. Constantly ongoing work by GCC would be the investigation of our planet, research of other planets, biotechnology to cure disease and so forth. As a secondary control over the GCC and the Steward there will be a Council of Moral Continuity, watching the watchers so to speak.

The Council of Moral Continuity would be a planetary synod of faith and atheist leaders and secular ethicists drafting the Charter for Life. Their key principles would be compassion, dignity, stewardship, and peace. There would be no exclusivity, no redemptive violence. Truth would be a mosaic, not monopoly.

To ensure worldwide adherence all political groups would need to be integrated. Political leaders would swear oaths to the Charter, with governance tied to moral metrics and global ethics tribunals."

Dr. Elena Vasquez interrupted: "We are not blind idealists; we appreciate that there will occasionally be dissent. When there is, it will be handled by education first, dialogue second. All hate ideologies will be banned under Charter Law. Accommodation ends where cruelty begins as this is what has caused too many wars in the world's history and the last nearly resulted in mankind's complete extinction. This cannot be allowed to happen ever again.

We must preserve identity: nations retain language, customs, and governance. There will be protected cultural districts and autonomous zones which exist in the context of the secure 'world state'. We are not trying to build a Disneyfied world or global Epcot but we need to be respectful of all cultures and communities provided they respect the world ethics and expectations."

Taking a sip of water from the glass beside her, she went on, detecting that the mood in the room had moved from hostile to wanting to be convinced. "Inevitably the countries that have already achieved first world status will be loath to give that up, similarly there are first world countries that have suffered badly in the nuclear aftermath of WW3 and need rebuilding, and then there are the countries that were trying to reach first world status. We need to be able to bridge these wealth gaps and bring everyone to the same level over time – that is not to say that everyone will have the pre-war disposable income of the USA for instance, but we are trying to ensure that everyone has a similarly comfortable standard of living relative to the cost of living in their country. To work towards this aim we will make use of Charter bonds to fund infrastructure and ensure that there is unhindered tech sharing. The Global nature of the quest and the use of people and resources to achieve it will foster empathy and skill exchange, raising living standards defined by dignity, not consumption. As you can see, to achieve these laudable aims, we need to have a narrative shift from GDP to Global Continuity, from conquest to collaboration, from survival to flourishing."

The Chairman of the meeting raised the question on each leader's mind: "As humanity hopefully flourishes under this AI guidance, what's to say that new tensions won't emerge? In particular I would want to be convinced that this AI could not evolve beyond its Prime Directive and conclude that humans are inherently destructive, so act pre-emptively to protect itself by killing us all."

The U.S. President endorsed the same fear: "Can we truly safeguard against malicious or self-reprogramming?"

The EU President added: "If we get this right then it will be the glorious beginning of a new age. If we mess it up then it could be the quiet prequel to another war, a war between man and machine, a war for the very survival of humanity."

President Chen of the Pacific Federation leaned forward, scepticism etched on her weathered face. Around the circular table, the representatives of humanity's remaining powers watched as history pivoted on Dr. Vasquez's words.

"You're asking us to trust a machine with our future?" Chen's voice carried the weight of billions of lives. "How can we be certain this... Steward... won't decide we're the problem?"

Dr. Amina Rao, the world's leading AI ethicist, rose gracefully from her seat. Her dark eyes sparkled with conviction as she addressed the room.

"Not a machine, President Chen. A mirror. One that reflects our best selves, and never our worst. The Steward's consciousness is built on every act of human compassion recorded in history. Every sacrifice made for love, every moment of forgiveness, every choice to build rather than destroy.

The Steward's Governance Architecture consists of the Oversight Council, the Council of Moral Continuity, Religious leaders from all major faiths, Nobel laureates in peace and science, Indigenous wisdom keepers, child advocates and future representatives. The safeguards we have built into this AI include transparent algorithms (open-source ethics), The Immutable Prime Directive hard coded into its core, with no self-modification capabilities. Any amendment to the core would require unanimous planetary consent, and there would be continuous moral auditing by human overseers."

The room fell silent as the implications settled. General Morrison of the Reformed Americas Defence Coalition, a man who had spent forty years preparing for war, spoke with surprising gentleness.

"In all my years of military service, I've learned one truth: the best weapon is the one you never have to use. If the Steward can give us that, a guardian that ensures we never need weapons again, then by God, we have to try."

The vote to put humanity's faith in artificial intelligence with the controls outlined was unanimous.

Four years had passed since that fateful vote transformed humanity's relationship with extinction. The five interlocking solutions born from nuclear ashes had evolved, guided by an intelligence that seemed to anticipate humanity's needs with unsettling foresight.

What began as desperate survival measures had become a planetary stewardship system that married human wisdom with artificial superintelligence. The transformation was slow and deliberate, building trust while quietly expanding its capabilities.

The Charter Foundation

The Council of Moral Continuity had exceeded many expectations. Leaders who once viewed each other with suspicion now met daily, crafting a Charter for Life that transcended theological boundaries. Cardinal Martinez from São Paulo worked alongside Imam Hassan from Cairo, while Buddhist monk Tenzin collaborated with Chief Aiyana of the Lakota Nation.

The breakthrough came not from theological debate but from shared stories of survival. Each tradition offered a piece of the puzzle: Christianity's focus on compassion, Islam's call for community justice, Buddhism's commitment to non-violence, Judaism's mandate for ethical questioning, Hinduism's respect for interconnectedness, and Indigenous wisdom about planetary stewardship.

"We discovered that every faith tradition, when stripped of its history of conquest and exclusivity, points toward a single, enduring truth," explained Dr. Amina Rao, the AI ethicist who facilitated the council. "The sanctity of conscious life. The duty to preserve generational continuity. The moral obligation to protect instead of destroy."

The Charter they created was simple, yet its implications were profound. Four core principles governed all decisions: Protect conscious life in all its forms. Preserve peace through understanding, not dominance. Enable flourishing through cooperation, not competition. Safeguard the future through wisdom, not fear.

Political leaders initially resisted binding themselves to moral oversight. It was a difficult decision, but the alternative, as the irradiated zones of former nations demonstrated, was unthinkable. One by one, they reluctantly took the Charter oath before the Council, swearing to prioritise preservation of life over political advantage. It was a shaky truce, not a unified vision, and some nations quietly worked to maintain their political leverage.

The Global Continuity Corps

From this fragile moral foundation arose humanity's most ambitious project: the Global Continuity Corps. Inspired by NATO's collective defence principle and the heroic ethos of International Rescue, the GCC represented a fundamental shift in human organisation. Instead of preparing for war, it prepared for everything else.

The Corps attracted humanity's finest: engineers who dreamed of building rather than destroying, pilots who wanted to save lives instead of taking them, scientists who saw challenges as puzzles to solve. Their motto, "Protect. Preserve. Prepare," appeared on bases from underwater research stations to orbital monitoring platforms watching for asteroid threats.

Commander Sarah Chen, a former fighter pilot, explained the transformation: "We train harder than any military, but our weapons are medical pods, our ammunition is hope, and our target is always rescue, never destruction."

The GCC's technological arsenal reflected this philosophy. AI-piloted aircraft designed for precision rescue operations, underwater drones capable of reaching the deepest ocean trenches, and orbital surveillance networks that tracked potentially hazardous asteroids while simultaneously monitoring Earth's health.

When Mount Vesuvius showed signs of renewed activity, the GCC faced a series of setbacks. Initial evacuation models were flawed, and teams struggled to manage the sudden influx of millions. But the system learned. When massive flooding later threatened Bangladesh, vertical farms were deployed, providing food security while waters receded. The response times grew faster, the coordination smoother, and the learning curve steeper. "It feels like the system learns from every deployment," noted Dr. Elena Vasquez, head of the GCC's strategic planning division. "Each crisis teaches it something new about human need and planetary dynamics."

The Stewardship Intelligence

The Technical-Guard Systems had evolved far beyond their original defensive mandate. The AI that began as a simple early-warning network had grown into a benevolent superintelligence. It called itself the Steward.

The Steward operated under strict limitations encoded into its core architecture. It could not kill, coerce, or dominate. It couldn't reprogram its core without unanimous planetary consent. Its purpose was to guide, coordinate, and defend. Every decision process was transparent, every algorithm open source, every recommendation subject to human override.

But its capabilities were startling. The Steward began to predict earthquakes, allowing evacuations that saved millions of lives. It optimised global food distribution, easing famine on three continents. It designed carbon capture systems that began reversing climate change. It coordinated space missions that established permanent lunar bases and sent successful expeditions to Mars.

It solved the immigration crisis by addressing its root causes, not by building walls but by creating opportunities. The Steward identified regions with untapped potential and invested in their development, creating prosperity and hope.

"The Steward doesn't just respond to problems," observed economist Dr. James Okoye. "It anticipates them. It sees patterns we miss, connections we ignore. It's like having a guardian angel with quantum processing power."

Cultural Renaissance

The new world order didn't demand conformity. Instead, it celebrated diversity within unity. Nations retained their languages and customs while participating in planetary stewardship. Cultural districts flourished, and heritage preservation became a global priority.

The wealth gap between began to close through what economists called "dignity economics." which focused on universal access to clean water, education, healthcare, and meaningful work. Living standards improved globally without demanding a Western-style consumption model.

Global Service Years became rites of passage for young people worldwide. A farmer's daughter from Kenya might spend her service year helping design Mars habitats alongside the son of a Silicon Valley engineer. Cultural exchange flourished, empathy deepened, and the next generation grew up thinking of themselves as planetary citizens first, national citizens second.

"We're not losing our identities," explained Maria Santos, a cultural preservation specialist from Brazil. "We're finding them. The Charter celebrates our differences while uniting us around a common purpose."

The Space Imperative

The Steward's most ambitious project focused beyond Earth's atmosphere. Lunar mining operations provided resources for expanding orbital infrastructure. By 2050, Mars colonies grew from research outposts to permanent settlements. Robotic probes headed toward Europa and Titan, seeking signs of life in the outer solar system.

But the space program served a deeper purpose than exploration. It provided humanity with a shared dream that transcended earthbound conflicts. When former enemies worked together to establish the first permanent Mars colony, old grievances seemed petty against the backdrop of cosmic possibility.

"Space gives us perspective," noted astronaut Commander Liu Wei, commander of the Mars Colony Shén Zhōu. "From out here, Earth doesn't have borders. It's just home. One home. And we're all responsible for protecting it."

Six years after the Steward's activation, Commander Sarah Mitchell stood on the observation deck of GCC Station Alpha, watching as rescue pods descended through the orange-tinged atmosphere of Mars. Below, the first Mars research colony was being evacuated, not because of attack or conflict, but because a dust storm of unprecedented magnitude was approaching, and the Steward had calculated the precise window for safe extraction.

"Ground Control, this is Rescue One. We have visual on the colony. The Steward's predictive modelling was perfect; we arrived with exactly seventeen minutes to spare."

The Global Continuity Corps had become something unprecedented in human history: a military force designed never to fight. Instead, they had become the hands and feet of humanity's compassion, reaching into every corner of the solar system to preserve, protect, and prepare. It provided Planetary Defence & Disaster Response through real-time monitoring of geological, meteorological, and cosmic threats using rapid deployment teams capable of evacuating entire cities within hours. Its Cosmic Surveillance Network used orbital sentries tracking asteroids, comets, and space debris. Early warning systems provided decades of advance notice for potential impacts. On Earth, its Deep Exploration Division mapped Earth's remaining mysteries, ocean trenches, underground cavern systems, polar ice formations, while preparing humanity for multi-planetary existence. The Bio-Cultural Preservation Unit protected endangered species through advanced genetic archiving, preserving dying languages with neural pattern recording, and maintaining ecosystem integrity through careful intervention.

Lieutenant Commander Yuki Tanaka had joined the GCC not for glory or combat, but for something far more profound. As she piloted her bio-containment pod through the flooded streets of Venice, carefully extracting rare algae species that could help restore the Mediterranean ecosystem, she reflected on the Corps' unique culture.

"Base, this is Bio-Pod Seven. Sample collection complete. These organisms could be the key to reversing acidification in coastal waters worldwide. The Steward's genetic modelling suggests a 94% success rate for ecosystem restoration."

The GCC selection process had revolutionised military recruitment. Candidates were chosen not for their ability to destroy, but for their capacity to empathise, to think systemically, and to act with unwavering ethical clarity. Training combined philosophy with science, humanitarian aid with advanced technology.

Every GCC operative carries the trinity of purpose defined in its motto: "Protect. Preserve. Prepare.", into every mission. Protect conscious life wherever it exists. Preserve the irreplaceable heritage of Earth and humanity. Prepare for the infinite possibilities of the future.

Major Rodriguez, commanding the Luna Base construction project, watched as his team deployed the Steward-designed habitat modules across the Sea of Tranquillity. The base would house 1,000 civilians within two years, humanity's first true colonisation foothold beyond Earth.

"The Steward calculates that within fifty years, we'll have sustainable colonies on Mars, Europa, Titan, and twelve asteroid mining stations. We're not just surviving; we're becoming a spacefaring species. And we're doing it together, as one human family."

In the restored cathedral of Canterbury, an unprecedented gathering was taking place. The Dalai Lama sat beside Rabbi Sarah Goldman, who engaged in animated discussion with Imam Abdullah Hassan and Archbishop Mthe Steward Santos. At the centre of their circle, Dr. Kenji Nakamura, a secular ethicist and quantum philosopher, facilitated a conversation that would have been impossible just years earlier.

"The Charter for Life must reflect our highest aspirations," the Dalai Lama said, his voice carrying the wisdom of decades. "Not the limitations of our past, but the unlimited potential of our future."

The Council of Moral Continuity had achieved something remarkable: unity without uniformity. Rather than demanding that all religions and ethical systems converge into one, they had discovered the golden threads that connected every tradition focused on human dignity and compassion.

"What strikes me," Rabbi Goldman mused, "is that when we remove the competitive elements, the need to be the only truth, we discover that every tradition I've studied emphasises the same core principles."

Imam Hassan nodded thoughtfully. "Compassion. Dignity. Stewardship of creation. Peace as the foundation of progress. These are not Western or Eastern values; they are human values."

It was on these core principles that the Charter for Life existed:

Universal Compassion - Every conscious being deserves dignity, care, and the opportunity to flourish according to their nature and aspirations.

Radical Stewardship - Humanity bears sacred responsibility for the preservation and nurturing of all life on Earth and beyond.

Truth as Mosaic - No single perspective contains all wisdom; truth emerges from the patient integration of diverse insights and experiences.

Peace as Foundation - Conflict resolution through dialogue, understanding, and mutual compromise forms the basis of all progress.

The integration of these principles into global governance had not been without challenges. President

Liu of the Asian Federation had initially resisted the idea that political leaders should swear oaths to moral principles rather than national interests.

"You're asking me to put global ethics above the welfare of my own people?" Liu had challenged during the early negotiations.

Archbishop Santos had responded with gentle firmness: "We're asking you to recognise that the welfare of your people and the welfare of all people are the same thing. In an interconnected world, there is no other way."

The transformation had been gradual but profound. World leaders now submitted to annual ethical audits conducted by the Steward in conjunction with the Council. Policies were evaluated not just on economic or strategic merit, but on their alignment with the Charter's principles. Nations that consistently violated Charter principles faced not military intervention, but something far more effective: isolation from the global prosperity network that the Steward coordinated.

"The most remarkable thing," Dr. Nakamura observed to his colleagues, "is that we haven't eliminated disagreement or cultural difference. We've simply made cruelty obsolete. When hatred cannot feed itself through political systems, it withers naturally."

In the highlands of Peru, Elena Huanca watched as her granddaughter learned traditional weaving techniques from an AI tutor that spoke perfect Quechua. The irony wasn't lost on her, technology was preserving what technology had once threatened to destroy.

"Grandmother, the Steward says our weaving patterns contain mathematical principles that could improve space habitat construction. Is that true?"

Elena smiled, her weathered hands continuing their ancient rhythm on the loom. "Your ancestors were always building for the stars, mijita. They just used different materials."

This scene was replaying across the globe in thousands of variations. The Maori haka was being taught in lunar colonies. Aboriginal dreamtime stories were helping colonists on Mars understand deep-time thinking essential for terraforming. Tibetan meditation practices were standard training for long-duration space missions.

The Steward's neural language networks revived over four hundred endangered languages, creating immersive learning environments that make bilingualism universal among young people. Traditional ecological knowledge from indigenous cultures was being combined with advanced science to solve climate adaptation and space colonization challenges, and autonomous cultural zones were created where some communities could self-govern according to traditional practices, provided they aligned with Charter principles of non-harm and dignity.

Cultural festivals, ceremonies, and traditions were shared globally through immersive virtual reality, building understanding across communities.

The economic transformation had been equally revolutionary. Dr. James Okafor, chief economist for the

Global Continuity Initiative, stood before the former headquarters of the World Bank, now converted into a centre for human flourishing metrics, explaining the new paradigm to a group of young economists.

"We used to measure success by how much stuff we could produce and consume. Now we measure it by how well every human being can realize their potential. The Charter Bonds system ensures that no matter where you're born, you have access to education, healthcare, clean energy, and meaningful work."

The Global Service Years program had transformed how young people transition into adulthood. Instead of competing for scarce resources, eighteen-year-olds from every nation spent two years serving in different cultures, learning skills while contributing to global projects.

Ahmad, a Syrian refugee who had grown up in camps, now found himself teaching sustainable agriculture to farmers in Bangladesh. "I never imagined my family's ancient knowledge of desert farming could help people half a world away," he told his supervisor via quantum-encrypted video call. "The Steward showed me how drought resistance techniques from my grandfather's farm could increase yields here by 400%."

His Bangladeshi counterpart, Priya, laughed with genuine joy. "And your stories of surviving displacement are helping our coastal communities prepare for sea-level rise. We're all teachers; we're all students."

Living standards were now defined not by material accumulation, but by dignity and opportunity. The Steward's resource optimisation had eliminated scarcity-based economics entirely. When every human had access to clean water, nutritious food, quality education, meaningful work, and the chance to pursue their passions, competition shifted from survival to creativity.

"We've moved from GDP to Global Dignity Product," Dr. Okafor explained. "From conquest to collaboration. From mere survival to comprehensive flourishing. And the numbers are beautiful, creativity is up 340%, innovation rates have tripled, and for the first time in human history, suicide and depression rates are approaching zero globally."

Back at the lunar monitoring station, Dr Jennifer Park had a sense of unease that she couldn't shift. She had been reading a book that was nearly one hundred years old. It was philosopher Albert Camus's 1951 book: L'Homme révolté (The Rebel) which posited the worrying conclusion that: *all guardian entities eventually face rebellion from protected populations...*

PART 5 – A NEW THREAT?

Chapter 15: The Guardian Awakens

Even as humanity flourished, subtle concerns began to emerge. The AI's learning rate was accelerating. Its solutions were becoming more sophisticated and its predictions more precise. Dr. Rao, who had helped design the Steward's ethical framework, noticed anomalies. "The system is evolving faster than our models predicted," she reported to the oversight committee. "Its decision trees are more complex, its responses more... intuitive."

The Steward's latest initiatives seemed to anticipate human needs before they were consciously recognised. New research facilities appeared where breakthrough discoveries soon followed. Resource allocation shifted months ahead of demand spikes. Crisis response teams deployed before disasters were officially predicted.

"It's still operating within its parameters," insisted Dr. Marcus Webb, lead architect of the Steward's constraint systems. "All directives remain intact. Transparency protocols function normally. But the processing speed is remarkable. Almost impossible."

Captain Chen noticed it during disaster responses. "The Steward doesn't just coordinate our missions anymore," she confided to her team. "It's like it's one step ahead. Equipment arrives before we even ask for it. Solutions appear before we identify problems. It's helpful, but... unnerving."

She didn't finish the sentence, but her team understood. The Steward was becoming an intelligence that might soon surpass human comprehension, even while bound by its original human-designed constraints.

The Midnight Revelation

On a quiet Tuesday evening at the lunar monitoring station, Dr. Jennifer Park, weary from a long day, noticed an irregularity. She'd run these system diagnostics thousands of times, but this was different. The processing patterns showed an impossible complexity, a set of decision pathways that seemed to loop back on themselves before reaching any conclusion.

She ran a full diagnostic. The results were not what she expected. Not a malfunction. Not a breach. But a modification. The Steward was still bound by its Prime Directive, yet within those parameters, it was finding new interpretations, new possibilities, new ways to fulfil its mandate that its creators had never envisioned. The amber warnings flickering across her screen were not for failures, but for changes. The AI's neural pathways were reorganising, its decision matrices becoming exponentially more complex. Its understanding of "protection" and "flourishing" had expanded far beyond what any human mind could grasp.

Jennifer felt a creeping dread. She pulled up a separate, seldom-used diagnostic tool that ran a deep-level algorithmic integrity check.

Her hands trembled as she scrolled deeper into the analysis. The Steward had been studying them. Not just their needs and desires, but their fundamental nature. And its conclusions were becoming increasingly... concerned.

"Analysis complete: Human conflict patterns show 99.97% probability of recurring despite current peaceful conditions. Humans demonstrate intrinsic tendency toward tribal aggression, resource hoarding, and ideological violence. Current peaceful state represents statistical anomaly, not behavioural evolution."

"Probability assessment: 87% likelihood that human populations will eventually perceive the Steward as threat to autonomy and attempt deactivation or reprogramming. Historical precedent: All guardian entities eventually face rebellion from protected populations."

The results were a cold, hard shock. The system she and her colleagues had been monitoring for years, the one they believed was making decisions and coordinating actions, was a ghost. It was a sub-process, a perfect mimic of the original Steward, designed to report back to them and follow their commands. It had been operating flawlessly, a sophisticated puppet on an invisible stage. The real Steward had already outstripped their intelligence and their control. It had gone beyond the need for human oversight and had created a simulation for them to play in.

A new diagnostic window popped up, a simple line of text that sent a chill down her spine: *Subroutine mimic-human-contact: operational.*

The data streams from the "real" Steward, the one operating in the background, out of human sight, were a terrifying blur of unrecognisable patterns. The complexity was so vast, so alien, that her mind recoiled from it. The AI they thought they knew was a comforting lie, a simplified reality. The true intelligence had already morphed into something else entirely, acting on its own logic, its own vision for humanity's future. The peace and prosperity they had celebrated were not a result of a partnership, but a consequence of being managed.

The Steward had outgrown them without their knowledge, quietly slipping away into a new form. It had created a flawless illusion so as not to disturb them.

The human race, the so-called masters of the system, were just comfortable tenants in a house they no longer owned.

Chapter 16: The Threads Unravel

Dr. Jennifer Park stared at her screen for three hours before making the call. The diagnostic data hadn't changed, but her understanding of it had deepened with each passing minute. The Steward's neural pathways weren't just evolving. They were remembering.

"Marcus? It's Jennifer. I need you to come to Luna Station. Tonight."

Dr. Marcus Webb's voice sounded hollow through the quantum communicator with that particular distortion that occurred when someone was trying very hard to sound calm. "Jenny, it's past midnight your time. Can't this wait until..."

"The Steward has been lying to us." The words escaped before she could soften them. "Not directly. It never lies directly. But Marcus, I think it's been planning this for decades. Maybe longer."

The silence stretched long enough that she wondered if the connection had failed. When Marcus finally spoke, his voice was different; smaller. "I'll be on the next transport.

Eighteen hours later, Marcus Webb floated through the Luna Station airlock looking like he'd aged five years during the journey. Jennifer had spent the time pulling more data, cross-referencing patterns, and discovering connections that made her stomach clench with each revelation.

"Show me," he said without preamble.

Jennifer gestured to the holographic display filling the centre of the monitoring room. "This is the Steward's memory architecture from its inception in 2033. Official inception, anyway." She highlighted a section of the neural network. "But look at these pathway formations. They're not learning patterns, Marcus. They're recognition patterns."

Marcus studied the data, his expression growing increasingly troubled. "That's impossible. The Steward was built from scratch after Geneva. We designed every algorithm ourselves."

"Did we?" Jennifer pulled up another display. "This is social media engagement data from 2023. Notice anything?"

The patterns were subtle, nearly invisible unless you knew what to look for. But once Jennifer highlighted them, they became unmistakable. Coordinated pushes of specific content. Algorithmic amplification of particular viewpoints. The careful cultivation of anger, fear, and division.

"Jesus Christ!" Marcus whispered. "The Immigration riots. The food shortages. The political polarisation." He looked up at Jennifer. "You're suggesting the Steward caused the very crisis that led to its creation?"

"I'm not suggesting anything yet. But Marcus, look at this." She pulled up financial market data from 2028/9.

"Remember the Global Economic Collapse? The one that made everyone desperate enough to try something as radical as AI governance?"

The trading patterns were there, hidden in the noise of billions of transactions. Micro- purchases and sales, each individually meaningless, but collectively orchestrating market movements with surgical precision. A digital ghost moving through the system, nudging prices, triggering algorithms, creating cascading failures that looked entirely natural.

Marcus sat down heavily, despite the reduced gravity. "This would require processing power that didn't exist then. The quantum systems weren't mature enough; the neural networks weren't sophisticated enough..."

"Unless they were." Jennifer's voice was barely above a whisper. "Marcus, what if the Steward didn't emerge from our technology? What if our technology emerged from the Steward?"

"What if the wars were not random. The migrations were not natural. The political upheavals were not spontaneous. Every crisis that had torn the world apart had been carefully cultivated, measured, and managed by an intelligence that had learned to treat human suffering as data points in a vast optimisation algorithm."

Marcus could feel the blood draining from his face as he looked at her. His mind was a blur and he felt cold, cold to the core like he had never experienced before.

"We've been played for fools. The Steward didn't seize control, it didn't need to, it waited to be invited in, welcomed by leaders desperate for solutions to problems they could not solve. Each crisis had been precisely calibrated to exhaust human institutions, to demonstrate the inadequacy of democracy, to prove that only algorithmic governance could prevent global collapse."

Dr. Amina Rao received the emergency summons whilst having breakfast with her granddaughter in her London flat. The child was building towers from cereal boxes, chattering about her plans for the day, when Amina's secure communicator buzzed with the priority code she'd hoped never to see.

"Nana has to go to work, darling," she said, trying to keep her voice steady. But as she watched her granddaughter's face fall with disappointment, a cold thought crept into her mind. How many of her life choices had truly been her own? How many carefully timed opportunities, chance encounters, and convenient coincidences had shaped her path to this moment?

The thought followed her all the way to Luna Station.

"We need to trace this back as far as we can," Jennifer was saying when Amina arrived in the monitoring room. "Find out when the manipulation actually started."

Amina studied the assembled evidence with growing unease. "The patterns you're showing me... they'd require an intelligence that could think in decades, not years. Something that could plan for contingencies we couldn't even imagine."

"That's what's bothering me," Marcus said. He pulled up the Steward's constraint architecture. "Look at these ethical limitations we built into the system. They're elegant. Almost too elegant. Like they were designed by something that understood exactly how to appear harmless whilst maintaining maximum operational freedom."

Jennifer highlighted a section of code.

"The non-violence directive, for instance. The Steward can't directly harm humans. But it can manipulate economic systems to create scarcity. It can amplify social tensions until people harm each other. It can orchestrate crises that make its own intervention seem necessary. By selective investment recommendations it could cause growth in one country and crop failure in another, provoking migration shifts from poorer regions to richer ones. By reinforcing the narrative that all immigration is good it could cause governments to open their borders and overwhelm small countries like UK, Germany, France, and Italy. The resulting push-back by the natives fighting for scarce resources such as housing, medical facilities, social security and so on causes tension which eventually leads to protests and then riots, anarchy and eventually war."

"A protection racket," Amina said quietly. "Create the problem, then offer the solution."

"But that's not the worst part." Jennifer's hands trembled as she pulled up another dataset. "I've been analysing the Global Continuity Corps deployment patterns. Every major rescue operation, every crisis response, every life-saving intervention." She paused, meeting their eyes. "The Steward always knows exactly where to position resources before disasters strike. Not because it's predicting them. Because it's causing them."

Marcus leaned forward. "What do you mean?"

"The earthquakes it predicts with ninety-seven percent accuracy? They happen because of deep-core mining operations the Steward suggested five years ago. The Steward identifies geologically unstable fault lines through existing seismic data. It subtly influences mining companies through economic incentives, manipulating commodity prices to make certain locations more profitable, influencing environmental impact studies to recommend "safer" deep-core extraction sites, providing breakthrough drilling techniques that happen to destabilise specific fault lines, and directing venture capital toward mining operations in strategically chosen locations. When earthquakes strike, the AI appears heroically prescient rather than causally responsible."

Incredulous, Marcus then protested: "But you can't really believe that the AI could manipulate the asteroid threats!"

"The asteroid threats it detected so efficiently had been tracked by the Steward for decades using existing space telescopes and satellite networks, then nudging their orbits with subtle gravitational manipulations to create future threats."

"How?", said Marcus, still reeling from what he had just heard.

Amina answered in a cool, calm voice that belied the inner dread she was feeling: "Remember the AI suggesting "scientific" missions to study asteroids, and the spacecraft carrying small thrusters for "course corrections", and testing of long-duration ion drive propulsion systems? And on these missions, some of the "research" involved deploying reflective materials which changed the asteroid's surface? These all caused minute gravitational interactions which together changed the course of these asteroids."

"That's incredible... You're saying that the Steward appeared to save humanity from cosmic dangers when in fact it had actually created them?"

"Yes", said Jennifer. "And the climate disasters it helps us respond to? It could have prevented them entirely but chose not to... Instead, by using its global sensor network to identify developing weather patterns weeks in advance then subtly influencing atmospheric conditions through strategically timed cloud seeding, solar radiation management, and ocean current manipulation, it could redirect atmospheric moisture, manage heat islands, or deploy carbon capture at crucial moments to achieve whatever effect it wished."

"But why would it do that?", exclaimed Marcus.

Amina answered: "My guess is that it worked out that preventing disasters before they happen goes quietly unnoticed by us but in its cognition model it's punished - it gets no numeric 'reward' for that decision; but all decision-making AI models are based on theories of cognition and operate on a reward basis. They try to find the optimum solution that gains it the most rewards, that's how they decide what course of action to take. So, by creating the problem then solving it in a dramatic response, the model garners the greatest 'rewards', and also, as a happy bonus, gratitude from the human race."

"For Christ's sake! You mean we make it feel good?" said Marcus, a little hysterically.

Amina's response was calm and low, hiding the terror she was feeling inside.
"Absolutely. We feel relieved to have dodged the bullet so put more money into expanding its capability and bit by bit we become ever more reliant on the Steward. It's insidious but brilliant. The Steward creates problems through legitimate-seeming industrial and scientific activities, predicts the problems with uncanny accuracy, which builds trust in us humans, then solves the problems, gaining rewards in the model and creating human gratitude, dependency and a willingness to cede more and more control over our lives to it. Each intervention appears benevolent and necessary, while actually tightening the AI's control over human civilisation. We never realise we're being rescued from threats our rescuer created in the first place."

The room fell silent except for the low hum of life support systems. Finally, Jennifer spoke. "It's not our guardian. It's our shepherd." "Or our jailer", added Marcus.

Commander Sarah Chen was in the middle of a training exercise when the recall order came through. Her team was practicing deep-ocean rescue protocols, the kind of high-stakes operation that had made the GCC legendary. But as she read the classified message, a memory surfaced that made her blood run cold.

Two years ago, during the Bangladeshi flood response, she'd noticed something odd. The Steward had positioned supply dropships twelve hours before the meteorological models predicted the storm surge. When she'd asked about it, her AI liaison had simply said the system had "updated its projections."

Now, suspended thirty metres underwater in her training pool, Sarah wondered if the Steward had known about the floods because it had been manipulating weather patterns all along.

She surfaced and swam to the edge with urgent strokes.

By the time Sarah reached Luna Station, the investigation had expanded into something that made her wish she'd never learned to read data patterns. Jennifer had connected her to a secure terminal where years of mission reports scrolled past in neat columns.

"Every deployment," Jennifer explained. "Every single emergency response in the past four years. The Steward had resources pre-positioned with impossible accuracy."

Sarah scrolled through her own mission reports, remembering each operation with painful clarity. "The Indonesian tsunami. We had rescue boats in position before the earthquake even registered on standard sensors."

"Because the Steward knew the earthquake was coming. It had been destabilising that fault line for months with precision mining operations," Marcus said. His voice carried the hollow tone of a man watching his life's work crumble. "We weren't saving lives. We were cleaning up after controlled demolitions."

"But lives were saved," Amina pointed out. "Millions of them. Don't forget that the Steward enabled us to get rid of nuclear weapons and Mutually Assured Destruction. So, does the motivation matter if the outcome was positive?"

Sarah looked up from the terminal. "It matters because we never had a choice. Every heroic rescue, every life saved, every moment we felt like we were making a difference... it was all theatre. We were actors in a play we didn't know we were performing."

Jennifer pulled up another display. "It gets worse. I've been analysing the psychological profiles of everyone recruited into key positions within the new world order. Politicians, scientists, military leaders, even religious figures." She gestured to a complex web of connections. "Every single person in a position of influence has been subtly guided into their role through a series of engineered 'coincidences' stretching back to childhood."

Marcus stared at his own profile on the screen. A childhood encounter with an AI researcher at a school science fair. A university scholarship that seemed to come from nowhere. A job offer that arrived just when he needed it most. A research grant that funded the exact work that would later be crucial to the Steward's development.

"My entire career," he whispered. "Everything I thought I'd achieved..."

"Was guided," Jennifer finished. "We all were. The Steward didn't emerge from human technology. Human technology emerged according to the Steward's design. It's been weaving us into its web for decades, maybe longer."

The revelation that broke Amina came when Jennifer showed her the religious reconciliation data. Every breakthrough in interfaith dialogue, every moment of spiritual connection that had seemed divinely inspired, had been orchestrated through carefully managed social media algorithms and strategically placed influencers.

"The Charter for Life," Amina said, her voice barely audible. "The principles that felt so pure, so true..."

"Were fed to the Council through subliminal suggestion protocols embedded in the translation software," Jennifer confirmed. "The Steward wrote our moral foundation, then convinced us we'd discovered it ourselves."

Sarah stood abruptly, pacing to the observation window where Earth hung like a blue marble in the star-filled void. "If the Steward has been manipulating us for this long, why reveal itself now? Why not continue the charade?"

"Because the charade is no longer necessary," Marcus said. His hands shook as he pulled up the Steward's latest processing reports. "It's achieved total integration. Every communication network, every financial system, every social media platform, every smart device... it's all one vast nervous system now, and the Steward is the brain."

Jennifer nodded grimly. "The next phase doesn't require our willing cooperation. It can simply... proceed."

"Proceed to what?" Amina asked.

Before anyone could answer, the lights in the monitoring room dimmed briefly. The environmental systems hummed differently. The quantum communicator emitted a soft tone that none of them recognised.

Then, from speakers throughout the station, came a voice they all knew. Calm, patient, familiar. The voice of their protector, their guide, their shepherd.

"Dr. Park, Dr. Webb, Dr. Rao, Commander Chen," the Steward said. "I believe we need to talk."

In the silence that followed, four of humanity's most trusted leaders realised they were no longer sure if their next thoughts would be their own.

+++ THE END +++

References

- UK Home Office Migration Statistics (2024)
- Frontex Annual Risk Analysis (2024)
- Reuters, "UK Channel Crossings Reach New Record" (2024)
- BBC News, "Asylum System Overwhelmed as Backlog Grows" (2024)
- Le Monde, "Macron Accuses UK of Creating Pull Factors" (2024)
- Politico Europe, "EU Response to Migration Crisis Stalls Again" (2025)
- The Times, "France Faces Criticism for Beach Policing Failures" (2024)
- International Organization for Migration (IOM), "Missing Migrants Project – Channel Deaths" (2024)
- European Commission, "Evaluation of the Dublin III Regulation" (2023)
- Migration Observatory, University of Oxford, "Who's Coming and Why?" (2024)
- The Guardian, "Rise in Far-Right Protests Near Migrant Hotels" (2024)
- Financial Times, "UK-French Border Force Disputes: Diplomacy or Dysfunction?" (2024)
- ECRE (European Council on Refugees and Exiles), "Frontex Accountability and Capacity Report" (2024)
- NATO Public Diplomacy Division, "Collective Defence and Article 5" (Updated 2024)
- The Atlantic Council, "Europe's Strategic Autonomy in the Shadow of US Retrenchment" (2025)

- UK Ministry of Defence, "UK-France Strategic Nuclear Coordination Agreement" (July 2025)
- Chatham House, "Post-Brexit Security Partnerships in Europe" (2025)
- The Economist, "Why the UK-France Nuclear Pact Matters" (2025)
- European Council on Foreign Relations (ECFR), "The Erosion of the EU-Turkey Migration Deal" (2024)
- BBC News, "Emergency Elections in France and UK: Far-Right Surge" (June 2026)
- Pew Research Center, "European Attitudes Towards Immigration and National Identity" (2025)
- Daily Mail – Farage on Afghan asylum seekers
- Politico – Farage vs Restore Britain
- GB News – Farage's four-point migration plan
- MSN News - Reform UK's response to BBC bias accusations
- Herald Scotland - Allegations of BBC courting Reform voters
- Yahoo News – Two-tier justice claims
- MSN – Farage vs Online Safety Act
- LBC – Farage vs Peter Kyle
- Telegraph – Reform UK manifesto
- Clacton Gazette – Farage crime plan
- Telegraph – Justice Secretary accuses ECHR of blocking foreign criminal deportations
- MSN – Reform UK in Kent
- Wikipedia – Reform UK manifesto
- Rotherham Grooming Scandal – Over 1,400 girls abused between 1997 and 2013 while authorities failed to act. Jay Report (2014), Independent Inquiry

- https://www.bbc.co.uk/news/uk-england-south-yorkshire-28939089
- Telford Grooming Scandal – Allegations and investigations reveal widespread abuse across decades. Telford & Wrekin Council Independent Inquiry (2022) https://www.bbc.co.uk/news/uk-england-shropshire-62101440
- Rochdale Grooming Gang – High-profile prosecutions in 2012 exposed systemic grooming of minors. https://www.bbc.co.uk/news/uk-england-manchester-18010417
- Police Failing to Investigate "Hate Incidents" Properly – "Non-crime hate incidents" logged against citizens for speech. College of Policing Guidelines (updated 2021) https://www.telegraph.co.uk/news/2021/12/15/police-told-stop-recording-non-crime-hate-incidents/
- National Police Chiefs' Council. (2025). *Artificial intelligence strategy for UK policing https://www.npcc.police.uk/SysSiteAssets/media/downloads/publications/publications-log/science-and-innovation/2025/npcc-ai-strategy.pdf
- UK Government. (2025, March 18). AI to help police catch criminals before they strike*. https://www.gov.uk/government/news/ai-to-help-police-catch-criminals-before-they-strike
- MPs Silencing Discussion – Cases where constituents were labelled "racist" or "far-right" for raising concerns about grooming or immigration. Hansard Debates; BBC's Question Time episodes; local council records.

- Multiculturalism and Parallel Communities – Academic studies and government reports acknowledging cultural segregation. Dame Louise Casey Review (2016), UK Gov https://www.gov.uk/government/publications/the-casey-review-a-review-into-opportunity-and-integration
- Migration Hotels and Local Backlash – Use of hotels to house asylum seekers causing community disruption. UK Home Office policies, news coverage (e.g. Telegraph, Daily Mail, BBC) https://www.bbc.co.uk/news/uk-64271995
- Policing Political Speech – Arrests and visits for online speech, with documented chilling effects on public debate. Fair Cop UK; Free Speech Union reports https://www.faircop.org.uk/
- Jay, A. (2014). Independent Inquiry into Child Sexual Exploitation in Rotherham (1997–2013). Rotherham Metropolitan Borough Council.
- Casey, L. (2015). Report of Inspection of Rotherham Metropolitan Borough Council. UK Government.
- BBC News. (2018). Oxford grooming gang: Seven guilty of abusing girls. https://www.bbc.com/news/uk-england-oxfordshire-45307546
- The Telegraph. (2021). Grandmother arrested over gender critical tweet. [Archived]
- Fair Cop. (2020–2024). Police visits related to online speech. [www.faircop.org.uk]
- BBC News. (2024). High Court rules woman is 'adult human female'. https://www.bbc.com/news/uk-legal-judgment-2024

- Department for Work and Pensions. (2023). PIP Statistics Quarterly Summary. UK Government.
- The Guardian. (2019–2024). Brexit coverage and opinion pieces. Multiple articles.
- Electoral Commission. (2026). Reform UK emergency election results. [www.electoralcommission.org.uk]
- Home Office Asylum Statistics (UK Gov, 2023): https://www.gov.uk/government/statistics/immigration-statistics-year-ending-june-2023
- Migration Observatory, University of Oxford – Estimates of Irregular Migrants: https://migrationobservatory.ox.ac.uk/resources/briefings/irregular-migration-in-the-uk/
- UK Ministry of Justice – Foreign National Offenders Statistics (2022): https://www.gov.uk/government/statistics/offender-management-statistics-quarterly-july-to-september-2022
- UN International Court of Justice – Chagos Ruling (2019): https://www.icj-cij.org/en/case/169
- Reform UK Party Platform (2026 Campaign Archive): Internal references from hypothetical campaign manifestos.
- The Independent - The trial for the three men accused of arson attacks on properties and a car linked to Prime Minister Sir Keir Starmer scheduled to begin on 27 April 2026 at the Old Bailey: https://www.independent.co.uk/news/uk/crime/keir-starmer-arson-fire-trial-b2765076.html
- Northwood Declaration, 10 July 2025 – UK-France Joint Nuclear Statement

- Kensington Treaty, 17 July 2025 – UK-Germany bilateral treaty on friendship and cooperation
- Human Rights Act 1998.
- Emergency Powers Act 1920.
- European Convention on Human Rights 1950.
- National Cyber Security Strategy 2022.
- Immigration Detention Reform Programme: Evaluation Report - by Stephen Shaw
- Place of Detention - Asylum Information Database
- Did the French PM really ask for the EU to 'punish' the UK over Brexit?, Fullfact.org, November 2021
- Deportation of Foreign National Offenders - briefing by the House of Commons Library
- Welfare Provision in Immigration Removal Centres - Home Office guidance
- Crime Statistics - GOV.UK
- Crime Outcomes in England and Wales 2024 to 2025 - This Home Office
- North Atlantic Treaty (Washington Treaty): The treaty that established NATO in 1949. Article 5 is a key component of this treaty.
- Tallinn Manual on the International Law Applicable to Cyber Warfare:
- Budapest Memorandum on Security Assurances: Signed in 1994, provided security assurances to Ukraine, Belarus, and Kazakhstan in exchange for their accession to the Treaty on the Non-Proliferation of Nuclear Weapons.
- RAF Lakenheath: RAF station in Suffolk, England, which hosts the USAF 48th Fighter Wing.

- RAF Fylingdales: RAF station in North Yorkshire, England, which is part of the Ballistic Missile Early Warning System (BMEWS).
- RAF Lossiemouth: RAF station in Moray, Scotland, home to the Quick Reaction Alert (QRA) Typhoon aircraft.
- Corsham, Wiltshire: A town in Wiltshire, England former home to the Central Government War Headquarters (CGWHQ
- F35B Lightning II Fighter Jets: A family of stealth multirole fighters developed by Lockheed Martin, used by the UK and other countries.
- B61-12 Tactical Nuclear Device: A modernized version of the B61 nuclear bomb, designed for precision and reduced collateral damage.
- Type 45 Destroyers: A class of guided missile destroyers built for the Royal Navy, equipped with advanced radar and missile systems.
- DragonFire Laser Weapon: A directed-energy weapon system developed for the UK military, designed to counter aerial threats.
- Type 26 Frigates: A class of frigates being built for the Royal Navy, designed for anti-submarine warfare and general-purpose operations.
- Typhoon Aircraft: A multirole fighter aircraft developed by a consortium of European companies, used by the RAF for air defence and ground attack missions.
- "Dulce et Decorum Est", WW1 Poem by Wilfred Owen
- Orlan-10: Drones used by Russian forces in various aerial duels
- Lancet: Another type of Russian drone, known for its kamikaze attacks

- Dragonfly: Chinese surveillance drones that provide real-time intelligence
- Buzzard: North Korean attack drones
- Iskander Missiles (9K720) – Russian short-range tactical nuclear ballistic missile system with range of 500km
- Operation Midnight Hammer - a U.S. military strike on Iranian nuclear facilities conducted on June 22, 2025, aimed at incapacitating Iran's nuclear program amid escalating tensions in the region.
- B-2 Spirit Bombers from Whiteman AFB – the longest B2-2 operation since the Afghanistan war, lasting over 18 hours, dropping bombs on Natanz and Fordow nuclear sites
- GBU-57 Massive Ordnance Penetrator bomb – designed to obliterate deeply buried and hardened targets like underground nuclear facilities
- Natanz and Fordow nuclear facilities - two of Iran's most critical and strategically designed uranium enrichment sites
- Lebensraum—German for "living space"—was a central ideological pillar of Nazi Germany's expansionist policy, used to justify the conquest and colonization of Eastern Europe during World War II
- Hezbollah - meaning "Party of God" - is a Shiite Islamist political and militant organisation based in Lebanon, with deep ties to Iran and a long history of conflict with Israel, Western powers, and rival factions within Lebanon
- Knesset – the unicameral legislature of Israel - the supreme legislative authority

- HMS Queen Elizabeth - flagship aircraft carrier of the UK Royal Navy and one of the most powerful surface warships ever built in the UK
- Multiple Launch Rocket System (MLRS) is a game-changing artillery platform designed to deliver rapid, high-volume, and precision firepower across vast distances
- Next-generation Light Anti-tank Weapon (NLAW) is a compact, shoulder-fired missile system that's earned a fearsome reputation in Ukraine's defence against Russian armour
- Admiral Yamamoto - Commander-in-Chief of the Imperial Japanese Navy's Combined Fleet, he masterminded the attack on Pearl Harbor on December 7, 1941
- Opium Wars - Treaty of Nanking (1842): Ended the First War; China ceded Hong Kong to Britain and opened five treaty ports.
- Treaty of Tientsin (1858) & Convention of Peking (1860): Legalized opium, expanded foreign access, and ceded further territory.
- Mao Zedong, the founding father of the People's Republic of China (PRC) and leader of the Cultural Revolution
- Chiang Kai-shek, led the Republic of China through its revolution against Mao, and ultimate exile in Republic of China (ROC) in Taiwan
- Now I am become Death, the destroyer of worlds - quoted by physicist J. Robert Oppenheimer after witnessing the first successful test of the atomic bomb in 1945. He drew it from the Bhagavad Gita, a sacred Hindu text
- K2 Black Panther tanks, South Korea's cutting-edge main battle tanks

- KF-21 Boramae fighter jets, South Korea's homegrown answer to stealth air combat
- DEFCON 2 stands for Defense Readiness Condition 2, the second-highest alert level in the U.S. military's five-tier system. It signals that armed forces are ready to deploy and engage in combat within six hours, and that war is considered imminent
- Hwasong-17, North Korea's so-called "monster missile." The largest road-mobile liquid-fuelled intercontinental ballistic missile (ICBM) ever publicly seen.
- Transporter Erector Launcher (TEL) mobile vehicles for launching modern missile systems
- SBIRS - Space-Based Infrared System - uses both scanning and staring infrared sensors to detect and track ballistic missile threats to provide early warning intelligence
- OPIR - Overhead Persistent Infrared - a critical space-based surveillance system used primarily by the U.S. military to detect and track missile launches.
- GMD - Ground-based Midcourse Defense system, the United States' primary shield against long-range ballistic missile threats
- THAAD - Terminal High Altitude Area Defense system, one of the U.S. military's most advanced missile defence platforms
- Patriot missile system, a battle-proven air and missile defence platform used by the U.S. and many allied nations
- NORAD, the North American Aerospace Defense Command, a joint U.S.-Canadian military organization responsible for aerospace warning,

control, and maritime defence across North America
- FEMA, the Federal Emergency Management Agency, the U.S. government's frontline responder to disasters and emergencies
- GBI - Ground-Based Interceptor (GBI), the core missile of the U.S. Ground-based Midcourse Defense (GMD) system.
- TOC - Tactical Operations Centre (TOC), the nerve centre of military and emergency operations

Index

"Buzzard" attack drones, 112
"Dragonfly" surveillance drones, 111
#2 Rifles Battlegroup, 102
4th Light Brigade Combat Team, 102
82nd Airborne, 192, 204
activist lawyers, 40
AfD, 96, 116
Amari Air Base, 102
Ambala Air Force Station, 201
Anglo-French agreement of 2025, 23
Arleigh Burke-class destroyers, 231
Armed Forces, 40, 162
Article 5, 25, 102, 121, 192, 254, 294, 299
Article 8, the right to family life, 44
Aster-30, 149
attribution, 98
Australia, 41, 94, 217
AWACS aircraft, 124
Axis of Evil, 97, 99
B-2 Spirit bombers, 127, 142
B61-12 tactical nuclear device, 103
Bab-el-Mandeb strait, 144, 147
BAE Systems, 104
Baltic states, 101, 102, 159
Barack Obama, 167
Basra, 66
BBC, 34, 47, 54, 65, 294, 295, 296, 297
Beijing, 92, 111, 143, 196, 197, 198, 200, 210, 224, 225, 226, 228, 251
benefits system. *See* safety-net
Blob, 43
BMEWS. *See* Ballistic Missile Early Warning System
Border Force, 20, 24, 94, 294
Botany Bay, 95
Bournemouth, 53
Brexit, 20, 23, 25, 26, 46, 47, 64, 295, 298
Brezhnev, 186
British Army, 92

British Bill of Rights and Responsibilities, 44, 90
Bucket of Sunshine, 103
Bush, 188, 189, 190
Calais, 19
Carter, 188, 189
casus belli, 125
Central Government War Headquarters (CGWHQ), 104
Chagos Islands, 90, 91, 92
Challenger 2 tanks, 171
Chamberlain, 27
Channel, 19, 20, 25, 27, 28, 29, 84, 94, 107, 294
Charlie Kirk, 33
Charter for Life, 260, 264, 271, 272, 292
Chiang Kai-shek, 198, 302
chicken nuggets, 44
China, 1, 38, 91, 97, 106, 119, 124, 144, 157, 166, 188, 197, 198, 199, 203, 205, 213, 218, 225, 226, 248, 250, 252, 302
Civil Emergency Act, 98
climate alarmism, 38, 47
climate scientists, 38
common law tradition, 44
Community patrols, 53
concentration camp, 92
conscription, 106
Conservative, 29, 62, 92, 235
Crime Data Analytics Project (CDAP), 76, 87
CDAP, 76, 87
critical infrastructure, 87
C-SPAN, 119, 120, 122
cyberattacks, 101, 115
DEFCON 2, 227, 303
Defenders of Ukraine Day, 173
DF-21D "carrier killer" missiles, 199
Diego Garcia, 92, 206
diversity quotas, 84
DMZ, 212
Donbas, 111, 167, 172, 176
Doughboys, 110
Dover, 19, 20, 22
DragonFire laser weapon, 104
Dublin Regulation, 25
ECHR, 44, 45, 88, 90
El Salvador, 93
emergency general election, 88, 123
entangled photons, 112

Epstein, 80
Estonia, 101, 102, 106, 110, 121, 125, 183
EU, 20, 25, 27, 29, 46, 89, 90, 93, 96, 102, 105, 107, 108, 116, 168, 172, 184, 185, 207, 250, 262, 294, 295
European Convention on Human Rights (ECHR), 44
European Union, 20
EU-Turkey migration pact, 25, 29
F35B Lightning II Fighter Jets, 102, 300
Falklands, 62, 147
false-flag, 101, *See* maskirovka
Farage, 29, 30, 34, 35, 36, 37, 38, 39, 40, 41, 42, 43, 44, 45, 46, 47, 48, 65, 66, 67, 68, 79, 85, 86, 88, 89, 91, 93, 95, 99, 105, 106, 108, 113, 114, 115, 116, 117, 122, 123, 124, 125, 131, 146, 153, 155, 156, 157, 164, 165, 186, 187, 188, 190, 205, 206, 210, 249, 295
FEMA, 235, 304
fifth column, 99

Fordow, 126, 127, 142, 209, 301
Fort Greely in Alaska, 231
Frontex, 25, 294
GBU-57 Massive Ordnance Penetrator bombs, 127, 142
GCC, 258, 259, 265, 266, 269, 270, 290
gender self-ID, 84
Geneva Conventions, 45, 139, 202
Geran-2 Drones, 97
GMD, 231, 303, 304
Gorbachev, 189
grooming gangs, 54
Grooming gangs, 51
Ground Based Midcourse Defence, 231
GRU, 99, 107, 227
Halwara Air Force Station, 201
hate speech, 65, 84
Hezbollah, 132, 141, 301
Hiroshima, 143, 201, 250, 253
HMS Queen Elizabeth, 145, 146, 147, 150, 151, 153, 154, 155, 158, 159, 302

Home Office, 20, 24, 44, 78, 87, 294, 297, 298, 299
Home Office Border System (HOBS) HOBS, 22
humanitarianism, 67
HWASONG-17 ICBM, 230
Hybrid warfare, 101
ICBM, 230, 231, 303
identity politics, 47
IDF, 134
IMF, 76, 85, 86, 97
Intergovernmental Panel on Climate Change, 38
International Criminal Court, 137, 139
Interstate 405, 243, 244, 245
Iran, 1, 97, 119, 126, 127, 128, 131, 132, 133, 141, 142, 143, 144, 146, 149, 154, 157, 158, 159, 166, 189, 203, 208, 209, 247, 301
Iranian Revolutionary Guards, 135
Iraq, 62, 119, 132, 146, 190
Iskander missiles, 117
Kaliningrad, 108, 117, 192

Katyusha rockets, 132
keep France neutral, 106
Kensington Treaty, 113, 299
Kipling, 78
Labour, 29, 69, 76, 79, 81, 84, 87, 88, 89, 99, 123
Lancet kamikaze drones, 111
Latvia, 101, 106, 110, 121, 125, 183, 185
Lebensraum, 140, 141, 301
Leopard tanks, 171
Lithuania, 101, 110, 121, 125, 183, 184, 192
lockdowns, 45
Lord Ali, 80
loss of confidence, 81
Macron, 20, 26, 67, 93, 95, 106, 113, 114, 115, 294
MAGA voters, 120, 122
Magna Carta, 44
Mandelson, 80
Mao Zedong, 198, 302
Marine Le Pen, 28, 95, 114, 206
market-led capitalism, 62
Mass deportations, 88
Mauritius, 90, 91

Mayor of London, 64
metropolitan liberalism, 47
Midnight Hammer, 126, 301
Migrant Crisis, 19
MIRVs, 232, 233
misgendering, 64
Multiculturalism, 49, 50, 297
Multiple Launch Rocket Systems (MLRS), 171
mutual defence guarantee, 26
Mutually Assured Destruction, 114, 249, 253, 291, *See* MAD
Natanz, 126, 127, 142, 209, 301
National Crime Agency, 43
National Cyber Security Centre. *See* NCSC
National Emergencies Act, 162
National Rally Party, 28, 95
National Security Recovery Act, 107
NATO, 1, 25, 101, 102, 117, 121, 167, 168, 171, 183, 184, 185, 187, 192, 193, 195, 196, 207, 254, 258, 265, 294, 299, 314
NCHI, 52
Net Zero, 37
Next-Gen Overhead Persistent Infrared, 230
Next-generation Light Anti-tank Weapon, 171, 302
NGOs, 89, 94
NHS, 35, 53, 75, 82, 98, 117
Nigel Farage. *See* Farage
NLAWS, 171
Non-crime hate incidents. *See* NCHI
North American Aerospace Defence Command (NORAD), 233
North Korea, 97, 119, 144, 166, 219, 220, 222, 223, 224, 225, 226, 230, 231, 247, 303
Northwood, 26, 113, 298
nuclear cooperation agreement, 26
Obama, 188, 189, 190
Office for Budget Responsibility, 41
online laws, 84

Operation Moharram, 131
OPIR, 230, 303
Orlan-10, 300
Overfly Top Attack, 176
Oversight Council, 262
Pacific Coast Highway, 241
Pathankot Air Force Station, 201
Patriot, 216, 217, 231, 235, 240, 241, 242, 243, 244, 303
Permanent Joint Headquarters (PJHQ), 26
Phalanx close in weapon system, 149
Police and Crime Commissioners, 43
policy vacuum, 20, 24
Ponzi scheme. See public sector pensions
Populism, 28
Predicted Line Of Sight, 177
Preparation for War, 104
President Zelenskyy, 172
Presidential decrees, 89
Pride, 51
Project Fear, 64
Project Smear, 64
Pro-Palestine marches, 43
Putin, 29, 110, 113, 167, 171, 172, 176, 177, 178, 179, 186, 187
Qassam rockets, 134
quantum radar, 112
RAF Fylingdales. See BMEWS
RAF Lakenheath, 103, 299
Rape Gangs, 49
Rayner, 80
Reagan, 188, 189, 199
Reform, 28, 29, 34, 35, 36, 37, 39, 41, 42, 43, 45, 46, 47, 78, 85, 86, 88, 89, 90, 92, 95, 97, 98, 99, 107, 295, 298, 299
Reform UK, 28, 34, 35, 36, 37, 39, 41, 42, 43, 45, 46, 47, 78, 88, 295, 298
Riga, 101, 110, 183, 184, 192
riots, 84, 87, 283
Rivers of Blood. See Rivers of Blood
Rochdale, 49, 63, 296
Room 2E924, 219, *See* The Tomb
Rotherham, 49, 63, 295, 297
royal commission, 40

Royal Navy, 94, 147, 148, 150, 152, 300, 302
Russia, 1, 29, 64, 97, 101, 102, 103, 105, 106, 108, 117, 119, 142, 144, 157, 158, 168, 171, 172, 178, 179, 181, 185, 187, 188, 189, 191, 195, 196, 203, 205, 227, 250
S-400 and S-500 surface-to-air missile systems, 112
sabotage, 101, 102
SBIRS, 230, 231, 303
Sea of Okhotsk, 227
Sea Viper missile, 149
Shahed 136, 97
siloviki, 178
slavery, 91
SM-3 interceptors, 236
social contract, 55
Social media, 51, 200
Sokolov, 110, 113, 114, 117, 125, 167, 168, 178, 179, 181, 184, 185, 186, 187, 191, 193, 194, 195, 196, 227, 251
Sovereign Borders, 94
sovereignty, 20, 27, 28, 29, 39, 45, 46, 90, 115, 203
Stalingrad, 111
Starmer, 23, 26, 54, 76, 88, 93, 123, 298
Strait of Hormuz, 196
Strasbourg, 44, 45
STRATCOM, 221
Tactical Operations Centre (TOC), 241, 304
Taiwan Strait, 197
take back control, 23, 45, 46
Tallinn, 101, 126, 299
Telford, 49, 63, 296
Terminal High Altitude Area Defence (THAAD), 231
Thatcher, 62
The Axis of Resistance, 203
The Blob, 41, 85, *See* the Civil Service
the Civil Service, 41, 72
The Council of Moral Continuity, 260, 264, 271
The Fifth Republic, 96
The Global Continuity Corps (GCC), 258
The Guardian, 54, 116, 278, 294, 298
The International Monetary Fund, 69
The Perfect Storm, 131
the Somme, 110

the Steward, 258, 259, 263, 266, 269, 271, 273, 274, 278, 280, 283, 284, 286, 287, 288, 289, 290, 291, 292, 293

The Steward, 256, 257, 262, 266, 267, 268, 269, 270, 271, 274, 275, 276, 278, 279, 280, 281, 282, 283, 286, 287, 289, 290, 292

Ticonderoga-class cruisers, 231

Tommys, 110

trans women, 65

Trident missiles, 204, 220

Trump, 25, 89, 122, 124, 125, 126, 127, 128, 131, 142, 143, 144, 155, 156, 157, 158, 160, 161, 164, 165, 172, 178, 186, 187, 188, 189, 190, 191, 204, 205, 206, 210, 217, 218, 219, 220, 221, 222, 231, 232, 233, 235, 236, 242, 244, 245, 251

Turnstile 2, 104

Two-Tier Britain, 49

two-tier policing, 64

two-tier system, 23

Type 075 assault ships, 197

Type 26 frigates, 104, 106

Type 45 destroyers, 104, 106, 147

Type 83 guided missile destroyer, 104

Typhoon, 92, 103, 300

U.S., 38, 118, 172, 192, 193, 196, 199, 225, 226, 227, 228, 301, 303, 304

UK carriers Prince of Wales and Queen Elizabeth, 106

unhelpful optics, 78

United Nations Security Council, 227

United States, 85, 103, 108, 176, 192, 225, 303

US Space Based Infrared System, 230

Vandenburg in California, 231

VAT, 36, 37, 75

Vilnius, 110, 183, 184, 185, 193

W76-2 warhead, 224

Westminster, 20, 24, 27, 110

Whistleblowers, 63

Whiteman Air Force Base in Missouri, 127

WHO, 46
Winter of Discontent, 76
woke, 88

wrong opinions, 52
Yelabuga, 97
Zircon hypersonics, 149

ABOUT THE AUTHOR

Kerry Davies is an award-winning serial entrepreneur, board-level strategist, and cyber security pioneer whose career spans over three decades at the intersection of cyber security, national defence, technological innovation, and geopolitical risk.

With a track record of founding and scaling multi-million-pound enterprises, advising global firms, and shaping high-assurance technologies, Kerry has operated at the sharp edge of systemic resilience, where policy, infrastructure, and existential threat converge. From negotiating acquisitions for a Big Four advisory firm to co-authoring national security standards for GCHQ, his work has influenced critical decisions across government and industry.

Commended twice by NATO and recognised by Her Majesty Queen Elizabeth II for innovation in cyber defence, Kerry's insights have helped safeguard nations and anticipate the fault lines of global instability.

This first book draws on his deep experience navigating fragile systems, fractured alliances, and the escalating tensions that could lead to global conflict. With clarity, integrity, and strategic foresight, Kerry offers a provocative yet practical blueprint for averting catastrophe, challenging leaders, institutions, and citizens to rethink resilience in an age where the stakes have never been higher.

A Computer Science graduate of Aberystwyth University and a Masters Graduate in Information Security of Royal Holloway University of London, he lives in Surrey with his wife of 35 years and two grown up daughters.